Part of Me

THE SEASIDE CHRONICLES

Part of Me

THE SEASIDE CHRONICLES

KELLY ELLIOTT

Part of Me
Book 2 Seaside Chronicles Copyright © 2022 by Kelly Elliott

Cover Design by: Hang Le
Interior Design & Formatting by: Elaine York, Allusion Publishing
www.allusionpublishing.com
Developmental Editor: Kelli Collins
Content Editor: Rachel Carter, Yellow Bird Editing
Proofing Editor: Erin Quinn-Kong, Yellow Bird Editing
Proofing Editor: Elaine York, Allusion Publishing
www.allusionpublishing.com

For more information on Kelly and her books, please visit her website www.kellyelliottauthor.com.

Dear Reader,

A note to you before you begin the book. The Seaside Chronicles is NOT a stand-alone series. They are interconnected stories with the siblings' stories being carried throughout the series. The books are best read in order or you may find yourself confused, and this writer does not want that to happen!

You can find out more about the books at the link below.
https://kellyelliottauthor.com/library/#seaside

Now...let's begin with Gannon and Adelaide's story, shall we?

Chapter One

Sutton
End of Senior Year

'd always heard that when you meet your soul mate, the one you were meant to spend the rest of your life with, you would feel it in the very depths of your soul. That your two hearts were forged in the same fire. I never felt that with Jack Larson, my now ex-boyfriend. I cared about him, but when his eyes met mine across a room or he smiled at me, something was...missing. Jack had a way of making me feel like I was the lucky one to be with him. It wasn't a partnership. He was quick to point out my faults, and then fast to explain that he didn't mean to hurt my feelings. It was clear that he would never change. It would always be his needs above anyone else's. That wasn't a soul mate.

My older sister, Adelaide—whom everyone called Addie—and her ex-boyfriend, Gannon Wilson, were soul mates. Everyone could see that. Jack and I...were far from it.

And here I sat, alone on a beach, after Jack had informed me that he wanted to call things off. We were both on our way to college, and he felt like he needed to explore other...*options* was the word he'd used. I should have been sad, but I wasn't. Once again, he'd been cruel with his words, like always.

He'd actually wanted to have sex only minutes before, even with everyone gathered around the dune at the bonfire. *Everyone.* Including my sister, Addie, and Gannon—who was home on leave from the Navy, along with his older brother, Brody. There was no way I was doing that with Jack. Plus, I wasn't ready. At least, I wasn't ready to take that step with *him*.

I heard someone walking toward me, and I quickly wiped my face.

"He's not worth a single tear, Sutton."

Looking up, I saw Brody standing there. He smiled, and my stomach flipped while my chest fluttered. When his eyes met mine, my heartbeat picked up. The way he made me feel was like nothing I'd *ever* experienced with Jack. Not one single time. What did that say about me and Jack?

I was the first to admit that I'd had a crush on Brody for as long as I could remember. But when I saw him show up with Gannon tonight—with his nearly black hair shaved in a military buzz cut, and his body more muscular and hardened—my entire insides felt like they melted on the spot. I knew Jack had seen my reaction, and it was the reason he'd pulled me aside and tried to pull the whole "we need to sleep together before we leave for college" stunt. I also knew in my heart that sleeping with Jack wasn't what I wanted, and if there was one thing I could control in our relationship, it was if and when I gave him my entire self.

I cleared my throat and looked up at Brody. "I'm not crying over him. Only the words he spit out."

Jack had said that I wasn't worth the wait and that we were over. His words weren't said in anger, really, but from somewhere deep inside of him. It had hurt only because a part of me knew it was a sign that he'd always known, like I did, that we were never really in love.

It was hard to love someone when you'd already given your heart to another man, regardless if that man realized it or not.

Brody sat down and handed me the beer he'd been drinking. I took a sip and handed it back, then rested my head on his shoulder. He was four years older than me and had joined the Navy right after he'd graduated from high school. I remembered sitting in my room and crying for hours because he was gone. I would no longer be able to see that crooked smile of his or the dimple in his cheek. Or those beautiful hazel eyes with the gold flecks sprinkled in as if they were a gift from above.

For as long as I could remember, I'd sworn I was in love with Brody. Then I'd met Jack, and I really *had* liked him. He'd been so sweet at first, and in a strange way, he'd reminded me of Brody. He'd made me forget that my heart was broken after Brody had left Seaside.

At first, things with Jack had been good. He had a sense of humor, was a charmer, and had a way of making me smile...when he wanted to. Of course, looking back now, I realized it had all been an act to get me to sleep with him. He'd probably had plans to break up with me regardless if I'd slept with him tonight or not. I'd never felt real love for Jack, only Brody. I knew that was why I wasn't heartbroken, but simply relieved.

Of course, Brody had no idea about my feelings for him. He'd never seen me as anything other than a kid, flashing me an occasional sweet smile, or giving me a pat on the head as he said hello.

Until tonight.

Brody hadn't come back home in over a year. When he'd walked up to the bonfire and had spotted me standing there, it was clear he no longer saw the little girl he'd remembered. His gaze had traveled down my body slowly, and I had thanked the stars above I'd worn the black shorts and tank top that Adelaide had talked me into. My body had developed a lot since the last time I'd seen Brody, and it was obvious he'd noticed. The way his eyes had taken me in sent a shiver racing through my body and had caused a feeling deep in my stomach I'd never experienced before.

"He's an asshole, Sutton," Brody said now. "And if you're not ready yet, any decent guy who cares enough about you would wait."

I swallowed the lump in my throat. "It's not that I'm not ready. It's just...I don't want my first time to be with Jack."

Brody stiffened next to me. "Why not?"

Turning to look at him, I worked up the courage I needed to admit my feelings. This would be the last time I'd see Brody for months. Maybe even longer. He was set to leave again soon, heading out on a ship for his first tour of duty. "Because I want my first time to be with someone I love and care for deeply."

Under the light of the moon, I saw Brody's eyes search my face. "You don't love Jack?"

I slowly shook my head. "I've never loved him."

Then I did something I never thought I'd do. I kissed Brody Wilson.

I fully expected him to push me away or tell me to stop. But he didn't. Instead, he brought his hand up behind my neck and deepened the kiss.

Jack had *never* kissed me the way Brody did. It was powerful. Emotional. Amazing. I swore I felt that kiss to the tips of my toes.

I let out a soft moan, and Brody tugged on my hair, pulling my head back so he could take in more of me. Our tongues danced in a beautiful rhythm, and I was positive no man would ever kiss me like this again. I would remember it for the rest of my life. Even when I was an old woman in my bed, drawing in my last breath, Brody's kiss would be seared into my memory.

When he finally pulled his mouth from mine, we were both panting.

"Sutton," he whispered.

Before he could say another word, I quickly moved to straddle him. I knew we could be caught at any moment, but I didn't care. This was my chance, and I was going to take it by the reins and go for everything I wanted.

I'd finally kissed Brody, and Lord above, he'd kissed me back.

"Brody, please," I whimpered as I lowered myself onto him. I could feel he was hard, and that did all kinds of things to me, but most of all, it gave me the courage to show him...tell him what I wanted. He had always treated me like a kid sister. Now...now his body clearly said that was no longer the case. And that thrilled me.

He cupped my face in his hands and brought my mouth down to his. This time, the kiss felt different. Searing and full of want and desire, and my goodness, did my body react to it in the most amazing ways.

"What are you doing to me, Sutton?" he whispered, leaning his forehead against mine after he broke the kiss.

"I want you, Brody. Please."

He drew back and slowly shook his head. "I'm not doing this on the beach. That's not how your first time should be. And it should be with someone—"

I pressed my fingers to his lips to stop him from talking. "Don't. Please don't, Brody. I don't think I could stand to hear you say it. Not like this, not right now."

Shaking his head as if confused, he placed his hand on the side of my face. "You said you wanted your first time to be with someone you loved."

I bit down on my lip and looked away before I met his eyes again. It didn't take him long to figure it out. A plethora of emotions crossed his face as his eyes widened, and he softly said my name again.

"Sutton, sweetheart."

I squeezed my eyes shut because I knew I couldn't look at him while I uttered my next words. "I know you don't love me back, and that's okay. I mean, unless you don't want me, then..."

I opened my eyes in time to see Brody close his. I could see the pained expression on his face before he opened them and our gazes locked again. Something was different. He looked...conflicted.

"I want you more than you could know, Sutton. I have for a long time."

Butterflies danced in my stomach as his words sank in. "You... you have?"

He nodded and ran the back of his fingers down my cheek.

Brody wanted me.

Smiling, I slid my shaking fingers through his hair and pressed my mouth to his once more. The kiss was slower, sweeter than before. It filled my body with a feeling I had never experienced. It was like a warm blanket on a cold winter night, and somehow I knew everything would be okay because of this kiss. That what happened next would forever change our lives.

"Then take me, Brody. I want it to be you. Please."

Before I knew what was happening, Brody stood, lifting me right with him. He gently placed my feet on the sand, then took my hand and started to walk down the beach, away from the bonfire.

"Where are we going?"

"To our fishing hut."

Shivers ran through my body, and I knew it wasn't from any chill in the air since it was a hot August night.

Brody and Gannon's parents owned two houses in Seaside. Their main house was on Captain's Row, which wasn't that far from my parents' house. They also had a smaller place on the beach that included a fishing hut on a private pier over the water. I had been to it a few times. It was really nice, unlike some local fishing huts. The last time I'd been in it with Addie, it had a card table, a bar, and a sofa inside. I knew, from what Addie had told me, that Brody and Gannon hung out there a lot.

"Why don't we go to the beach house?" I asked as we started down the pier toward the hut.

Brody looked at me and winked. "Gannon and Addie are there."

That caused me to swing my head around and glance back over my shoulder. "Oh," I said softly, seeing a faint light coming from the house. Addie and Gannon's relationship was...complicated, to say the least. They had mutually agreed to break up after high school since Gannon was going into the Navy and Addie was heading off to college. But when they were in town at the same time, they were on again. And that meant sneaking off to do whatever it was they did when they were alone.

Brody pulled out his keys and unlocked the door to the hut, then motioned for me to go in. I wondered how many girls he'd brought here to have sex. I knew he wasn't a sweet, innocent boy, but the thought of other women having him first made me jealous, and I hated that feeling. I worked at pushing the emotion away. This wasn't the time or place for that.

Brody turned on a light and smiled. When he spoke his next words, my eyes went wide. It was as if he'd read my mind.

"I have to tell you, Sutton, I've never brought a girl here. And if Gannon knew what we were about to do, he'd be pissed. This place is like a sanctuary for him. No girls allowed. Well, not unless they're fishing."

I knew I had a wide grin on my face. Of course, Brody probably thought I was smiling because of what Gannon would say if he knew what we were about to do.

Taking a few steps closer to me, he pushed a lock of my brown hair behind my ear. "Are you sure about this, sweetheart?"

I blinked rapidly in an attempt to keep my tears at bay. It wasn't because I was scared or worried; I was on the verge of crying because Brody had called me sweetheart, and not in a casual, friendly way.

"I've never been so sure of anything in my life. I want my first time to be with you, Brody."

A brilliant smile appeared on his face, and he reached for my tank top and pulled it over my head. He placed it on the table, then stared hotly at my white lace bra for a few seconds before he started to slide my shorts off.

"What all have you done?" he asked as I stepped out of the shorts. He ran his hands up my bare legs, causing me to tremble with anticipation.

"Wh-what do you mean?" I asked, watching him place a kiss above my belly button. I sucked in a breath and nearly let out a moan. Jack had never touched my body like this. It was almost like Brody was worshiping me.

"Sex-wise. What have you done?"

I licked my dry lips and fought to keep my voice even and casual. "Not much. I've only ever dated Jack, and he...well, he likes to kiss."

"Has he made you come with his fingers or mouth?"

I felt my eyes widen. Brody was so blunt with his questions, but that was probably a good thing. Better to get straight to the point. "Um, his fingers a few times, but..."

He looked up at me. "But what?"

Shrugging, I replied, "He gets mad when I don't want to go further. He usually wants me to play with *him*, then he occasionally makes me come with his fingers. We've never had oral sex."

A look of anger washed over Brody's handsome face, but it quickly disappeared. "He's an idiot."

Laughing, I nodded. Honestly, I didn't know what else to do.

Something changed in his eyes, and I swore they got darker. Or the lights in the cabin dimmed, I wasn't sure which.

He ran his hands back up my legs, then hooked his fingers into my panties and slowly pulled them down. Both of our breathing picked up, and I was positive he could hear my heart pound. It was so loud in my ears, I almost missed the low growl that came from the back of Brody's throat as he stared at me.

Licking his lips, he stood and looked directly into my eyes while he unclasped my bra, letting it fall down my arms to rest next to the panties I'd stepped out of moments ago.

"I'm going to be the first man to make you come with my mouth— and you have no idea how that makes me feel."

I chewed on my lip, feeling the pulse between my legs grow stronger. The urge to press my thighs together was nearly unbearable.

"Oh," I whispered. My cheeks heated, knowing I was so inexperienced when it came to things like sex and foreplay. Brody was probably used to being with women who knew what to do, how to touch him to make him feel good. I had no idea what to do, and even if I did, I was so nervous I probably wouldn't remember any of it right now.

"Sit down, sweetheart."

His voice was barely a whisper. I sat down on the sofa, and Brody dropped to his knees. I watched his face as he took in my naked body. I wasn't the least bit embarrassed, and that struck me as odd. With Jack, I was always so conscious of my nakedness, and found that I often wanted to keep something on. A shirt, my bra...some kind of a barrier.

"You're so goddamn beautiful, Sutton."

His words made my heart slam against my rib cage. He leaned in and cupped one of my breasts with his hand and feasted on my nipple. I gasped in pleasure and found myself arching into him. Needing more. *God*, I needed more.

"Brody," I whimpered while his other hand moved down my body and between my legs. I spread them wider, giving him access.

When his finger slipped inside of me, he moaned and drew back to look at me.

"You're so wet, sweetheart." His voice sounded strained, and he closed his eyes for a moment as he pushed his finger in again, then pulled it out. "I need to taste you."

Before I could even respond, he spread my legs wider and licked between my lips, then sucked on my clitoris. I nearly jumped off the sofa.

"Oh God!"

He looked up again and smirked. "You taste like heaven. Did you like that, Sutton? Do you like me tasting you like this?"

All I could do was manage a weak, "Yes."

"Do you want more?"

Nodding, I whimpered when no other words would come out.

Brody put his head back between my legs, and I watched as he feasted on me like I was his favorite dessert. I brought my hands to his head and pulled him closer. More. I needed more...yet, it was almost too much. The buildup wasn't taking long, and I arched my back. I couldn't stop my hips from moving. Brody reached up and pinned me down with one hand as he pushed his tongue inside me, and I cried out.

"Brody! Yes. Oh God."

I'd had orgasms before. Jack had used his hand, but it was always rushed. As soon as I came, he'd put my hand on his dick and tell me to get him off again. There was never anything romantic about our intimacy. I'd asked him once about oral sex, and he'd said he wasn't into it. Giving *or* receiving. So I had never brought it up again. But I'd heard my friends talk about how earth-shattering the orgasms were that happened when a guy gave you oral. And they were not kidding. It felt as if I was floating out of my body and watching myself on the sofa.

He licked me again, and then pushed his fingers inside me. I felt a slight burn when he seemed to be spreading me open wider. I hissed, and he put his mouth back on me, this time sucking hard on my clit.

"Oh my God. Brody! Yes! *Yes!*"

From the tips of my toes, I felt the orgasm building. It started off as a slow roll before breaking free and racing through my entire body. The moment it unleashed, I had to put my hand over my mouth to keep from screaming.

It was pure pleasure mixed with a bit of pain when Brody added what I guessed was another finger.

The orgasm rolled through my body like a freight train out of control. I wasn't sure if it would ever stop. At one point, I tried to push Brody away, but he kept going. He pulled out every ounce of that orgasm until I was panting and staring up at the ceiling while stars danced around the room.

He stood and quickly got undressed. Reaching into his wallet, he pulled out a condom.

"Do we have to use one?" I asked.

Brody stilled. "Sutton, I'm not sure I'll be able to pull out."

"I'm on the pill."

A look of longing washed over Brody's face. "I've never had sex without a condom."

I tried not to look disheartened. I really wanted to feel all of Brody without a barrier. I wanted to be connected as one, especially since this was my first time.

He obviously saw the look of disappointment on my face. "Are you sure, Sutton?"

"I've never been so sure of anything!" The smile that appeared on my face made him chuckle. "I want to feel all of you, Brody."

He closed his eyes and cursed. "I'm not going to last long, being bare inside of you."

Reaching down, he picked me up and carried me over to the single bed that was in the corner of the hut. He pulled the covers down and gently placed me on the mattress. With his hand on the side of my face, he said, "I need to make you come again."

I wasn't about to argue with that. "Okay," I panted out.

"When I push inside you for the first time, it's going to hurt, but it should go away pretty quickly. If you need me to stop, you'll tell me?"

Nodding, I ran my hands down his chest. "I promise I'll tell you if it hurts."

He leaned down and captured my mouth with his. The kiss was amazing. I could taste myself on his tongue, and that caused a rush of wetness to coat the finger that Brody slipped inside of me. He moaned, and that made *me* moan. I couldn't have pictured my first time being any better.

It didn't take long before I was crying out Brody's name again. Before my orgasm stopped, he moved between my legs and slowly pushed inside of me.

Pain and pleasure mixed together to create one amazing cocktail. I dug my fingers into his ass, and he stopped pushing into me.

"No!" I called out. "Don't stop. Please don't stop!"

Slowly, Brody filled my body completely. It was the most glorious feeling I'd ever experienced. He was huge and so hard, yet we fit together perfectly.

"Hang on, sweetheart."

He thrust slightly, and I let out a squeak when more pain hit me. Brody buried his face in my neck. "I'm so sorry, Sutton. I'm sorry."

I wrapped my arms and legs around his body. "It's okay. I'm okay. It's fading away. Don't stop, Brody. You feel so good."

Moving in and out slowly, Brody lifted his head and our eyes met. "I've never felt *anything* like you, Sutton. You're so tight...so perfect. It feels so fucking good!"

I lifted up and pressed my mouth to his. He rocked in and out of me in the most sensual way. Each time he pushed in, he hit a spot that made my toes curl. I needed more of that. More of him.

"Harder, Brody."

He picked up his pace, and I felt like a completely new woman.

"Yes! I want it harder. Fuck me, please."

Dropping his head again, he whispered, "Fucking hell, Sutton. It's so damn hot to hear you talk like that."

"Brody!" I cried out as he gave me what I wanted. "Yes. *Yes.* Oh, Brody. Faster! Harder...I can feel it...oh God!"

Brody moved his hips faster, pulling out and driving back into me. Yet I could tell he was holding back a bit, afraid to hurt me. I wanted all of him. The sound of his body hitting mine was the most erotic thing I'd ever heard, and I couldn't get enough of it.

"Sweetheart, I'm getting close. Fuck, Sutton..."

He reached between our bodies and pressed his thumb against my clit, and I exploded. His name fell from my lips like a prayer as he moved even faster. I could feel him grow bigger inside of me, and I smiled when he found his release.

"Sutton! Oh God." He closed his eyes, and the look on his face was so beautiful, I nearly started to cry. "Christ, I'm coming. Oh God, that feels so good!"

I reached up and cupped his face with my hands, locking our eyes as he came inside of me.

When he pressed his mouth to mine, I swore I felt something pass between us. In that very moment, with Brody deep inside of me, I never wanted the feeling to end. I wanted to stay this way forever, the two of us as one for the rest of eternity.

Our breathing slowly returned to normal while Brody placed light kisses all over my face and neck. When he lifted up, I wrapped my arms around him. "Not yet. Please, don't leave me yet."

Smiling, he rested on his elbows and stared down at me. "That was amazing, Sutton. I've never..."

His words trailed off, and I wanted to know what he'd been about to say.

"You've never what?"

"It's never been that good."

I smiled, running my fingers over the soft fuzz of hair at the base of his neck.

He kissed the tip of my nose. "Are you sore?"

"No." I trailed my fingers down the side of his handsome face. "I've never felt more alive."

Brody drew in a deep breath and slowly exhaled. He gently pulled out, then moved behind me. He wrapped his arms around my body and drew me closer.

He let out a long sigh. "I wish we could stay like this forever, but life is going to knock on that door any moment."

I lazily moved my finger up and down his arm, tears stinging the backs of my eyes. When Brody kissed my shoulder, I turned in his arms to face him. "Thank you."

He let out a soft laugh. "The one thing you do *not* have to do is thank me, sweetheart. Trust me, it was my pleasure."

I felt my cheeks heat as I looked up at him. "Was I... I mean, did I do everything right?"

Brody blinked at me a few times before he took his finger and traced it over my brow. "I don't like it when you frown. And why in the hell would you think you did anything wrong?"

Shrugging, I fought with whether or not I should bring up Jack. Brody and I had spent the most amazing time together, and I didn't want to ruin it. "I'm often told I do these kinds of things wrong."

It was his turn to frown. "By that jackass? Don't listen to him, Sutton. You're the most amazing woman I've ever met."

My heart beat rapidly in my chest, and I looked away, trying to hide my face. I knew I was blushing hard because I could feel the heat on my cheeks.

Using his finger, Brody lifted my chin until our eyes met. "I'm the one who needs to be thanking you, Sutton. You gave yourself to me, and I'll never forget this night for as long as I live."

He leaned closer and brushed his lips lightly over mine. I was so taken by the moment, I let the words I held so close to my heart slip free.

"I love you."

He stilled. His eyes searched my face, and I watched as he worked to swallow. Then I saw it. He was shutting down, pulling back from me.

"I didn't mean to say that out loud," I said. "And I don't expect anything from you. Please know that."

Brody forced a smile. "We should get dressed before we're gone too long and people notice."

I blinked rapidly to hold back the tears that threatened to come. "But..."

The words I wanted to say seemed stuck. Brody kissed me once more, though this time it felt like a goodbye kiss.

He sat up and crawled over me. Turning, he reached for my hand and helped me stand.

In silence, he helped me get dressed. I felt numb, and everything inside of me screamed to push his hands away. To tell him I could get dressed on my own. But another part needed to feel his touch. How messed up was that?

I sat on the sofa and watched as he quickly got dressed.

"Ready to head back?" he asked, not looking at me.

Standing, I shook my head. "No. What just happened, Brody?"

"Nothing."

Tilting my head, I regarded him. "Nothing? How can you say that?"

He scrubbed a hand down his face. "I don't mean that in the way you think, Sutton. That was amazing. Making love to you was... amazing."

I felt myself frown. "Then what happened?"

He looked away and stared off into space. "Nothing, it's just...I can't be with you."

I took a step back at his cold words. It was clear he'd instantly put a wall up after I'd uttered those three words. "Ever? Are you saying this meant nothing to you, and we won't ever..."

He looked away and rubbed at the back of his neck before he focused back on me. "Sutton, I'm in the Navy. I'm never home. You're heading off to college. This...it wouldn't work. It wouldn't be fair to you."

The second I felt a tear slip free, I inwardly cursed. I quickly wiped it away. "How can you simply walk away from what just happened between us? I know you felt what I felt, Brody. I saw it on your face. Felt it in the way you kissed me and moved inside of me. I may not have ever had sex before, but I'm positive that was something beyond *amazing*."

"I'm not good for you, Sutton. You deserve someone who'll love you and give you everything you've ever wanted. Someone who deserves to hear those words from you."

A quiet sob slipped free before I covered my mouth with my hand. Brody hadn't felt *anything*. Had I been the only one to feel the love between us?

I was suddenly embarrassed—and I needed to get as far away from Brody Wilson as I could. I pushed past him and started for the door.

He reached out a hand to stop me. "Sutton, don't do this. Don't make this more than what it was and ruin what we shared."

Spinning around, I glared at him. "Me? I'm the one who's ruining it? I gave myself to you, thinking you wanted me as much as I wanted *you*."

"I did!"

"Was that it? All you wanted was to fuck me?"

He flinched. "That's not what happened between us, Sutton, and you know it."

"Then how can you brush me aside like this?"

"Because I can't be with you! I can't give you the things you want, and maybe it was selfish of me not to tell you that first. To not tell you that I want you, but I can't give you anything more than *me* right now."

My tears fell freely now. "That's the problem, Brody, you didn't give me *you*. You gave me your body." I stared up at him, knowing I had a pleading look on my face. "Why can't you be with me? Why won't this work?"

He closed his eyes, a pained look on his face before he opened them again. A chill ran through my body when I saw his blank expression and the void in his hazel eyes. The next words out of his mouth broke me into a million pieces.

"Because I don't love you."

Chapter Two

Sutton
Present Day — April

I hit the light switch and sighed when nothing turned on. "What in the hell, Jack. Did you purposely break everything in the whole damn house?"

"Checked everything upstairs. Looks like you've got a few issues, but it shouldn't be anything too bad," Harlee said as she approached and followed my gaze. "It doesn't work?"

With a shake of my head, I let out a breath. "Nope. Getting Jack to fix anything was always an issue, but I swear he did all of this on purpose. There weren't this many things wrong with the house when we lived here together."

It had been eight months since I'd left my husband. We'd been married for six years, almost seven. To be honest, I wasn't sure how I'd managed to stay married to him for that long. It had been a mistake to even get married in the first place, but there was no use crying over spilled milk. Still, if I could have one do-over in my life, it would be Jack Larson.

I'd left for the University of Maine with a broken heart. Not caused by Jack, but by Brody. After an amazing evening in his family's fishing hut, he'd rejected me. I'd felt lost and confused...and who had showed up at my dorm only a week after school started? Jack.

He'd begged me to forgive him. Told me things would be different, that he wanted to be with me forever. Realizing I'd never have a future with the man I really wanted, I gave in and went out to dinner with Jack. From that point on, we dated throughout college. He'd asked me to marry him right before we'd both graduated. My heart had begged me to say no, but my head had convinced me that Jack would make a good husband. He was reliable, had a steady job waiting, and he wouldn't stand in the way of me opening up my own business in Seaside. He'd checked almost every box on paper.

The fact that I knew deep in my heart I didn't love him should have been the first clue that I was making a mistake. The fact that no one in my family cared for Jack should have been clue number two.

I was hell bent though, and looking back, I knew it was because I'd still been angry with Brody—even though it had been four years. I had given myself to him. Was prepared to wait for however long he'd needed. But then he'd said those four words.

"I don't love you."

Everything had changed after that. Love was for fools, and I no longer believed in the ridiculous idea of soul mates. There was no happily ever after; at least, there never would be for me. So, I had married a man I'd loved, but wasn't *in love* with. I'd stayed with him for over six years and had ignored the fact that there was a serious problem in our marriage. Jack had never laid a finger on me, but his emotional abuse had finally gotten so bad, I knew I had to leave.

When I'd found him with another woman, I'd filed for divorce so fast, no one saw it coming except for Jack. He'd known I was unhappy. Hell, *he* had been unhappy too. But when I'd filed for divorce late last summer and moved back in with my parents, Jack had suddenly seemed more angry than anything else. He'd harassed me nonstop, until I'd finally taken out a restraining order against him. After my father had his heart attack, the last thing I wanted was for Jack to cause more issues in our family.

As soon as the divorce was final, Jack had taken off for France, where his father had another business.

Once I'd left him, everyone I knew told me their true feelings about him, and they all asked me over and over why I'd stayed with

Jack for as long as I had. Stupidity. Fear of failure. A deep worry that I wouldn't be able to make it on my own. But they were all silly reasons I'd talked myself into believing, keeping me in a loveless marriage way longer than I should have been.

Now my divorce was final, and I had been granted the house. Though I didn't want it, to be honest. Jack had never made a fuss about giving me the house. He'd actually freely handed it over to me. The judge had also ordered him to sell his half of my boutique, Coastal Chic, to me and only me. But so far the asshat had either been ignoring my lawyer's emails and calls, or he was dead.

There was no way I could be so lucky that it was the latter.

I know. I know. It was a terrible thing to think, but…it was also the truth.

"Do you want me to help you make a list of things that need fixing?" Harlee asked.

Glancing around the bare house, I shook my head. I had gotten rid of every single piece of furniture. Every painting that Jack had bought and hung up. Every ugly-ass curtain he'd demanded we buy. All of it was gone. The entire house was empty, and I was starting over from scratch. I didn't want a single reminder of him in this place.

Jack took what he wanted, and the rest I'd had hauled away and donated to charity. Right down to the godawful ugly gold silverware he'd insisted we put on our wedding registry.

I turned to my best friend, Harlee Tilson. I wasn't sure what I would have done the last few years without her or my two sisters, Palmer and Addie.

With another quick look at the empty walls, I asked, "How about we go get some paint and get rid of this awful beige? This place needs more color."

Harlee's eyes lit up. I hated to paint, but Harlee lived for it. I was also positive I could talk my sister Palmer into helping by simply offering her free food and beer.

"That sounds like a lot more fun," Harlee said.

I laughed as I grabbed my purse, and we headed out the door to the hardware store.

"You know, if you stare at that wall long enough, you might be able to make it move with your mind."

My entire body tingled at the sound of Brody's voice. I forced myself to put on a small smile and looked at him over my shoulder. He was standing there with a basket in his hands and that damn crooked grin of his. Every time I saw Brody, he got more and more handsome. I was honestly surprised he was still single. Of course, he was only thirty-two and, according to our local gossip column, not in a rush to settle down anytime soon.

"I'm trying to figure out what I need to fix a light switch." I gestured to the hardware shop's plethora of light-switch options.

He raised a brow. "At the shop?"

"No," I said, turning to face him full on. "The house. I moved back in, now that the divorce is final."

Brody gave me a small nod. "I can, um, stop by and take a look at it if you want?"

I chewed on my lip as I thought about whether that would be a mistake or not. It had taken me several years, but I'd finally gotten over my anger from the night I'd given him my virginity. Since Brody had returned to Seaside after being discharged from the Navy, we'd both silently ignored what had happened between us.

We were still friends...and that bugged the shit out of Jack. I'd never told him who I'd given my virginity to, but I had a strong feeling he'd always suspected it was Brody. He'd never asked, and I'd never offered up the information. It was another wall between us in our marriage.

I sighed and shook my head. "I'm going to see about hiring a handyman. There's a pretty long list of problems that I need to have fixed."

Brody took a step closer. "Don't do that. Let me swing by and take a look at the switch."

With a reluctant nod, I glanced over his shoulder to see Harlee walking up. "Hey, did you order the paint?"

She smiled at Brody. "Hey, Brody, how are you?"

He returned her grin. "Hi, Harlee. I'm doing well. You?"

"I'm good. Excited I get to help Sutton paint her entire house!" She looked over at me. "And to answer you, yes. Paint is being mixed now."

Brody focused back on me. "Painting the house, huh? Do you guys need help?"

With a shake of my head, I replied, "No."

At the same moment, Harlee gave an excited, "Yes!"

Brody raised his brows. "I don't mind helping."

I smiled. "Having you look at the light switch is a great help already."

Harlee huffed. "Oh man, there is *so much* to do in that house. Jackass left it a mess."

Laughing, Brody reached behind me and plucked something off the wall I'd been staring at. "When's a good time for me to stop by?"

"Um. Well, anytime that's good for *you*," I said. "I close the store at four during the off season, so anytime you want. Or whenever you're free, I mean."

"I'm off today. Why don't I meet you there and take a look at things... unless you need to get back to Coastal Chic?"

Before I could utter a word, Harlee spoke up. "Sutton closed the store for a few days. We can totally meet you at the house in, like, maybe thirty minutes?"

I stared at my best friend with an open mouth. When I realized Brody was waiting for me to agree, I cleared my throat. "Yeah, sure. That works. Give us about thirty minutes to pick up the paint and some other supplies."

He winked, and I suddenly became hyperaware of my entire body, including the way my nipples tightened and my stomach fluttered.

"Sounds good," he said. "See you ladies then."

My heart hammered in my chest as I watched him turn and head back down the aisle.

Without even knowing what she'd done, Harlee turned to face me. "This is awesome! Maybe Brody knows someone who can help get some of the bigger issues fixed. And if he can help paint, we'll knock it out even faster."

I didn't pull my eyes off his retreating back as I replied, "I'm sure he has more important things to do than help us."

Harlee laughed and began heading down the aisle. "Are you saying our project house won't be fun?"

It was my turn to laugh. "Project house? That's one way of describing it, and no, I don't think this is going to be fun. If I was smarter, I'd put it on the market and sell it."

Harlee grabbed my arm and pulled me to a stop. "I thought you loved that house."

I shrugged. "Once upon a time, I did."

I saw pity in her eyes. "I'm sorry, Sutton."

"I'm not. The only thing I'm sorry about is the years I wasted on Jack. It's time to move on—and that's exactly what we're going to do. Come on, let's go get that paint."

Doing a little happy dance, Harlee started for the paint counter, an extra pep in her step. I glanced around the hardware store and paused when I saw Brody near the front, checking out. He was laughing at something the cashier said. Then he looked over at me and our eyes met. It was only for a fleeting moment...but I found myself replaying it over and over in my head as Harlee and I headed back to my house.

Brody walked through the entire house, adding to my list of all the things that needed fixing. As I stared at one of the wires in a light switch that had obviously been cut, it was all too clear that my ex had done a good portion of this to cause me heartache.

I hope you choke on water, you asshole.

Brody frowned and looked over at me. "Sutton, it's going to cost you a fortune to hire someone to do all of these repairs. Let me do it."

I shook my head. "I'm not going to let you do all of this for free."

He exhaled, rolling his eyes. "Fine. Then you can pay me in home-cooked dinners."

I folded my arms over my chest. There was no way I was going to allow Brody to do all that work for a few meals. And the last thing I wanted was to be indebted to anyone. "Home-cooked dinners?"

"Yeah."

"How about I pay you twenty bucks an hour, and I throw in a home-cooked meal every now and then? That's all I can afford right now."

Brody's brows furrowed slightly before he relaxed his features. "We'll work it all out. I'm going to head back to the hardware store and pick up a few things while you ladies start painting."

"I'll go for you!" Palmer shouted as she looked up at us from where she was perched on the floor. She was cutting in around the baseboards with white paint and had more paint on *her* than she did on the wall.

Brody laughed. "I take it you're not a fan of painting?"

Palmer stood, shook her head, and handed Brody the paint brush. "I used to love it. Now it's too damn tedious. I'll trade you. You give me the list, and I'll get everything for you."

He reached into his back pocket for his wallet.

"No, you're not paying for it, Brody," I said, pushing his arm down.

"Let me buy some of this stuff up front." He pulled out an American Express card. "You can pay me back later."

I started to argue, but Palmer had already taken the card from Brody's hand. "Let him pay for it, Sutton. He makes a lot more money than you do. You're barely breaking even at the store."

My face, neck, and ears felt entirely too hot. I shot my sister a dirty look. What she said about the store was true, but I didn't want Brody to know that.

Brody chuckled. "I always thought you were the smartest, Palmer."

She gave him a wink. "You always did call 'em like you see 'em."

I rolled my eyes. "Go to the store, and get back here. You're not getting out of painting."

Chapter Three

Brody
Two Weeks Later

Newsflash—I wanted to kick in Jack Larson's face with steel-toed boots.

I'd never liked the guy. Hated that he'd convinced Sutton to marry him, and couldn't stand the idea that he'd had something I'd wanted for as long as I could remember. If that wasn't enough reason to hate the guy, the fact that he'd purposely caused a lot of the issues in Sutton's house made me want to hurt him even more. I'd lost count of how many times I'd cursed his name over the past two weeks.

I looked up at the newly installed ceiling fan and light, then smiled when I flipped the switch and it turned on.

"It looks beautiful, Brody!"

I turned to see Sutton walking into her bedroom. She was covered in light blue paint, and it took everything I had not to laugh.

"You're the one who picked it out," I said.

She smiled as she looked up at the new fixture. "It looks good in here, though, doesn't it?"

I nodded and slipped my hands into my jean pockets. "It looks great. I also like the color of the walls."

Sutton glanced around the empty bedroom with satisfaction. She had painted the walls a soft gray. "Thanks. I ordered white furniture, so hopefully it will look good together. I figured I'd better at least buy a bed to sleep on."

Her entire house was empty. And when I say empty, I mean completely void of *anything*. She had sold or donated every single thing Jack had left behind.

"What about the living room and the kitchen?"

She shrugged. "When I can afford it, I'll buy stuff piece by piece. My mom's going to give me her dining room table, so that will help. She's getting a new one."

All I could do was nod. It killed me that I had money sitting in the bank and could buy Sutton whatever she wanted, filling this house without even blinking. Years of being a bachelor, of living on base or stationed on a ship and then staying at my folks' beach house, had allowed me to put most of my money away. I'd invested a lot of it and had ended up purchasing the beach house from my parents for next to nothing. Perks of buying from family. Now I made good money and had few bills to pay.

"It's a pretty big house to furnish, so I'm sure it'll take time," I said, looking around the room.

She smiled softly, but it didn't quite reach those beautiful green eyes of hers.

Sutton and Dickhead had bought this house only a couple of years ago. It was a four-bedroom, three-bath colonial. It had a ton of character with beautiful hardwood floors and a kitchen that would make any chef's panties melt.

"I really like the yellow you painted for the downstairs," I said. "It's cheery."

Her eyes lit up and the corners of her mouth rose. "It is, isn't it? It makes me happy, and Lord knows I was never happy in this..." She let her words fade away when she realized what she was about to say.

My chest felt tight as the guilt hit me once again. Sutton hadn't been happy with Jack. Everyone saw it, myself included. I *hated* that I was the reason she'd most likely ended up with him. Because of one stupid decision when I was simply too afraid to admit my own feelings. Instead of being honest with Sutton, I'd pushed her away—and straight back into Jack's arms.

"I know tomorrow is Sunday and all," she said, "but I was going to attempt to hang up some beadboard in a couple of the bathrooms. You wouldn't be available to help, would you? I'll pay you. Harlee and Palmer are both busy. I'd ask Brax, but you know my brother, he's almost always out with a charter."

The tightness in my chest faded a bit. "I'd love to help, and no, you're not paying me. You could buy pizza and have some beer on hand, though."

The smile that always melted my heart appeared on her beautiful face. "Pizza and beer, it is."

I'd never laughed so much in my entire life as I did watching Sutton try to hang up wallpaper.

When the large piece she was attempting to hang fell back and covered nearly her entire body, I had to step in. "Maybe wallpaper hanging isn't your thing, Sutton."

She blew a piece of hair out of her eyes and sat down on the floor of the laundry room. "This is for the birds. The beadboard last week was so much easier."

"Do you really want this wallpaper up?" I asked, trying to smooth it back onto the wall.

Exhaling, Sutton stood and placed her hands on her hips as she studied the laundry room. "Actually, I think a nice coat of seafoam green would look beautiful in here."

I bit the inside of my cheek to keep from laughing and turned in a circle. When the paper I'd just hung fell halfway off the wall, I replied, "I agree."

We both laughed as Sutton pulled the paper off and crumpled it up.

"How about you shower to get all that glue off of you, and I'll go grab us some lunch," I said. "Then we can head to the hardware store."

With a little smile, she nodded. "Chinese?"

Over the last few weeks, we'd shared countless meals, either cooking together at Sutton's or ordering takeout. A few times, we'd eaten at her parents' restaurant. "That sounds good. Text me what you want."

As I started to head out of the laundry room, Sutton reached for my arm, bringing me to a halt. "Brody?"

"Yeah?" I turned and looked into those gorgeous eyes that had captured my heart so many years ago.

She chewed on her lower lip for a moment before she spoke. "Thank you for all your help. I really appreciate it."

"It's my pleasure."

Dropping her hand, she headed toward the steps while I made my way to the back door. I'd been parking at the back of her house in the hopes that no one would notice how often my truck was there. So far, we'd managed to stay under the radar—which was crazy, since the local newspaper had a gossip column that seemed to know what everyone was doing in town at any given moment.

After stopping by my place to check on a few things, I swung downtown, picked up the Chinese food, and headed back to Sutton's. When I pulled up at her curb, I frowned when I saw a BMW parked out front. I parked behind the house and then made my way in through the back door.

I should have knocked before I walked in. It was a dick move not to. But curiosity won out over politeness. Or maybe part of me feared it was Jack who'd stopped by unexpectedly.

"What do we do now?" I heard Sutton ask.

"We alert the court that he still hasn't reached out to you about buying his share of the store. Since the judge ordered it, he legally has to."

"Isn't there a time limit on it?"

I peeked around the corner to see Sutton's divorce lawyer, Ted Johnson, sitting at the table Sutton's parents had dropped off yesterday.

"There is. Or was. He's already surpassed it. He keeps having his lawyer file extensions since he's working out of the country."

"Why should that matter?" Sutton asked.

"Well, he *does* need to be here to sign the paperwork at closing."

"Can't we do DocuSign or something like that?"

Ted shook his head. "I'm afraid not. We need him to come back to town."

"That's the *last* thing I need."

I'd been standing in the back hallway, so I took a few silent steps backward so I could open and shut the door loudly. Then I proceeded to casually walk into the kitchen. Sutton and Ted both looked up.

"Brody, it's good to see you," Ted said.

I set the food down and reached out to shake his hand. "Ted, how are you doing?"

He smiled. "Can't complain."

When Ted glanced between the two of us, Sutton quickly jumped in with an explanation for why I was there. "Brody's been kind enough to help me with some things around the house that need fixing."

Ted nodded. "That's nice of you, Brody." Then he said to Sutton, "I'm sure that's helping keep costs down, since you need to keep that money untouched in your bank account."

"What money?" I asked without thinking.

Ted cleared his throat and looked at Sutton with an expression that said he was sorry for letting it slip.

She turned to me. "Um, part of the divorce settlement is that Jack has to let me buy him out of his half of the store. We worked out an amount, and my mom and dad helped me come up with part of the money. I had to have it in my account before the divorce was final. It's pretty much all the savings I have left, plus what my parents helped with."

Anger boiled up inside of me. Instead of signing over his half, like a decent man would do, the dickhead was literally taking all of Sutton's money and then some.

"When is it happening?" I asked, even though I knew the answer.

Sutton shrugged. "We've been running into some issues."

"He won't come back to Seaside for us to close on the sale," Ted explained.

I frowned. "Sounds like Jack."

Ted started to gather up his things. "Remember, if he does come back, Sutton, you still have the restraining order in place. He needs to communicate with *me*, not you."

She nodded, and I felt my stomach lurch at the words "restraining order." It had clearly gotten so bad that she didn't want her ex anywhere near her.

Sutton walked Ted through the house, and I trailed behind them.

Before leaving, Ted raised his hand toward me. "See you around, Brody."

"Yeah, good seeing you, Ted."

Sutton said her goodbyes, shut the door, and turned to me with a fake smile on her face. "I'm starving."

She started for the kitchen, and I gently reached for her hand and brought her to a stop. "Restraining order?"

Her cheeks turned bright red.

"Did that bastard hit you, Sutton?"

"No," she said quickly. "But...he was verbally abusive, and let's say he changed toward the end of our marriage—especially after I found out about his affair. He started to threaten me, and...he made some comments that scared me."

I balled my free hand into a fist. "What kind of comments?"

"It doesn't really matter, Brody."

She tried to walk off, but I stepped in front of her. "It matters to *me*, Sutton. What did he say to you?"

With a one-shoulder shrug, she attempted to downplay it. "He said I was making a mistake, that he'd make me regret leaving him. Then he accused *me* of having an affair."

Laughing, I asked, "With who?"

When she wouldn't meet my gaze, I knew the answer. My stomach felt sick, and I had to force down the bile at the back of my throat. "Me?"

She looked up and nodded. "He was always jealous of you, and he used to accuse me of..."

"Of what?"

With a quick shake of her head, she let out a bitter laugh. "It really doesn't matter. It's over, and I just need him to sell me his half of the boutique so I can be done with him for good."

I let her go by me as she walked back toward the kitchen. I pushed a hand through my hair and cursed under my breath. *This is all my fault.*

What in the *hell* had Sutton gone through because I'd been too scared to admit my feelings?

Chapter Four

Sutton
June

"What is it with you and lights?"

Excitement filled my chest at the sound of Brody's voice. I looked down from the ladder I was standing on and laughed. "I can't figure out why this light stopped working."

He winked. "Good thing I'm here. And I brought food."

My pulse picked up some as I continued to stare at him. Why was his wink so freaking sexy?

"You brought me lunch?" I asked, finally climbing down the ladder.

"I did, indeed. I ran into Palmer at Seaside Grill, and she said she'd left your shop to grab lunch for you guys. Then she got a call from the vet's office, asking if she could come in and cover for Judy at the front desk since she's not feeling well. So, I offered to bring you lunch."

He handed me a brown bag, and I took it from him with a smile. "Thank you so much, Brody. It was sweet of you to bring it by."

"No problem."

I walked over to the counter and opened the bag to find a turkey and swiss on rye with a bag of chips and a small piece of pie. The sight made my stomach growl.

"Where's your breaker box?" Brody asked.

"It's in my office, right behind my desk."

He nodded and headed that way as I dug into my lunch. A short while later, Brody walked back out into the store. He glanced around the place, and I wondered what he thought of it.

Whenever I looked at my little boutique, I was filled with a sense of satisfaction. I'd worked so hard to open this shop, and it was my pride and joy. My favorite part of the store was the front window display. I'd decorated it with an old dresser that Palmer had painted white and distressed. Each drawer was open, holding different items. Next to the dresser was a display of hats. I *loved* hats. All different kinds of hats. Next to those, I'd placed a beautiful piece of artwork that a local artist had made.

When you first walked into the store, the check-out counter was on the left wall. I used different pieces of vintage furniture throughout to display clothes and other items for sale. I had a beautiful baby blue armoire where I displayed scarfs and other accessories. I'd picked up the large vintage table where I displayed sale items at an estate sale not that long ago. To me, it was boring to walk into a store and see the usual racks of clothes.

A large, beautiful white rug sat in the middle of the store and added a touch of warmth. On the wall opposite the check-out counter were two dressing rooms. Toward the back were a few steps that led to a small seating area and more storage. There was also a cute little loft that I wanted to do something fun with at some point. I hadn't had any great ideas for it yet, which was a good thing because my budget was stretched thin these days.

Finally, there was a large stockroom, my office, and a full bathroom. The theme throughout was coastal chic, hence the name of the shop.

Brody's voice broke through my thoughts. "Looks like the fuse blew. I can swing by and pick up a new one. Your toilet is running as well."

"Yeah, I've got that on my list of things to fix."

"I'll pick up a new float. I tried adjusting it, but I think it's best to replace it."

I wiped my mouth and placed the napkin back in the cardboard box that contained the other half of my sandwich. "I feel like I'm totally taking advantage of you...but can we add something else to your list?"

He laughed. "What else do you need?"

"Well, there's a plug in my office that's never worked."

He nodded and pulled out his phone to start making notes. "I'm going to head to the store. If you think of anything else, text me."

I followed him to the door. "You may have opened Pandora's box. There are too many little things around here that need to be repaired."

Brody stopped, turning to face me. "Did that asshat you married ever do *anything*?"

I looked over my shoulder at the store. "No. He never really wanted anything to do with Coastal Chic," I said before focusing back on Brody. "He said it was my *little pet project.*"

His brows shot up. "Pet project? What the fuck was wrong with that guy?"

Laughing, I replied, "Everything."

With a shake of his head, Brody continued out the door. I watched him walk to his truck and climb in. I pressed my hand to my stomach, drawing in a deep breath to settle the flutters there.

"He's a friend who's helping me out. It doesn't mean anything," I told myself.

It was the mantra I'd been repeating for the last couple of months. Brody had helped me with the house so much, fixing countless things. He's painted, installed new floors, helped when furniture was delivered. And all the while, I'd been fighting the same attraction that had been there for as long as I could remember.

I smiled as I thought about how he'd even helped me stencil a saying along the top wall of my dining room. He'd been spending nearly every weeknight evening at my house, and some Saturdays as well. I was starting to get used to him being there—and that was something I had to put a stop to. I didn't need Brody coming to my rescue every time something went wrong. And if I missed another

Saturday lunch with Harlee and my sister, they'd start asking questions. That was the last thing I wanted.

Once he drove off, I turned and headed back to my lunch. I stared at my sandwich and mumbled, "You may not need him, Sutton. But you certainly want him."

The bell above the door rang, and I quickly turned around. I let out an anxious breath when a customer walked in.

"Hi! Welcome to Coastal Chic," I said, putting my lunch under the counter. Two more women walked in, and as I helped my customers select outfits for an upcoming boat party, I forgot all about Brody.

At least for now.

Two months later - August

I stood in my office, took a deep breath, and then exhaled. Life had been going great lately, so I should have known something bad would happen.

My older sister Addie had moved back to Seaside from Boston. She and Gannon were officially back together. My parents were over the moon, and my father was doing amazingly well. His heart attack earlier this year had really scared all of us and was one of the main reasons Addie had come back home. Well, that and the fact that Gannon was out of the Navy and had been home for a couple of years. Their story was a romance novel in the making. After all these years, fate had brought the two of them back together.

Soul mates.

I closed my eyes and cursed inwardly. Yep. Everything had been going far too well.

Fuck. Fuck. Fuck.

Now Jack was back in town.

On the surface, it was another good thing. It meant he could finally sell me his half of the boutique. But it was also bad. Knowing he was here made my skin crawl.

A light knock at the office door pulled me from my thoughts. I spun around and saw Harlee standing there.

"Hey, are you okay?"

I forced my voice to stay calm. "Yeah, just trying to figure out how to get things organized."

"Are you really going to turn the back room into a...fun house?"

Laughing, I leaned back against my desk and folded my arms across my chest. I'd had lunch with Harlee and my sister Addie earlier, and Harlee had suggested I carry—of all things—dildos in my shop. Coming from her, it was funny as hell—and brilliant.

If the gossip column ever got wind of the naughty side of Harlee, the anonymous writer would be all over it. At the moment, they were focused on Addie and Gannon. Which was fine by me. When Jack and I were going through our divorce, we were the subjects of that column one too many times. It came out every Thursday, and even though people pretended not to care, everyone rushed to read it.

The last time I was mentioned, post-divorce, the writer had called me out for selling "old lady clothes." I'd been angry and hurt at first...and then realized they were spot on. For years, I'd been so afraid of what Jack would say if I carried anything too sexy that I'd played it *way* too safe.

As soon as the divorce was final, I'd gotten in touch with a friend from college who was now a big fashion designer in New York. Together, we'd designed some new items for me to exclusively carry in the shop. They were mostly summer-chic outfits, but we'd played around with a few pieces of lingerie as well. I hadn't really thought much about carrying a larger selection...until the conversation at lunch today.

"I think your idea of carrying sexier clothes, as well as toys, is a good one," I said to Harlee.

Her eyes lit up. "Oh my God! You're really going to do it?"

I laughed again. "I think so."

Harlee pulled me away from the desk and hugged me. "I think that's *amazing*, Sutton! And it'll be good for you to get in touch with that inner goddess we all know is hiding in there."

"Are you quoting the gossip column?"

She laughed. "I guess I am. But at lunch, I was being serious when I mentioned working here part time to help out. I'd really love it."

I raised my brows. "Are you sure you want to sell sex toys? After all, you're the unofficial Princess of Seaside."

Harlee rolled her eyes. "I'm not sure who put me up on that pedestal."

Reaching for her hand, I gave it a squeeze. "You deserve the recognition. You do so much for this town, Harlee."

She smiled sweetly. "Thanks, Sutton. Moving on...let's take a look at the back room and make a game plan."

"Sounds good."

After measuring the space and drawing out different layouts, Harlee and I finally came up with a configuration for the new sexy area of Coastal Chic. I was planning on incorporating pieces of white furniture with one round display in the middle.

"Okay, so...the toys. Do we put samples on display?" I asked, studying the back room.

Harlee glanced around. "I mean, wouldn't you want to pick one up and hold it? Check out the vibration level and all that?"

I closed my eyes. "I can't believe I'm really going to sell vibrators in my boutique." My eyes snapped back open. "Wait—you *touch* them before buying them?"

Harlee slowly tilted her head and asked, "Have you ever used a vibrator, Sutton?"

I laughed. "God, no. If Jack found out I'd used one, he would have been pissed. He was more of an it's-all-about-me kind of guy."

She rolled her eyes. "I hate that man so much."

"Join the club."

"Anyway, I think we should keep the toys in a more private space. I mean, the sexier clothes and lingerie will be in here, but what if we..."

She trailed off in thought—then we simultaneously looked toward the loft area tucked beneath the roof. It was a storage space now but could easily be turned into a spot for the toys.

"Are you thinking what I'm thinking?" I asked as we looked at each other.

"The pleasure loft of Coastal Chic."

We both fell into a fit of laughter. The kind of laughter that makes you cry and gasp for breath.

"I'm totally going to call it that from this point on," Harlee said, letting out a long sigh.

I wiped away my tears and drew in a few deep breaths.

"So—what's going on between you and Brody?" she asked.

And just like that, my smile disappeared. I stared at her. The change of subject was so sudden, I wasn't even sure I'd heard her correctly. "I'm sorry?"

She rolled her eyes. "Sutton, you should have seen how embarrassed you were when Brody walked up to our table today while we were talking about vibrators."

I was positive my eyes were as wide as saucers. "You were talking about *dildos*, Harlee! You asked him what he thought of sex toys."

She waggled her brows. "Did you see the way he looked right at you when he said they were fun to use on partners? Oh, I have an idea! Why don't you ask Brody to help you test them out?"

My mouth fell open. "I told you at lunch that Brody and I are only friends, Harlee."

Before she could say another word, the bell above the door alerted us to a customer.

"Oh! Let me go test out my sales clerk skills," she said.

Thankful that I had literally been saved by the bell, I stepped toward the short hallway and motioned for Harlee to head out to help the customer. I turned back toward the back room—and came to an abrupt halt. "Brody!"

He flashed me his innocently boyish smile. "Am I interrupting something?"

I slowly shook my head. "Nope. Nothing. Harlee's going to be working here part time. I'm, uh, I'm going to be, uh...changing up the use of this back room."

The way he was looking at me made my entire body shiver. "And what are you going to be doing with it?"

I felt my cheeks flame. "I'll be carrying a special line of...um... lingerie. Some that I helped design with a friend of mine from college."

His brows shot up. "You designed lingerie?"

"Well, I *helped*. She did most of the designing. We also did some super cute summer outfits. And, um, well, Harlee and I were thinking that the upstairs loft might make a good spot for the, um..." My voice trailed off.

"For the what?" he asked with a smirk.

"Ahh..." I glanced up and stared at the loft space. The image of Brody using a vibrator on me immediately popped into my head, and I licked my suddenly dry lips.

He smiled, still staring at me. "Where you'll be carrying the orgasmatrons?"

I brought my hands up to cover my face and groaned. "I can't believe she said all of that in the middle of my parents' restaurant!"

Warm fingers touched mine as Brody pulled my hands away from my face. He placed a finger on my chin and lifted it until our eyes met. "You don't have to be embarrassed to talk about things like that, Sutton. Not with me."

The way his voice sounded, all deep and husky, nearly had me offering to be his test subject for every vibrator I could find. I blinked a few times, then cleared my throat. "Yes, well...Harlee and Addie seem to think it would be a great idea to carry vibra—um...personal pleasure...toys."

Oh, dear God, this was humiliating.

He dropped his hand to his side. "Do you like them?" he asked in that same seductive voice, sending chills up and down my spine and giving me that wonderful visual again.

I opened my mouth, then snapped it shut.

"Sutton?" Harlee called out before walking into the room. "Oh— hey, Brody. What are you doing here?" she asked, shooting me a sideways look.

"Just stopped by to make sure everything was okay and that Sutton didn't need help with anything."

Harlee stepped closer to me, smiling coyly. "Do you? Need help with anything, Sutton?"

If looks could kill, Harlee would be dead at my feet. "Nope!" I said in a fake cheerful voice. "Everything is great. Fine. Perfect! No issues."

"A customer is asking about a piece of art you have hung up."

Smiling, I replied, "I'll be right there."

She looked between us once more before turning on her heels and heading back out to the front.

"Do you need anything built for your space upstairs?" Brody asked.

I chewed nervously on my lip. "I think so. Probably. I'm not sure yet, since I don't... I'll need to talk to Harlee about it. It was her idea."

Brody chuckled. "It's a *great* idea."

I crinkled my nose and watched as his expression softened. "You think so? You don't think I'll be judged for carrying them, do you?"

"Who gives a fuck what you sell? It's your store, and you can carry anything you want." He looked thoughtful. "Maybe to test the waters, you should have a little party up there."

"A party?"

He nodded. "Yeah. I've heard women have those types of parties. But keep it on the down low, or the gossip column will have something new to write about."

I placed my hands over my heated cheeks and groaned. "God, no."

We both laughed, and an awkward silence settled between us. "Well, I'd better go help Harlee with the customer," I said.

He nodded. "I'll head on up to the loft. Send Harlee up when she's done. She can tell me her ideas, if she has any."

"Brody, I don't expect you to—"

He pressed his finger to my mouth to silence me, then adjusted his hand so he could run his thumb over my lower lip. My knees wobbled, and I nearly reached out and held on to him before my legs went out from under me. "I know, Sutton. I *want* to help you. Plus, it gives me an excuse to be here."

What did that mean?

With a nod, I rushed out of the back room and attempted to calm my racing heart, trying hard to push that conversation from my mind.

Chapter Five

Brody

"Did you get everything boarded up at Sutton's?" asked her dad, Keegan.

"Yeah. Brax and Gannon are going to Brax's place, and I wanted to stop by and see if you needed any help here at the restaurant." There was a hurricane coming, so that meant storm shutters on all the windows, and anything on the floor that could be damaged in a potential flood needed to be picked up and stored somewhere high.

Keegan glanced around the dark restaurant. With all the windows boarded up, it looked pretty gloomy. "We're good here. I'm heading home to work on the windows at the house."

"No need, Gannon and Brax boarded them all up this morning," I said.

"They did?" Barbara, Sutton's mom, asked as she stepped into the main dining area. "What about your parents' house, Brody? And your own?"

"We boarded up the beach house as soon as we found out about the storm, and we put the shutters up on Mom and Dad's house yesterday."

Barbara wrung her hands together. "I hate storms."

Keegan put his arm around his wife. "We all do. I just hope Gannon is safe out there."

I nodded. When my parents found out Gannon was working during the storm, I'd thought my mother was going to come undone. I couldn't imagine having two sons who both worked in jobs that weren't exactly on the top of the safety ladder.

Trying to ease Keegan and Barbara's mind, I said, "He'll be fine. It's not his first time in bad weather."

Barbara forced a smile, but it didn't reach her eyes.

"You'll be staying at your house with Brax and the girls?" I asked.

"Yes, but only with Braxton. Adelaide called earlier and said she, Palmer, and Sutton would be staying at Harlee's. I don't think they want her to be alone. I invited all of them to the house, but I think the girls want to have a bit of a slumber party. Maybe keep Adelaide's mind off of Gannon bringing in those ships out in the storm."

"That's a great idea, and the four of them will have fun together. I have no doubt they'll keep Addie's mind occupied," Barbara said.

Keegan huffed. "I'm going to worry sick about them. I wish the girls would come to the house."

Placing my hand on his shoulder, I gave it a slight squeeze. "They'll be fine, Keegan. Harlee's house is a good ten feet above sea level, and they're already saying the storm is weakening."

He nodded. "Thank you, Brody. And thank you for stopping by. You be sure to tell Gannon to be careful."

"I will. And no problem. If you're good here, I'll head on over to Braxton's place and help him and Gannon get ready."

Barbara gave me a hug. "Thank you, sweetheart. Go on and take care of what you need to. We're all good here at the restaurant."

"Backup generator ready in case we lose power?" I asked.

"Good to go," Keegan said with a smile.

The Seaside Grill was a staple in town. Keegan and Barbara had owned it for as long as I could remember. It was where we'd hung out in high school—and still did now. At least three days a week, I met Gannon and Braxton here for breakfast. The Bradley kids had all grown up working at the restaurant. Even my first job had been working here as a busboy.

Barbara and Keegan were like second parents to me. It had nothing to do with the fact that Addie was dating Gannon. Or that Braxton was my best friend. They had always treated me and Gannon as their own. As such, they'd always held a special place in my heart.

"Be sure to keep in touch, and let me know if you guys need anything, okay?" I said.

Keegan reached for my hand and gave it a shake. "Will do, son. Stay safe."

"Always do," I said before I turned and headed out of the restaurant and got in my car to make my way to Braxton's. It wouldn't take me long to get there, but he lived closer to the water, and I knew he had a lot to prepare at his place.

Ten minutes after leaving the restaurant, I pulled up at Braxton's house. It was a small, two-bedroom Nantucket-style cottage. The gray clapboard gave it that New England look. Of course, Braxton's sisters had had a hand in helping him decorate the house when he'd first moved in. The front of the house was landscaped with beautiful flowers. The small front porch held two white rockers and a small table. The inside of the house had white beadboard all throughout. I was also positive Braxton hadn't picked out a single piece of furniture, leaving it all up to Palmer and Sutton. And boy did they have fun spending their brother's money furnishing the house.

I lifted my hand to knock on the door, but it opened before I could. "Hey, did you bring beer?" Brax asked.

Laughing, I walked into his house. "No, was I supposed to?"

"Dude, you never come empty-handed. I thought that was an unspoken rule."

I rolled my eyes and started for the kitchen, where Gannon was sitting. The entire first floor was open so you could see everything. The small living area had white, beachy-type furniture. In between the living room and kitchen was a large wooden table with white chairs. The kitchen cabinets were all white with touches of blue to give the space a more masculine vibe.

"How much more do you guys have to do?" I asked.

"We need to board up the front of the house, and then we are good," Braxton said as he tossed me a beer. "My mom called and said you stopped by the restaurant. Thanks for doing that for me. I appreciate it."

"No problem. You know your mom and dad are like my second parents."

"You're not staying at the beach house, are you?" Gannon asked.

"No," I said with a shake of my head. "I'll be at Mom and Dad's."

"What about the fishing hut?"

"Taken care of," I replied before I took a sip of beer.

Braxton sighed. "I hate storms. That's the *only* thing I hate about living on the coast."

"What about your boats?" I asked.

"All secured. Hopefully the swells aren't too bad, but with the new floating docks they should be okay regardless. As long as they actually stay secured."

Silence filled the room as the three of us glanced at each other. I looked down at the beer in my hand and exhaled the breath I'd been unconsciously holding in.

"Gannon—" I started before he interrupted me.

"I'll be fine, Brody. This isn't my first time doing my job during a storm."

"Hurricane," Braxton interjected.

Gannon shot him a side-eye look. "A hurricane that will most likely be downgraded to a tropical storm."

"The swells will still be pretty bad. I want you to be extra careful," I said.

Braxton laughed. "Yeah, my sister will kill you if you end up dead."

Gannon shook his head. "I have no intentions of letting that happen. You on call tomorrow?"

Braxton nodded. "Yeah, for the next three days."

Braxton and I were both on the search-and-rescue team in Seaside. We all rotated shifts when there was a major storm coming in. If anything happened—like say, my brother slipped and fell off the ladder while boarding a cargo ship—then we would be called in along with the Coast Guard. The search-and-rescue team was created fifty years ago after a fishing boat started to take on water. The

Coast Guard was on another rescue and couldn't make it to them fast enough, so the pilots' association, along with a few others, put together this volunteer group. It was a pretty intense training program.

Gannon glanced at me, and I shook my head. "Not on call this time."

He simply nodded. "Well, I need to get to the station. You guys got this?"

Brax nodded. "We're golden here, dude. Head on out."

Gannon stood and grabbed a backpack he'd placed on the floor.

"Gannon," I said quickly as I stood. "Be careful."

He smiled and pulled me in for a hug and a pat on the back. "I'll be safe."

Braxton and I both watched my brother head toward the front door. Before he walked out, he looked back and waved his hand. "Don't get too drunk, Brax. Don't need you having a hangover tomorrow."

"That, I can promise you, will not happen."

Once the door shut, I turned back to Braxton. He lifted his brows and gave me a questioning look.

"What?" I asked with a soft laugh.

"Have you talked to Sutton yet?"

My smile faded. "I wish I never told you what happened."

He scoffed. "It wasn't hard to piece together, Brody. You and my sister disappeared off that beach, and you both came back looking like something happened between you. And then she locked herself in her room for days to cry, and you didn't come home for your whole allotted leave. I knew she wasn't crying over Jackass."

I sighed and pushed my hand through my hair. "We're friends, Brax. Things are good between us now. I'm not sure bringing up the past is a good idea."

"So you're going to ignore the fact that you're in love with my sister, and she loves you too?"

"She *loved*...past tense. She married Jack."

He scowled. "Because you broke her heart. Told her you didn't love her. I still want to beat your ass for that."

"Trust me, I've paid for it time and time again."

Brax lifted his beer to his mouth and took a drink. "Why don't you tell her how you feel, Brody? I see the way you two look at each other."

How could I explain it to Braxton when I had no idea how to explain it to myself? I could deny my feelings for Sutton all I wanted, but I knew deep down that I was still in love with her. She was the only one in my dreams, and in my heart, and had been for years.

"Dude, tell her you ran because you were scared."

I looked up at Brax. "What?"

"You don't think I know how you felt, Brody?"

My brows drew down in confusion. "Sounds like you're speaking from experience. Who?"

He looked away as he said, "It doesn't matter."

I stared at my best friend for a good minute before he spoke again.

"It's like you're silently fighting each other," Braxton said when he focused back on me. "She's free, Brody. You're here now. Why keep denying your feelings?"

Shaking my head, I exhaled. "You didn't see her face, Brax, when I told her I didn't love her. I...I took something special from her, and then I freaked. I purposely hurt her to push her away. It's unforgiveable."

"I think that's for her to decide. Just tell her everything, dude. She's either going to forgive you or she's not. Either way, you'll still be friends."

I swallowed the lump in my throat and stared down at the bottle of beer in my hand. "Will we? Because I pushed her away, she ended up marrying that asshole. He treated her like shit, Brax. He put her through hell, and it was my fault, because I was too scared to admit my feelings for her."

"You still are."

Standing, I walked into the living room. Brax followed. "What if..." My voice trailed off as I sat down on the sofa, put my beer on the coffee table, and scrubbed my hands down my face.

Brax looked at me thoughtfully. "When I was about to tell my father I wasn't interested in taking over the restaurant, I almost changed my mind."

"What do you mean?"

"I almost told him I'd do it. I was afraid to admit that taking over for him and Mom wasn't part of my life plan. I was afraid to tell him that I'd saved up enough money to buy my first fishing charter boat. I told my mom first. She was understanding. Then I asked how she thought Dad would take it. She said he'd be hurt, but he'd understand. So, I asked her if Dad would be angry with me for not following in his footsteps. And what if I was making a mistake. She laughed and said that if she ever heard me utter 'what if' like that again, she'd slap me."

I laughed.

He smiled and rubbed the back of his neck, caught up in the memory for a moment. "*What if* is a cop-out, Brody. You can 'what if' all you like, and it's not going to change anything. What if she doesn't love you? What if she never stopped loving you? What if she hadn't married Jack? What if you'd met someone else and fallen in love? Fuck the 'what ifs.' Follow your heart."

"Are you following yours?"

Closing his eyes, he drew in a slow breath and then let it out just as slowly. "I fucked up, and my chances are long gone. I don't want to see that happen to you, *especially* because I know she still loves you."

Finishing off my beer, I set it on the table once more. "We better get to work on those shutters before it gets too dark."

Braxton shook his head, finished off his own beer, and stood. "I'd like to tell you that you're a stupid asshat, but that would be the pot calling the kettle black."

Chapter Six

Sutton

I sat on the widow's walk of my parents' house and stared out over the bay. So much had happened in the last few weeks. A major storm. Gannon nearly dying from falling off the pilot boat. Jack showing up every time I turned around. It was enough to make me want to jump in my car and drive until I got to the Pacific Ocean.

"Hey, are you okay?"

Glancing over my shoulder, I smiled to see Palmer there. "Yeah. Just needed a place to clear my head."

She sat down next to me and handed me a beer. "Thought you might need this."

I noticed my hand shaking as I reached for it.

"Are you going to tell Mom and Dad that Jack stopped by the boutique?" she asked.

"No, and don't you tell them either. Mom has enough to worry about with the restaurant and Dad's health. I've got it under control. I'm pretty sure they know he's back in town anyway. It is Seaside, after all."

Palmer didn't say anything, and when I looked at her, she gave me a sympathetic smile. "Sutton, I know you never told anyone how bad it was with him, especially toward the end. But I don't think you should try to handle this alone. Jack was... he was unhinged. I saw it with my own eyes. He was livid that you filed for divorce, even after you caught him with another woman."

I brought the beer to my lips and took a long drink.

"What were you and Brody arguing about the other day when I walked into the storage room?" she asked.

My body stiffened. "Nothing."

"You're such a terrible liar."

Turning to face her, I drew in a deep breath. "What if *they* find out he's been coming to the shop and write about it?"

Palmer's brows drew in. "The gossip columnist?"

I nodded. "I mean, they've been so occupied with Gannon and Addie lately, but what if..."

"Don't 'what if,' Sutton. You know what Mom says about that. Besides, would it really be that bad? Who cares if they write that Jack is back in town? Maybe it'll light a fire under his ass to sell you his half of the shop."

Dropping my head back against the chair, I let out a frustrated groan. "You're right, I know you are. I feel so lost and confused."

She reached for my hand. "Talk to me, Sutton. Please. If you would open up, maybe I could help."

I wiped a tear away as I looked out over the water.

"Does this have anything to do with how you feel about Brody?"

A bitter laugh slipped free.

She nodded. "I'll take that as a yes."

It was time to change the subject. "Hey, didn't Addie go in for her job interview with the hot new doctor?"

Palmer grinned. "Way to change the subject. And yes. She texted that he offered her the job. Gannon is taking her out tonight to celebrate."

I smiled. "I'm so glad they found their way back to each other. They were meant to be."

She nodded. "Soul mates."

My heart dropped, and I fought to hold back tears. "Do you think we'll ever be that happy, Palmer?"

After taking a sip of beer, she thought about her answer for a few moments. "I sure hope so. I look at how Addie beams when she sees Gannon, or when anyone even mentions him. I want that so much... but sometimes I wonder if not all of us are lucky enough to get a love like that."

All I could do was nod. After a few moments of silence, I asked, "You believe in soul mates?"

My little sister grinned. "I do. I mean, look at Mom and Dad. Addie and Gannon. Maybe the journey for some simply has more tears and hurt than for others. I can't imagine all that heartbreak leads you to nothing." She let out a soft laugh. "Maybe they come into our lives when we least expect it."

"So you have hope that you'll find your soul mate some day?"

Her eyes met mine. "My head tells me not to have hope, but my heart is telling me he's on his way. I just hope his ass shows up soon."

I couldn't help but laugh.

"What about you?" she asked.

Shrugging, I said, "I used to. But it's hard to believe in love when you've given your heart to someone and they simply tossed it aside."

She took my hand in hers. "Jack wasn't your soul mate, Sutton."

"I wasn't talking about Jack."

Squeezing my hand, she said, "Do you know that song 'One More Try,' by George Michael?"

"Yeah, what about it?"

Palmer stood. "Maybe you should listen to it and give it one more try." Leaning down, she kissed the top of my head and then headed down the steps and into the house.

By the time I managed to make it back downstairs, my parents were home.

"Sutton, what are you doing here?" Mom asked as she walked over and pulled me into a hug.

"I missed the widow's walk."

Dad laughed. "You always did love it up there."

Mom gave me an assessing look. "Is everything okay?"

Nodding, I forced myself to smile. "Yes. Everything's perfect. Why are you two home so early?"

"You didn't get a text from Gannon?"

Confused, I said, "No. My phone has been in my purse down here."

A wide smile erupted on my mother's face. "Well, we knew it was coming, but Gannon is going to ask Adelaide to marry him tonight. He wants everyone to be there."

"Oh my gosh! That's amazing!" I said.

Dad grinned, and I could see the happiness all over his face. "I always did like that boy."

My mother laughed. "You're just glad he came and asked for her hand in marriage first."

I smiled. "Palmer said he was taking Addie out for dinner tonight to celebrate her new job."

"Yes, the doctor's office did hire her," my mother confirmed. "She was over-the-moon happy about it, and Gannon is using that as an excuse to take her out and propose."

"Yeah, I bet Addie's thrilled."

My mother took one look at me in my shorts and Def Leppard T-shirt and raised an eyebrow. "Sweetheart, you better get home and change if you want to be at the restaurant in time. Gannon wants everyone there before they arrive so we can watch the proposal."

I looked down at my outfit. "What time do I need to be there?"

"He plans on bringing her to Pete's Place by seven."

Glancing at my watch, I gasped. "I better get going."

A couple of hours later, I stood on the outside deck of Pete's Place and sipped on champagne as I listened to the sounds of the water in front of me and everyone celebrating Gannon and Addie's engagement behind me.

I shivered the second I felt Brody's presence. I didn't need to turn around to know it was him. I knew he was there.

"What a night," he said.

Smiling, I glanced over my shoulder. "It was beautiful. I'm so happy for them."

He stood next to me, and for a few moments, we simply enjoyed the silence. "Has Jack come by the store again since last time?" he finally asked.

I stiffened at the mention of my ex-husband. "No."

Brody's eyes met mine. "Have you told your lawyer that he broke the restraining order?"

Nodding, I took a sip of my drink.

"And?"

"And I really don't want to talk about this right now, Brody. Not on such a happy night."

He sighed. "Sutton, I think you need to tell—"

Turning, I interrupted him. "Not here, Brody. Not tonight. Please."

His facial expression softened. "I'm sorry. It's just...he makes me... I don't know what I'm trying to say. I don't want to see you hurt in any way."

I raised a brow. "That's a change for you."

Brody's brows pulled down into a frown. "Excuse me?"

With a one-shoulder shrug, I turned back to face the water and downed the rest of my drink, setting the glass on the railing. I wasn't sure why I'd said that. Maybe a part of me was jealous that my sister had found her prince and was riding off into the sunset. Maybe I was simply in the mood for a fight. Either way, it had been a crappy thing to say. Yet, I couldn't seem to stop myself.

"What do you mean by that, Sutton?" he repeated.

"You didn't seem to mind hurting me after you took my virginity."

"Took it? You make it sound calculated, when we both know it wasn't."

With a sideways glance, I let out a humorless laugh. "You said all the things you needed to say to get me to sleep with you."

Brody moved a bit closer to me and lowered his voice. "Funny, I remember you crawling onto my lap and asking me directly."

I opened my mouth to argue with him, but I knew he was right. Here I had thought I had gotten over the hurt of that night, but clearly I hadn't.

When I didn't say anything, a look of hurt crossed his face. "Is that what you think of me, Sutton? That I lied to you in order to fuck you?"

I flinched but steeled myself. "I don't know, Brody. You tell me. I opened my heart up to you that night, and you took hold of it and crushed it. You're the reason I took Jack back."

The pain on his face made me yearn to retract my words.

Brody closed his eyes and slowly shook his head before he looked at me. His face had softened, and there was something in his eyes that made my heart race. Was he tearing up? I instantly wanted to say I was sorry. That I hadn't meant any of it. I wasn't in a good place right now.

Brody reached for my hand and started to say something when my father's voice broke through the moment.

"What are you two whispering about over here?"

Brody dropped my hand, and we both took a step away from one another. Before I could say anything, Brody spoke first. "Bachelor and bachelorette parties. What else?"

My dad let out a laugh and gave Brody a slap on the back. "You're next, Brody. Any special girl you've got your eye on?"

Brody glanced at me before focusing back on my father. My breath hitched in my throat, and I knew in that moment I would stay up all night analyzing the look he'd given me.

"I think we need to concentrate on Gannon and Addie for now," he said.

Dad smiled. "I, for one, am glad to see them back together." He looked at me. "What about you, pumpkin?"

I forced myself to smile brightly and keep my voice even. "I am too. If anyone deserves happiness, it's Addie and Gannon."

"You deserve it as well. Especially after being married to such a..." My father let his words hang in the air.

"I'm not looking for love, Dad. I don't seem to have much luck with it."

From the corner of my eye, I saw Brody look down at his drink.

"I hate to break up the fun conversation of parties," he said, "but Brody, I'd like to talk to you about that project you'll be working on for Sam Nelson."

"The concrete dock support for the new section of pier?"

Dad nodded. "Yes."

Brody turned to look at me, clearly not wanting our conversation to end. I, however, did. "I'm going to go admire that ring again," I said. "Enjoy your talk, gentlemen."

It wasn't hard to miss the disappointment on Brody's face, but I ignored it and headed toward Addie.

Brody clearly wasn't finished though. He reached for my hand, pulling me to a stop. "How about I stop by later this evening so we can finish our conversation?"

If I said no, my father would become suspicious. If I said yes, I was opening up the door for old wounds to reappear. I did what I thought was the right thing...for now. Plastering on a fake-as-hell smile, I replied, "Sure, sounds good."

I kissed my father on the cheek and turned toward my older sister, ignoring the fact that my heart had dropped to my stomach. I wasn't sure I could deal with Brody tonight, especially alone at my house. My emotions were all over the place.

Once I reached Addie, I hugged her and we quickly got lost in conversation, the previous one with Brody pushed out of my mind.

That was, until I got home an hour later—and the doorbell rang five minutes after I walked through the door. Had he followed me home from the restaurant?

I marched to the door and started to talk before I opened it. "I don't want to talk to you, Br—" My heart dropped at the sight before me. "Jack?"

He sneered at me. "Why am I not surprised you were expecting him and not me."

I scowled. "Probably because I have a restraining order against you, and you shouldn't even be on my front steps."

I started to shut the door, but Jack put his hand out to stop it. "Sutton, this game is getting old. I thought the time apart would give you some clarity."

Laughing, I gave him a look of disbelief. "Clarity? Nothing is more clear to me, Jack. I do *not* love you. I *never* loved you. I want you out of my life, and I want my store back!"

He raised a single brow. "Let me in so we can talk like adults."

"You can talk to my lawyer, Jack. If you don't leave right now, I'm going to call the cops."

"Are you sure you want to do that? Maybe what *needs* to happen is a tip to the gossip hotline. You know...something about how you cheated on me during our marriage."

My eyes went wide, and for a moment I internally panicked—until I pulled my shit together. "You have us mixed up, Jack. You seem to forget I have *proof* of your cheating. Your threats no longer work on me, so you might as well stop trying."

His eyes moved slowly down my body, and I had to fight the urge to gag. How had I ever married this man? Let him touch me?

"Sutton, don't behave like a child. Let me in so we can talk. We still have a chance to make it work. Why do you think I've been stalling on selling you the store for so long?"

I scoffed. "Oh, let me see. You've been stalling because it's the only thing you have over me now, and you love that. But if I have to take you back to court, I will."

"Last time I checked, you barely have enough money in the bank to make ends meet."

I was about to threaten him that I would scream if he didn't leave when I heard another voice call out from behind Jack.

"If you don't remove your hand from her door, I'll remove it for you."

Brody. I exhaled with relief.

Jack dropped his hand and turned to face him.

"If you don't mind, Brody, we're trying to have a conversation right now. Run along and go play with your underwater toys."

Brody casually shoved his hands into his dress pants pockets and laughed. He started up the steps and moved past Jack, knocking his broad shoulder into my ex before he stepped into the house. Turning, he leaned against the doorjamb.

"You never were very bright, were you, Jack? As someone who works with numbers on a daily basis, I'd assume you could work out how well paid I am."

Jack scoffed. "Sure, you are, Wilson. What do you make a year? Sixty, if you're lucky?"

"Jack, it's time for you to leave," I said, pulling on Brody's arm to get him fully into the house.

"You are so fucking off, it's unreal. But all you really need to know is this: if Sutton wants to take you back to court, I'm in her corner—and my money is hers."

Jack took a step back. "What the fuck does that mean?" He snapped his eyes to me. "Are you marrying him?"

I swallowed hard but kept my mouth shut. If Jack thought I was going to marry Brody, he might finally leave me alone.

Jack's face was white, and I could see the anger in his eyes. "You *can't* marry him, Sutton. You and I are meant to be together!"

Brody pushed off the frame and took a step back into the house, reaching for the door and slamming it shut.

It only took two seconds for him to turn and catch me when my legs gave out.

"Hey, it's okay. He's gone," he said.

I shook my head as tears started streaming down my face. "He's never going to leave me alone. *Never.* I didn't have my phone on me, or I would have called 9-1-1. They said they can't do anything unless they catch him in the act of breaking the restraining order."

Brody lifted me up into his arms before walking over to the sofa. He sat down, cradling me on his lap, and for the first time in years, I let myself fall apart.

In the arms of the man I was head over heels in love with.

Chapter Seven

Brody

wanted to kill Jack Larson. And if Sutton wasn't currently breaking down, I might have gone after his ass the moment I saw her first tear fall.

"Shhh, don't let him get to you like this, Sutton."

Her body trembled as she sobbed in my arms. "I...I...I hate him so much!"

I pulled her closer and kissed the top of her head. I wasn't sure what to say. I was the reason she was crying. Yes, Jack was the literal reason, but if I had been open about my feelings for Sutton in the first place, she never would have allowed Jack back into her life.

After a few minutes, she drew back, wiped her eyes, and looked at me. When her gaze fell to my lips, I nearly pulled her to me and kissed her. But that was the last thing she needed right now. I gently moved her off my lap and set her on the sofa. "Do you want something to drink?"

I couldn't read her face as she shook her head. "I'm not really in the mood to hash out our past tonight, Brody. If you wouldn't mind leaving..."

I let out a dry laugh. "I am *not* leaving, knowing that he's showing up at your house now, Sutton. We don't have to talk. But I'm not leaving."

Her eyes widened. "You can't stay here."

"Why not?"

Sutton quickly stood. "I don't really want people to think we're... we're..."

"Sleeping together?"

She shot me a dirty look. "I was going to say dating. No, I'll be fine. I'm going to call my lawyer and let him know Jack showed up at my house. They'll send the police over to his house to warn him to stay away from me."

"And didn't they do that the last time he showed up at the store? Sutton, the guy has some weird delusion that you two are going to get back together. He isn't right in the head."

She threw up her hands before letting them fall back to her side. "I don't really know what to do about that, Brody! I keep telling him there's no future for us."

"Then take the option off the table."

She opened her mouth to say something, then immediately shut it. "How do you suggest I do that? I can't really have him killed. I do like my freedom and all."

I felt the lump in my throat and pushed through it. It wasn't the way I had dreamed of doing this, but I didn't see another choice. "Marry me, and he'll leave you alone."

Sutton stared at me for what felt like an eternity...before she started to laugh. "Marry you? Are you high on something, Brody?"

I tried not to show how much her words hurt. "No, I'm not high, Sutton. I...I care about you, and I don't like seeing him do this to you. If we got married, then he'd be forced to accept that the two of you aren't getting back together. He'll sell you his half of Coastal Chic, and then we...we can get divorced...I guess."

"Oh, nice. So then I'd be twice divorced by the age of thirty. Lucky me."

"An annulment, then."

She stared at me with a surprised look on her face before she said quietly, "Because that makes it better."

I ran my hand through my hair and sighed. "Sutton, I'm just...I don't like seeing him hurt you—and before you remind me, yes, I know I hurt you as well. I was confused and scared, and we were so young back then."

She narrowed her eyes at me, and for a moment I thought she was going to unleash hell on me. Instead, she dropped back down to the sofa.

"God, I feel so tired suddenly. I'm exhausted."

I took her hand in mine. "If you let me help you, we can get through this, Sutton."

She exhaled and dropped her head onto my shoulder. "I can't think right now, Brody. I'm going to bed."

When she didn't move, I asked, "Do you want me to carry you up to your bedroom?" She didn't answer after a minute. "Sutton?"

A small snore escaped her lips. With a sigh, I scooped her into my arms and carried her up the stairs.

"Brody?" Sutton whispered against my chest.

"Yeah?"

"Will you still stay tonight? Please? I...I don't want to be alone if he comes back."

My heart damn near burst out of my chest. I wasn't sure what had changed her mind, and I wasn't about to ask. I took the moment and ran with it. "I won't leave, sweetheart. I promise."

Once we got into her room, I put her down on her bed. "Do you need help with anything?" I asked.

"No. I'm going to close my eyes for a little bit."

Only a minute later, she was breathing deeply, fast asleep. I wasn't sure how long I stood there and watched my sleeping beauty before I turned and headed to the guest bedroom. I stripped out of my clothes and took a long hot shower before crawling into the bed. After staring up at the ceiling for what felt like forever, I finally drifted off to sleep.

The Seaside Chronicle

September 3, 2022

Tied in Knots (Special Edition)

Seasiders!

A seagull has informed me that Gannon Wilson and Adelaide Bradley are getting married at the end of October. Can we say warp-speed matrimony? Word on the docks is a baby shrimp might be sautéing away, and that's the reason for the rushed wedding, but we'd like to think that they're just so in love, they couldn't wait to make it official. Curious minds want to know, are you Team Shrimp Jr. or Team True Love?

It's also been brought to my attention that some changes are happening over at Coastal Chic; more on that when we get the bait pulled back in—with some info on it, hopefully.

Speaking of Coastal Chic, has any other fish noticed how often Brody Wilson has been seen going in and out of the boutique? One can only imagine why our front-runner in the Catch of the Season competition might be visiting the shop so much. According to Sutton, he's only helping with some repairs around the shop. But if the older Mr. Wilson is indeed on the hook, hearts will be broken all over Seaside. Don't worry, we'll be sure to keep you updated here in the column.

Fair winds and following seas!

"Fucking hell," I mumbled as I reread the gossip column. The last thing I wanted was for Sutton to be talked about in that stupid column again.

I'd stopped and had dinner at my parents' house and heard all about how livid Gannon was that the column hinted that Addie was pregnant. I swiped the paper before I left, and now *I* was pissed that they'd insinuated that something was going on between me and Sutton.

I leaned back and looked down at the paper on my passenger seat. Maybe it was actually a good thing. If Jack read the article, he might believe that Sutton and I were together and simply keeping it on the down low.

Sutton, meanwhile, hadn't brought up how I'd stayed at her house, nor had she given me another chance to talk to her about what had happened between us so many years ago. She'd been weaving and bobbing, avoiding me anytime I even attempted to talk to her. It was getting old.

Starting my truck, I put it in gear and headed to Sutton's store. I had the day off, and she'd sent me a text that Addie wanted to meet with both of us to talk about the bachelor and bachelorette parties.

When I got to Coastal Chic, it was closed. I walked around the back and used the key Sutton had given me to head inside. She and Addie were in her office, talking all things wedding.

"Am I interrupting anything?"

Both women turned and glanced over their shoulders when I stepped in.

"No. We were looking at the seating arrangements for the reception," Addie said as she went back to looking at the chart in front of her. It had a bunch of round tables drawn on a large piece of paper. "Anyone we should avoid putting together on your side of the family?"

Laughing, I replied, "Not that I'm aware of. Might want to ask Gannon, though. We do have a great-aunt my father isn't very fond of. Something about her drawing on him with makeup while he was asleep, and he went to school without realizing. My grandmother said it was a good lesson for him. He started washing his face every morning after that little stunt."

Sutton giggled as Addie folded the paper and put it in a large folder.

"I'll double-check with your dad," Addie said. "Now, down to business. I want to have a co-ed bachelor and bachelorette party."

I blinked several times. "I'm sorry, what?"

"She wants to combine the parties," Sutton clarified. "And not only the bachelor and bachelorette parties, but the shower as well. Addie wants them all to be one big party."

I slowly shook my head. "Why?"

"I asked her that too." Sutton wore a pinched expression as she leaned against her desk. "You're robbing us of properly sending you off into married life."

Addie rolled her eyes. "Seriously? I'm *robbing* you of that?"

Sutton and I both nodded.

"Too bad. This is what I want. We're too close to the wedding, and running around to all these different events is going to add stress. And, if I'm being honest, I don't trust Brax and Palmer to get it done."

"Good call on Brax," I mumbled.

Sutton grinned and then looked at her sister. "Addie, I think if you thought about it a little more, you'd change your mind."

She shook her head. "I'm not changing my mind. It's one party. Period."

"What if I want to throw my brother a separate bachelor party?" I asked.

Addie tilted her head and gave me the sweetest smile. "If either of you even think of throwing a bachelor or bachelorette party, I'll send in a tip to the gossip column that you're having an affair."

Sutton gasped. "Adelaide! You wouldn't!"

Addie turned to her sister. "You bet your sweet ass, I would. No other parties. It's one co-ed party, a week from today if Gannon has the date off. Brody, do you have access to his schedule?"

I pulled up the schedule. "Next Saturday should work. He's free."

Addie clapped her hands together. "Perfect. Then you two better get busy! You only have a week to plan this thing!"

"Addie...a week? Come on. It could take a week to get everyone's information. Not to mention, who do we even invite?" Sutton stated.

Addie pulled out a sheet of paper. "I did all that work for you. Everyone's names, addresses, and emails are listed here. I'd suggest sending an evite, though you may have to call one or two people."

Sutton snatched the paper from her sister's hands and scanned it. "Theme?" she asked, continuing to look over the list.

"Theme? We have to have a theme?" I asked.

"No theme. The simpler, the better," Addie said.

I blew out a breath. "Dodged that bullet."

Addie rolled her eyes and focused on her sister. "We can have it at the event center above The Maine Bakery. I already booked it."

"Man, Addie, what do you even need *us* for?" Sutton asked with a laugh.

Addie started gathering up her things. "To plan all the other stuff. Like food, decorations, things like that. I've got to run. Talk to you two soon!"

"I'll let you out the front," Sutton said as she followed her sister out of her office and through the shop.

A few minutes later, Sutton walked back into her office and sat at her desk. "So, should we start to plan this party now or do you need to be somewhere?"

I watched her ruffle papers on her desk to avoid looking at me. "Sutton, we need to talk."

"If it's not about the party or the back room, I don't think we have anything to talk about."

I was hit with an instant headache, and I rubbed my fingers against my temples. "Fine, if this is how you want to handle it, I'll play along. What do you need me to do for the party?"

She smiled and looked up at me. "I'll make a list of things we need to get done, and we can split the tasks. I'll do half, you do the other."

"Okay, sounds good."

I turned and headed out of her office, making my way to the back room that Sutton was converting into more retail space. I quickly got to work on my list of things to do, getting lost in the music coursing from my AirPods.

A short while later, I turned toward the hall to see Sutton standing in the doorway, watching me. I pulled out one of my earphones. "Did you need something?"

She wrapped her arms around herself—and a feeling of dread hit me right in the stomach. She was on the verge of crying.

"What's wrong, Sutton?"

When she didn't say anything, I quickly moved across the room. "What's wrong?" I asked again, bending down to look at her. She'd *already* been crying. I cupped her face in my hands and silently pleaded with her to open up to me.

"He took the money."

"What?" I asked, confused.

She sniffled. "He took the money out of my account. Out of the business account. He took it all out!"

Rage washed over me. "I'm going to fucking kill him!"

I went to move past Sutton, but she grabbed my arm to stop me. "Wait! Don't, Brody. It'll only make things worse. I already called my lawyer, and he said he'll get it taken care of, though it might take some time. I have to pay bills, and I...I...I don't know what to do!"

I ran a hand down my face to keep myself calm. It didn't work, so I dropped my hand and cursed. "Goddammit, Sutton. Why won't you let me help you? *Please* let me help you."

She swallowed hard, then handed me her phone. I took it, reading a text message she'd pulled up from Jack.

> **Jack: Sutton, why are you making me do things to hurt you? The sooner you realize we're meant to be together, the faster we can put all of this behind us. Stop fighting it. Agree to re-marry me, and I'll put the money back in the account.**

I wanted to crush the phone in my hand. "That son-of-a-bitch."

"He's not going to stop. And if my parents find out about this, my dad is going to... oh God." She buried her face in her hands and started to cry again.

Wrapping my arms around Sutton, I held her until she got her emotions under control. When she stepped back, I reluctantly let her go.

She wiped her tears away, squared her shoulders, and said, "Okay."

"Okay, what?"

"I think the only way to get him to realize things are over is by, um...moving on."

I nodded and pushed a loose lock of hair behind her ear. "I think so too."

She lifted her eyes to meet mine. "Are you sure about this, Brody? If you marry me, then...you're giving up—"

I cut her off. "I'm not giving up anything, Sutton. There's *nothing* I wouldn't do for you."

The corners of her mouth twitched with a soft smile. "I don't know how long we'll have to stay married."

"I don't care."

She cleared her throat and took another step back. "Can you meet me next Monday? We can go and get a marriage license. I don't want to do anything until after the party on Saturday, and I don't want anyone to find out we got married until after Gannon and Addie's wedding. The last thing I'd want to do is steal my own sister's thunder."

I nodded. "What about Jack? He could easily tell people."

She closed her eyes. "Let's try to keep it between us for as long as we can. I have a feeling Jack won't want to spread that news around. He's always looked at you as his competition."

"Okay. Do you want me to give you some money until you can work things out with the lawyer?"

Her eyes filled with tears once again, but she somehow managed to keep them at bay. "I paid the rent, so I'm okay for at least a month, but I do have a large order of...items...that I placed for the loft area. I'm sure my friend in New York will understand if I have to delay her payment on the lingerie, but the other things...I'll need to pay for them before they ship."

A smile spread across my face. "So what you're saying is, you need me to lend you money to buy some *special items* that you'll be stocking?"

Her cheeks turned bright red. "Yes."

I nodded. "Let me know what you need."

She closed her eyes and sighed. "Brody, it's frickin' lingerie and dildos. It feels so weird having you pay for them! I mean, if it was office supplies, that would be one thing. But knowing you're buying sex toys is...too much."

My dick jumped in my pants. "You were the one who told me what the items were, Sutton. I would never have asked."

"Oh. I wasn't even thinking about that."

I laughed and kissed the top of her head, trying to ignore the fact that my cock was growing even harder. "Let me know how much you need, and we'll get it taken care of."

She nodded and drew in a shaking breath. "I hate that he makes me feel this way."

"What way?" I asked.

"Helpless. Dependent. He thrived on that when we were married, and I vowed to never let him make me feel that way again—and here I am."

"You're far from helpless, and you're not dependent on anyone."

"Really?" she asked with a disbelieving laugh. "Because I'm borrowing money from you and asking you to give up your life and marry me to keep my crazy ex-husband from tormenting me. That sounds a hell of a lot like being dependent on someone."

"To me, that sounds like Asshat is playing games and toying around with your life. It's not your fault he had access to the money. And trust me, marrying you isn't going to end my life."

Sutton turned and started toward her office. "Oh my God. I can't believe I'm getting married again. Two unwanted marriages. What are my parents going to think?"

My steps faltered at her words, but I ignored the stab of pain and followed her. "Hey, why don't you let me clean up my mess, then we can go and grab something to eat. My treat."

Sutton stopped right before she walked into her office. "Can we go somewhere with alcohol? I need a strong drink. Maybe ten."

I winked. "We sure can. Let's drop your car off at your house so I can be your designated driver, and you can drink all you want. How does that sound?"

"Good. It sounds good. And we can talk more about the party. I already have a list of to-dos drawn up."

"Okay, give me ten, and I'll meet you back in here."

She nodded.

As I turned around to go clean up, Sutton called out, "Hey, Brody?"

I turned to face her while still walking backward.

"I don't know how to thank you for all you're doing for me," she said. "And I don't know why you're being so nice."

Tell her, Brody. Tell her you love her. Tell her she means the world to you and always has.

I opened my mouth to reveal my true feelings, but then stopped. She had been through so much in the past day with all this Jack drama. Did she need the added weight of my feelings?

I smiled. "That's what friends are for, Sutton."

She smiled in return, then walked into her office.

I wanted to punch my fist into the wall, I was so pissed at Jack. Instead, I picked up my phone and sent off a text.

Me: Hey, it's Brody Wilson. You on a job?

Miles: Not at the moment. What do you need from me, Sir?

Miles had served under me in the Navy and was the best out there when it came to digging into people's lives. And their pasts. He always knew how to find information.

Me: I need info on someone. I'll send you all of his details on Monday. And I need you to work fast.

Miles: You've got it, Sir.

Staring at my phone, I drew in a deep breath and then let it out. "You won once, Jack. But you won't win this time."

Chapter Eight

Sutton

The Seaside Chronicle

September 6, 2022

Hot Off the Reel (Special Edition)

Seasiders,

News on the docks is Sutton Bradley may be adding new stock to her little boutique store, Coastal Chic, on the square. Now, I can neither confirm nor deny that it's sexy lingerie, but seeing as Ms. Bradley has been seen on more than one occasion in the company of Brody Wilson—who, let me remind you, was voted Catch of the Season—one can only come to a certain conclusion, and that is...

Love is in the air.

I, for one, would love to see Sutton move on from that terrible first marriage of hers, and in my humble opinion, Mr. Brody Wilson would do a fine job of making her forget all about what's-his-name.

Next on my list of to-do's for today...stop by Coastal Chic! Stay tuned for more on Lingerie Gate!

Fair winds and following seas!

I dropped my head to the desk and let out a moan. "This is not happening."

"What's not happening?" Harlee asked as she walked into my office.

I quickly lifted my head. "*Another* special edition of the gossip column came out. Whoever's writing this somehow found out I'm going to be carrying sexy lingerie!"

She smiled. "Hey! Free advertisement."

I shot her a dirty look. "Seriously? They're also hinting that something's going on with me and Brody."

She waved me off. "Please. Everyone is whispering about that anyway."

I stared at her. "They are?"

Nodding, she added, "Don't tell me the gossip column is what has you looking like you haven't slept in days."

"Gosh, thanks for that. No, it's, um, just that some stock I need is on back order."

Her brows shot up. "Not the dildos!"

Laughing, I stood up. "No, they're not delayed. And wait until you see some of the lingerie I've already gotten in. I'm really glad I took the leap with this back room like you suggested."

"Me too! I'm telling you, Sutton, I think you're going to be surprised by how many women will be buying this stuff. Who doesn't want to feel sexy, even if no one else can see your undies?"

Smiling, I leaned against my desk. "I've been invited to a fashion show for boutiques in New York this December. Do you want to go with me? I'd love to get your input.

Harlee's eyes lit up. "Are you serious? I'd love to come!"

"Great! We can have a girls' weekend. I'm planning on staying with my friend, Jill, and I'm sure she won't mind you staying there too."

"Is her place big enough?"

I nodded. "Trust me, she has a gorgeous apartment in New York. Kelly Ripa lives like three doors down from her."

"Oh, I love her! I'd kill to be in the audience for a taping of *Live with Kelly and Ryan*."

Reaching for my phone, I pulled up my texts. "I'll send her a message now and see if we can get tickets for that Friday or Monday."

Harlee clapped and did a little jump. "Perfect! So, what needs to be done today? I'm dressed in clothes I don't mind ruining, just like you said."

"Brody has done almost everything except for hanging a few shelves up in the loft. I thought we could paint the walls while it's still empty. Palmer's going to come and man the front of the store for me while we work."

Rubbing her hands together, Harlee said, "Let's get our paint on!"

We spent the next few hours painting the walls a light blue to give it that beachy feel, though the space still had a classy touch. Palmer dealt with the customers up front, so Harlee and I were able to finish painting the back room and the loft area.

When we finished, I turned to look at Harlee—and started laughing. "You're exactly like Palmer! You have more paint on you than the walls."

She looked down at her clothes, then back up at me, clearly confused.

I shook my head. "It's in your hair, all over your hands, and even on the tip of your nose! How is that possible?"

With a shrug, Harlee said, "I think I scratched my nose at one point."

Palmer walked into the room and gasped. "Wow! It looks so good in here. There's a delivery, Sutton, for some racks and two pieces of furniture. I told him to go around back."

"Thanks, I'll go meet him now."

Turning on her heels, my sister headed back out to the front of the shop. She looked adorable in a pair of overalls I sold in the store, along with a light green sleeveless shirt. Her dark blonde hair was pulled up into two pigtails.

"How is she still single?" Harlee asked.

I laughed and shrugged. "How are things going with you and Thomas?"

Harlee smiled, but it didn't reach her eyes. "We're doing well. Listen, I'm going to close up the paint lids and then head on out. Thomas is taking me to Pete's Place for dinner tonight."

I quickly gave her a hug. "Thank you so much! I owe you big time."

"Nah," she said with a wave her hand. "Give me free pleasure toys, and we're golden."

Laughing, I rushed through the room and out to the back door where I received the bigger deliveries for the shop. A young guy stood there with a clipboard in his hand. "Ms. Bradley?"

"That's me."

"I've got a delivery of four round racks and two pieces of furniture."

"Perfect. I'll show you where to put them."

A while later, I stood in the middle of my new room. Harlee had taken off after cleaning up the paint mess we'd made. The racks were all stored in the middle of the back room, away from the freshly painted walls. I couldn't help but smile as I took it all in. I was expanding the store, and that was an exciting thought. But also scary. Especially since my business bank account was sitting at zero.

"Looks amazing in here."

The sound of Brody's voice made me jump. "You scared me!"

He smiled. "Sorry about that. I like the color."

"Thanks. Harlee helped paint, and the racks were delivered a little while ago."

He nodded and looked around. "You excited about expanding?"

I gestured toward my office, not wanting anyone in the front of the store—or Palmer, for that matter—to overhear me. Once inside, I shut the door and walked around my desk. I needed to put some distance between myself and Brody. He looked too good in his jeans and tight T-shirt that said *Welders Do It Best*.

With a long sigh, I answered, "I would be more excited if my ex hadn't robbed me of all of my money."

"What did your lawyer say?"

"He said the next time Jack shows up, to call the police. Same thing he's *been* saying. Every time I call the police, though, he's gone before they show up."

Brody closed his eyes, and I could see the frustration on his face. "What about the money, Sutton?"

"The bank froze the account, and they're looking into it. Since he's still listed as part owner, they need to see the divorce ruling that says he has to sell to me. It's a big mess right now."

A look of anger passed over Brody's face. "He has the right to fucking drain the account and leave you stranded? How in the hell is that okay?"

I pressed my fingers to my temples to ease the instant ache building there. I had managed to not think about the whole Jack drama for most of the day, but all the stress was coming back now. "I don't know, Brody. My lawyer sent something to the court saying that Jack left me with no means to pay any bills. He's confident we'll be able to get the money back. Meanwhile, Jack thinks he has a hold over me."

"You haven't heard from him?"

"No," I said, my voice cracking with emotion. I'd been trying to put up a good front for the last two days, and it was beginning to take its toll.

Brody walked around the desk and reached for me. He pulled me up and drew me into his arms. "It's okay, Sutton."

I pushed him away. "It's not okay, Brody! My crazy ex-husband is back in town. He stole my money, and when my father finds out... I don't even want to *think* about what he'll do. He doesn't need this type of stress."

"We'll get it fixed. We've got the marriage certificate. As soon as you say the word, we can get married."

I swallowed the lump in my throat. But what would happen *after*? Would Brody want to consummate the marriage? How would things work? Where would he live? Oh God—what if he moved in with me? How in the hell would I be able to resist him, living under the same roof?

"Where will you live?" I blurted out.

The corner of his mouth twitched with a hidden smile. "I'm assuming I'll move in with you. The idea is to make Jack think he no longer stands a chance, right?"

"You want to move in with me? How in the hell am I going to explain that to my parents?"

"We can tell them whatever you *want* to tell them. The truth, a lie, or a combination of both."

"And? What do you expect from me?"

He frowned. "What do you mean?"

"Sex-wise. I mean, if we get married, would you expect me to have sex with you? Isn't that what all guys want?"

Jerking his head back, Brody stared at me for what felt like an eternity. His eyes fell to my mouth, and I could feel the instant pull between us. The sexual tension that had been building for months—and that we'd both been ignoring—seemed to catch fire. The idea of being with Brody again sent heat right to my core. My breathing sped up, and I had to work on making it steady.

He sighed, finally breaking the silence. "If you think I'm going to force you to sleep with me simply because of a marriage certificate, then you don't know me at all, Sutton. I'm not doing this to fuck you. I'm doing it because I care about you, and I want to help you."

I raised my brows. "Will you still be sleeping with other women then?"

"What?" he asked in a shocked voice. "Did you seriously fucking ask me that?"

There was a light knock on the door, and we both turned to see Palmer standing in the doorway of my office with a confused look on her face. "Um...I knocked, but it sounded like you were arguing so I don't think you heard me. Am I interrupting something?"

Brody said, "Yes," at the same time I answered, "No, not at all."

He tilted his head, gave me an incredulous look, then stormed around my desk and started to head out of the office.

Palmer watched him with wide eyes. "I don't know how to say this but...Jack is here."

Brody stopped and turned around. "He's here? In the store?"

Palmer nodded. "I told him he has to leave, but he said he has a right to be here."

"I'll take care of it," Brody said.

I stepped forward. "No! Brody, don't. You'll only make things worse."

"Then call the cops, Sutton. You have a restraining order against him."

"What?" Palmer gasped. "What did he do?"

"Palmer, not right now, okay?" I said as I made my way around both of them. "I'll take care of this."

"Jesus Christ," Brody said as he turned away from me in anger.

Palmer looked over at me. "Wow. He's pissed."

"If you don't mind sticking around for a bit, Palmer..."

She nodded. "Of course."

"Give me a minute alone with Jack. If he doesn't leave, will you come out? The last thing I need is for Brody to get involved."

She nodded and quietly listened as I called the police to inform them of the violation. Then I drew in a deep breath and headed toward the front of the store. Jack stood there with a smug look on his face.

"How dare you show your face here," I snapped.

He smirked. "It's half my store, Sutton. And by my calculation, I have a good four minutes before the police show up."

"Give me back my money, Jack."

"Oh yes, the money. My lawyer wasn't too happy with me. I'll tell you what, I'll redeposit the money if you give me one night with you."

A feeling of sickness rolled through my entire body, and it took everything I had not to gag at the idea of being with Jack again. "No."

"So you'd rather lose the boutique then?"

"Yes."

"I'm not asking you to fuck me, Sutton. Let's just go out to dinner and talk about my share of the store."

I pulled my shoulders back so I stood taller. "Go fuck yourself, Jack."

His brows pulled down some. "Did your little boyfriend cover the bills for you? Is that why you're so confident all of a sudden?"

I slowly shook my head. "I don't know why I ever married you. You make me sick, and the idea of spending a single moment alone with you repulses me. You have one minute to get out of this store before the police get here to arrest you for violating your restraining order."

"Even though I'm in my store?"

"It's not your store!" I shouted.

He laughed—and I instantly knew I'd made a mistake. He wanted to rile me up. That's why he was here. That was *always* how he'd gotten his kicks. The damn mind games.

A siren wailed in the distance, and Jack held up both hands as Palmer appeared at my side.

"Good seeing you, Palmer."

"Fuck off, Jackass."

He laughed again, then turned on his heels and rushed out the door. I quickly locked it and leaned against the glass as I attempted to get my heart rate back to normal.

When I opened my eyes, I saw Brody standing there. I could see the anger all over his face, but before I could say anything, Palmer started to speak.

"Okay, do you want to tell me what that was all about, Sutton?" she asked.

Brody turned and walked away.

With shaking hands, I called 9-1-1 back and told them Jack had left. The dispatcher told me the officers would still do a drive-by. I ended the call and drew in a slow, deep breath before exhaling it all out in one big whoosh.

I met my sister's gaze, and the only thing I could do was shake my head and let out a quiet, "Not now, Palmer. I can't. Not right now."

For once, my sister let something go. Her face softened as she said, "I'll finish closing up and meet you in your office, okay?"

I nodded. "Thanks, Palmer."

She reached for my hand and gave it a squeeze. "Of course. I love you, sis."

Fighting back tears, I drew in a shaky breath. "I love you too."

"Why are those two over there pouting?" Palmer asked as she walked up and handed me a glass of wine.

My eyes followed her gaze to where my brother and Brody were sitting alone at a table.

"Who knows with those two," I said before I took a sip of my drink.

"Apparently, Brody told Brax to invite some single women to this party."

That caused my heart to do a weird drop. Would he really do that? Was he hoping to get in one last weekend of meaningless sex before Monday, when we were set to head to the Justice of the Peace together? "Why?"

"Who knows. Maybe they both want to get laid."

I looked back over to the table and stared at Brody. He was listening to something Braxton was telling him, ignoring the party going on around him, his head bent and a look of concentration on his face. The idea that Brody might want to sleep with someone before he was officially off the market made me sick to my stomach.

"And where in the hell is Harlee?" Palmer asked. "I swear, if she snuck off with Thomas to have sex, I'm never talking to her again."

I sighed. "At least one of us is having sex."

Palmer huffed. "Right? At this point, I'm ready to pull that hot waiter over there into a closet and have my way with him."

I giggled.

Palmer turned to face me. "What did Dad want, by the way?"

"He wanted to make sure I was okay. Thanks for not telling him and Mom that Jack is back in town. I was hoping to keep it on the down low until after today. I want them to focus on Addie."

"I can't believe he emptied your bank account, Sutton."

After Jack showed up at the store, I'd broken down and told Palmer about the money he stole. It felt good to talk to someone other than Brody and my lawyer about it. I'd also gotten good news—the judge had ordered Jack to replace the money, plus the lost interest, which honestly was next to nothing. "He has until Monday to put it back or risk going to jail."

Palmer sipped her wine while we both looked around the room. As Addie had requested, the party was being held in the large space above The Maine Bakery. It was a cool and convenient event space to have in the middle of downtown. My folks had catered the food, and they'd let Ruby, their longtime employee, take care of all the planning, included managing the serving staff. I had to hand it to her, she was a natural. No wonder my parents loved her so much.

"I don't even know half of these people," Palmer said. "I honestly didn't think so many people would show up with such short notice."

I let out a laugh. "Please. They all want the free food and the gossip."

"True that."

We both sighed at the same time, then chuckled.

She looked over at the buffet table. "Oh, Lord. Looks like it's time to eat. Do you have a speech ready?"

I snapped my head up to look at my sister. "What do you mean, a speech?"

"Well, you're like the hostess. Don't you have to give a speech?"

I frantically looked around for Brody. "No, that's for the wedding. I mean, we don't give speeches at the...at the...whatever kind of party this is! Shower slash bachelorette slash bachelor party. No one gives speeches at those."

Palmer lifted her brows and gave me an are-you-sure-about-that look.

"Oh shit," I whispered as I stood, heading for Brody. "I have to go!"

"Good luck!" she called out.

I not-so-politely pushed my way through the crowd until I got to Brody's table. I grabbed his arm and pulled him up and into the nearest corner.

"Jesus, Sutton. If you want a moment alone, I'm sure I can find us a better spot."

I hit him in the stomach, causing him to let out a breath. "Are we supposed to give speeches?"

His face paled. "What? I can't give two speeches. I've only got enough material for the wedding speech."

I blinked at him. "Material?"

"Words, thoughts, well wishes, whatever the hell you want to call it. I feel like my brain is fried after putting together that damn slideshow you wanted to do." He yawned, and it made *me* yawn. "I'm still tired."

"What are you even complaining about? You fell asleep on my sofa an hour into it. I put the whole thing together while you snored next to me."

He pointed at me. "Hey, I can't help it if you have an incredibly comfortable couch. That thing is made for napping."

I rolled my eyes, then spotted my mother walking by. I grabbed her arm and pulled her into the little nook. "Mom! Are we supposed to give a speech?"

She looked from me to Brody, then started to laugh. "You both look white as ghosts. No, you don't have to give a speech. But I *would* suggest getting everyone's attention so you can start the slideshow."

"You can't do that?" I asked.

She shot me a stern look. "Sutton Bradley, you did not just ask me that."

"I believe she did," Brody said. It took everything I had not to elbow him in the side.

"One of you, the *hosts*, should get everyone's attention and introduce the slideshow. I'll leave it up to you to decide who it is."

The second she walked off, Brody and I turned to face each other. "Rock, paper, scissors?" he asked.

"Fine. One. Two. Three."

"Wait, wait, wait. Best out of three or one and done?"

"Um…" I glanced over my shoulder. Nearly everyone was almost seated. "One and done."

He nodded.

"One. Two. Three."

Brody did paper, and I threw out a rock.

"No! Dammit. You always do scissors!" I said.

He winked. "And you always do the rock." He motioned for me to lead the way. "Shall we?"

I huffed and started to stomp away like a child as Brody chuckled from behind me.

Once we got to the table where we'd be sitting for dinner, I picked up a water glass and tapped the side with a spoon. When I had everyone's attention, I thanked them for coming. Then Braxton cracked a poor joke and Palmer hit him in the stomach. When the video slideshow started to play, I sat down and let out a relieved breath.

Brody leaned in close to me. "See, that wasn't so hard."

I forced myself to smile as I replied, "Payback's a bitch."

He lifted his glass and took a drink. "I won fair and square."

"You cheated."

"How did I cheat? I can't help it if you're predictable."

"What?" I nearly shouted. Both sets of our parents turned to look at us. I flashed them a wide grin, then leaned in and whispered into Brody's ear, "After we get married, and you're sound asleep on that comfy sofa, I'm going to write on your forehead with a Sharpie."

He tried to hold in his laugh, and a snort came out instead. Drawing away, he looked at me and smiled. Not a lazy smile, but that crooked grin that made my insides melt. "So that's a yes, then."

I quickly looked away because I was positive it wasn't happiness I was seeing in his eyes. It was something deeper. Stronger. I just couldn't pinpoint it.

"Sutton?"

"I already agreed to it, Brody."

When he reached under the table and took my hand, squeezing it lightly, my chest tightened with a feeling I hadn't had in a very long time.

Hope.

Chapter Nine

Brody

S utton and I stared at the door of the Justice of the Peace's office for what felt like an eternity before I reached for the handle and opened it. Mindy Larson—no relation to Jackass Larson—looked up from her desk and smiled. I had called Mitch Murphy, our Justice of the Peace, on Friday to let him know we would be here this morning.

Sutton wanted to keep it simple, so I'd worn dress pants and a button-down shirt with a tie. She had on a cream-colored dress that hugged her body in ways that had me fighting an erection the entire drive over here.

We'd parked a couple of blocks away and walked to the municipal building. The entire time, Sutton kept glancing around to make sure no one was watching us.

"If you keep looking so suspicious, someone's going to think we're up to something, Sutton."

"Sorry! I just don't know who's a spy for that damn column. I don't want to read that we got married in this Thursday's edition."

"You won't."

She exhaled. "I wish I had your confidence."

Once inside, Mindy quickly pointed out that Sutton needed to have some flowers to hold. After all, it was our wedding day. Sutton tried to tell her it was okay, but Mindy insisted. It was, it turned out, why she kept fresh flowers in the office at all times.

I could see the small cluster of flowers shaking in Sutton's hands as Mitch read through our vows. Not going to lie: I had never pictured my wedding day like this. I wanted a wedding with my parents there and with Gannon standing up next to me. Though I'd always envisioned Sutton as the bride, even when she'd been married to Asshat.

But to sneak into the JP's office and do it in secret in an effort to keep Sutton's ex from harassing her...yeah, that wasn't how I'd wanted it to go down.

"Do you have a ring?" Mitch asked me.

"Um, yes."

Reaching into my pocket, I took out the ring box that held the engagement ring as well as the wedding band that my mom had given to me for my future bride. As I opened the box, I heard Sutton inhale sharply.

"Brody," she whispered.

I met her questioning gaze. "It was passed down to me."

Something subtle changed in her expression, but it was gone before I could read it. This had been my grandmother's ring. It meant the world to me, and if another woman was standing here, I wouldn't be using it. But it was Sutton. And every part of me screamed to tell her that.

Sutton gave me a wobbly smile, then handed Mitch the silver band I'd picked up when I was in Portland a few days ago. Mitch's hand was steady as I shakily put the ring for Sutton into his palm. I wasn't even sure what he said after that until he told me to pick up the ring and place it on Sutton's finger.

I took her hand in mine and slipped the ring on. A look of panic crossed her face as she stared down at the ring. It was pretty damn clear Sutton didn't want to do this. The thought of marrying me must repulse her because she looked as if she was going to be sick.

After I said my vows, Sutton slipped the band on my finger and somehow managed to get her vows out. She was blinking rapidly, fighting to hold back tears as she looked up and met my gaze.

She truly *didn't* want to marry me—and I wasn't sure how that made me feel. A small part of me had hoped that maybe we could use this as a way to grow closer. To maybe actually have a relationship. But it was clear from the look on her face that this was the last thing she wanted.

When she finished saying her vows, she withdrew her hand from mine.

"I now pronounce you Mr. and Mrs. Brody Wilson."

We looked at one another in a way I was pretty damn sure two people who had just gotten married shouldn't be looking.

Mitch chuckled. "Um, this is where you kiss her, Brody."

I snapped out of my stupor. "Oh, yeah...right."

Placing my hand on the side of Sutton's face, I leaned down and softly kissed her on the lips. For a second, I felt her lift up to deepen the kiss, but then she pulled back. I slowly drew away and our eyes locked. For the briefest of moments, I had a glimpse of the young woman who had given herself to me and whispered the words that scared the living shit out of me.

I love you, Brody.

But the woman standing before me didn't utter those words, even though I would have given everything to hear them again. Instead, she took a step back.

"Are you sure you want to keep this marriage under wraps?" Mitch asked.

We both nodded, though neither of us said a word.

Mitch sighed. "I won't ask any questions, but you'd tell me if anything was wrong, right?"

Sutton pulled her gaze away from me, shook her head, and said, "Everything's fine."

I fucking hated the words coming out of her mouth. Nothing was fine. It hadn't been for years, and it was my fault. I was the one who had caused all of her heartache.

Clenching my jaw to keep from saying what I really wanted to, I forced myself to smile and look at Mitch. With a carefree attitude, I said, "Everything's perfect, Mitch. Just. Perfect."

Sutton closed her eyes and turned her head before she took a few steps away.

Mitch smiled. "Okay, well, let's go ahead and get your marriage certificate all signed, and then I'll let you two go celebrate."

I placed my hand on Sutton's back and felt her entire body shiver. Jesus, did my touch make her that uneasy? Maybe this was a huge mistake. Maybe I should have gone to her parents and told them everything. Forced Sutton to face the problem of Jack head on and stop hiding behind excuses.

But it was too late now.

Mitch opened the door—and Sutton and I both came to a halt when we saw my brother and her sister standing in the outer office.

"Holy shit," Gannon said while Addie stood there with a stunned look on her face.

Mindy leaned toward Addie and said, "I'm going to guess you had no idea they were also here to get married."

Addie slowly shook her head as she brought her hand up to her throat. "No...idea...at...all."

"Wait—you two are here to get married?" Sutton asked.

"Um, hello, *you're* here to get married?" Addie replied. "I mean, there should be no surprise about me and Gannon, but you and *Brody*? How long have you guys been hiding this?"

"Brody?" Gannon asked, giving me a look of utter disappointment.

"Why are you getting married at a JP anyway? You're supposed to get married next month," Sutton directed at her sister.

Addie tossed her hands in the air. "We wanted to do something crazy and only for us. But it appears you beat us to it!"

Sutton shook her head. "No, Addie, that wasn't what I was trying to do. It's not what you think."

Addie laughed. "I'm sorry, two people usually only get married for one reason, Sutton. How could you hide this from me? From Palmer and Harlee? Mom and Dad?"

"We didn't get married because we love each other! I was forced to do it," Sutton practically shouted.

I closed my eyes and felt every ounce of hope I had slip right out of my body.

"Wait—forced?" Mitch asked.

I opened my eyes to see four people glaring at me. I held up my hands. "I didn't force her to do anything."

Sutton stumbled over her words. "No, I didn't mean it like that. It has to do with Jack, and it's a long story, but Brody did this to help me. He hasn't done anything wrong and would *never* force me into an unwanted marriage."

Gannon glanced down at Sutton's hand. "You're wearing our grandmother's wedding band."

Sutton's eyes went wide as she looked down at her hand and then back up at me. "This is your *grandmother's* ring?"

When she looked back at the ring and quickly wiped a tear away, it felt like someone had punched me in the stomach. The walls were closing in, so I did what I did best. "If you'll excuse me, I need some air."

Before I had a chance to leave, Mitch said, "You both need to sign the marriage certificate."

All I wanted to do was go get a drink. A strong drink. But I turned and followed Mitch over to Mindy's desk.

Mindy smiled at Addie and Gannon. "I know you didn't see the ceremony, but would you like to be witnesses?"

The next few minutes felt like a blur. I signed my name, Sutton signed hers, and somehow my brother and Addie signed as witnesses.

"How about we all go grab a late breakfast?" Addie said.

"I thought you and Gannon wanted to get married?" Sutton asked.

Gannon and Addie exchanged a look and then focused back on us. "I think we're okay waiting until our actual wedding day," Addie said. "Can we please go somewhere and talk? Maybe The Maine Bakery?"

I was about to decline when Sutton said, "Okay, we'll meet you there."

Fuck.

All I wanted to do was get the hell out of dodge. Seeing how much Sutton had fought to keep herself from running out of Mitch's office was enough to deal with for one day. Now I'd have to sit and hear about how awful it was to be *forced* into marriage to keep a fucking psychopath out of her life.

Outside, Addie kissed her sister on the cheek, then leaned up and kissed mine. "See you both there."

We watched as they walked away, hand in hand. Once they'd crossed the street, I started toward my truck.

"Brody."

I kept walking.

"Brody, please, will you slow down? I can't walk that fast in these heels."

Every part of me screamed to keep going. To not even get in my truck and just run as fast as I could. But I couldn't do that to Sutton. No matter how much my heart was hurting. I slowed, and she eventually caught up.

"I didn't mean for it to sound that way."

"It's fine, Sutton. It was pretty damn clear from the look on your face during the whole ceremony that you were repulsed by the idea of marrying me."

She stopped walking, and I did the same. Turning around, I saw a look of confusion on her face. "You really think that?" she asked.

"Do you deny it?"

She started fiddling with her dress.

"I'll take your silence as a no," I said. "I'm sorry that I wasn't the guy you dreamed of marrying. At least it's simply a business arrangement. Once Jack is out of your life, we'll get an annulment."

She stood there and stared at me. When she didn't say anything, I turned and started to walk away again, though I moved slower this time. I could hear her heels clicking on the sidewalk behind me.

Once we got to my truck, I opened the door and held out my hand to help her get in. She ignored it and climbed in, then stared straight ahead.

The drive to The Maine Bakery was about ten minutes. Neither one of us said a word until I parked and started to get out. Sutton's hand landed on my arm, and I stilled.

"I won't lie and say that it didn't cross my mind that we might be making a mistake," she said, "but it's not for the reasons you think, Brody. I'm not repulsed by the idea of marrying you."

All I could do was nod.

"It's just that...I thought the next time I got married, it would be—"

I feel my body deflate. "With someone you *wanted* to marry. Someone you loved. I get it, Sutton. It's fine. Let's go in and explain all this to Gannon and Addie before they come out here and drag us inside."

I opened the door and got out of the truck, then made my way around to open Sutton's door. When I did, she turned, and something about the way she stared at me made me pause for a moment.

"Do you really think of this as a business arrangement, Brody?"

"What would *you* call it, Sutton?"

She paused, then pressed her lips together in a tight line and got out of the truck. I placed my hand on her lower back and guided her to the front door. Once inside, we searched for Gannon and Addie.

"They must not be here yet," Sutton said.

"You guys can sit anywhere you want!" a young girl from behind the counter called out.

I nodded toward the back. "Let's try and find a spot where it'll be hard for people to hear us talking."

Sutton nodded and started to walk toward the outside patio. She pointed to a table in the corner as soon as we were outside. Once we were seated and had ordered our drinks, Addie and Gannon walked up.

We all waited for our drinks, then each ordered a little something to eat. Once the waitress brought our food and was out of sight, Addie glanced between me and Sutton.

"What the fuck? You two decide to get married, and it has to do with Jack being back in town, and no one thought to tell us? I mean, I knew *something* was going on between the two of you—"

"Excuse me," Sutton interrupted. "What do you mean, you knew something was going on?"

Addie rolled her eyes. "Sutton, please. Brody has been spending so much time at your place and the boutique. Why are you two hiding it? Even the gossip column is writing about it."

"Addie, we're not hiding anything," I said. "I'm legit helping her with things around the house and the store. Nothing has happened between us."

Her eyes bounced from me, to her sister, and back to me before finally settling on Sutton. "Well, maybe something *does* need to happen. It's obvious to everyone but you two that there's a connection here."

Sutton leaned in. "It's called friendship, Addie."

Addie laughed. "Oh, okay. Is that what you called it when you two hooked up before you went off to college?"

I immediately looked at Gannon. He held up his hands. "I didn't say a word to her."

"You knew?" Sutton asked Gannon.

Before he could say anything, Addie jumped back in. "No one told me anything. I guessed."

Sutton's mouth dropped open. "You little sneak."

Addie shrugged. "It's way past time the two of you fessed up to what's going on between you."

Dropping back in her seat, Sutton crossed her arms over her chest. It was clear she wasn't going to say anything, so that left me.

"Yes, Sutton and I have a past."

Sutton snapped her head over to look at me.

"What kind of a past?" Addie asked.

"Does it really matter?" Sutton probed.

"Considering you just married Brody, yes, I think it matters."

Sutton slowly shook her head.

I shot a quick look to Gannon, and he gave me a single nod. It was time to get everything out in the open. "We slept together the summer before Sutton went to college, when I was home on leave."

Addie's expression made it clear that she wasn't surprised. "Just once or…"

"Only the one time," Sutton said softly.

I cleared my throat and looked at Sutton as I spoke. "I, um…I got spooked by the way I felt...and I might have said something I didn't mean to Sutton in order to push her away."

"Oh my God. Is that why you married Jack?" Addie asked.

Sutton stared at me with an expression I could only describe as pure devastation. She almost looked like she wanted to slap me.

Addie leaned toward her. "Sutton?"

She turned toward her sister. "I guess it was part of the reason, yes. I thought Jack had changed and things would be different, but I was wrong. Once we got married, he slowly got worse, and the last few years of our marriage were a nightmare."

Gannon leaned in and lowered his voice. "He didn't hurt you, did he?"

Addie's hand flew up to her mouth as her eyes filled with tears.

Sutton shook her head. "No, not physically, but he got pretty verbally abusive. He was always controlling to a degree, but it started to happen more and more. When I caught him having an affair, it was the out I needed—so I jumped on it. But then Jack started to beg me for another chance. He called me nonstop and came to the store to disrupt my work so many times that I ended up having to get a restraining order."

"What?" Addie looked at Gannon and then me. "Did you guys know this?"

Gannon and I both shook our heads.

"Not at first, anyway," I replied.

Sutton sat back in her chair. "After I was granted the divorce, and he was ordered to sell me his share of the store, he left for France and has been stalling the sale ever since. Now he's back and he...he won't give up."

Gannon shot me a look that said he wanted to kill me. "Did you know all of this?"

"Not all of it, at least not until recently. Jack stole all of the money out of Sutton's business account."

"Oh my God!" Addie exclaimed. "Did you tell Mom and Dad?"

Sutton sat up and leaned toward her sister. "No—and don't you dare do it either. They have enough to worry about, and I will *not* be the reason our father has another heart attack."

"But they can help you financially," Addie said.

Shaking her head, Sutton wiped her tears away. "No, Addie. Mom and Dad are talking about retiring, and they need all the money they've saved for that. Anyway, it's okay. The court ruled that Jack has to deposit everything back into the account. Brody helped out by lending me enough to pay for some invoices that were due."

Addie and Gannon both looked at me. Addie offered a small smile before focusing back on Sutton.

"And my lawyer said if he continues to show up, I need to call the police."

Gannon spoke next. "So, if all that's settled, why did you and Brody get married?"

"Because he's not going to stop," I answered for her. "He doesn't care about the restraining order and in his sick, twisted mind, I think he actually believes that Sutton will take him back. He keeps ignoring the order, showing up at her business, at her house."

Sutton nodded. "If he knows we're married, maybe he'll leave me alone."

Gannon and Addie's eyes were back on me now as Addie asked, "So...what, you stay married until when? Jack finally gives up, gets remarried, moves away?"

Sutton and I looked at each other. Letting out a tired breath, Sutton answered, "We don't know. I was going to try to keep this on the down low until after your wedding. The last thing I want to do is steal your thunder."

"My thunder?" Addie asked, her eyes wide with shock. "Sutton, I couldn't care less. The only things I care about are your happiness and your safety! Gannon and I love each other and nothing is going to ruin our day."

"Well, we kind of ruined *today* for you guys," I interjected.

Gannon laughed. "That's true."

"That doesn't matter," Addie said. "But Sutton, you can't keep this on the down low. If you truly want Jack to realize that he's never going to get you back, you guys have to be open about the marriage."

"Open about the marriage?" Sutton and I both said at the same time.

Gannon nodded. "Yeah. You're going to have to, at the very least, act like a married couple."

I looked at Sutton. She was twisting her hands together in her lap. "What do we tell Mom and Dad?" she asked.

I gaped at her. "Wait, are you serious right now? You want to go public?"

Addie reached across the table and motioned for Sutton's hand. "You need to tell our parents, Sutton. And Ken and Janet deserve to know, as well, Brody. Could you imagine if they found out some other way?"

"Yeah, like in the gossip column," Gannon said with a snort. We all turned and glared at him. "Hey, I'm just saying. Whoever's writing that column knows everything. Don't be surprised if your fake marriage gets reported. Then what are you going to do? Brody isn't even living with you, Sutton."

Sutton and I exchanged glances.

Addie nodded, sitting back in her chair. "You're going to have to pretend to have a real marriage if you want Jackass to be convinced. Move Brody in, hold hands in public." Addie smiled. "Kiss. Come on, let's see you practice."

"You want us to kiss? Right now?" I asked.

Gannon winked. "What's wrong, Brody? You afraid to kiss your own wife?"

"Fuck off, Gannon. This isn't funny."

Addie pointed at me. "No, it isn't. This is very real and very serious. And the two of you made the very grown-up decision to get married. Not fake married, *real* married."

Sutton closed her eyes. "Oh my God, why didn't we think of a fake marriage?"

I shook my head. "Jack probably would've looked in the public records for our marriage certificate."

"He's right," Gannon said. "Come on, Sutton. It can't be all *that* bad being married to Brody. He's handsome, kind, and sort of funny. He's got money. And you already know how he is in bed."

Addie smacked him on the arm. "Gannon Wilson!"

"What?" he laughed. "It's all true."

"So, you think I'm handsome, huh?" I teased my brother.

Sutton sighed. "Can you be serious? Addie and Gannon are right. We need to tell our parents as soon as possible. We'll say we eloped because we didn't want to take anything away from Gannon and Addie's wedding."

Addie smirked. "How sweet of you to think of us, sis."

Sutton shot her sister the middle finger.

Gannon was sitting there with a shit-eating grin on his face.

"What are you smiling at?" I asked.

"I'm waiting to see you kiss your new bride."

Addie giggled. "Do it. Do it. Do it."

Sutton shook her head. "Now who's acting like a child?"

"Kiss him, for goodness sake," Addie demanded.

She rolled her eyes. "You really want me to kiss him?"

Addie clapped her hands. "Yes! And not a peck. A real, passionate, we-just-tied-the knot-and-can't-wait-until-our-wedding-night kind of kiss."

"Do you need me and Addie to show you guys how it's done?" Gannon smirked. "Passionate kissing, that is?"

Sutton and I both huffed and said, "No."

With a wave of her hand in our direction, Addie said, "Then go for it."

"Fine," Sutton responded.

Addie's brow rose. "Fine."

"*Fine*," Sutton stated as she folded her arms.

"Fine!"

"Oh, for fuck's sake, Addie and Sutton," Gannon cut in. "It's like watching a tennis match. Kiss her already, Brody."

I cleared my throat. "Fine."

The whole table groaned.

Sutton and I turned to face one another. I cupped the side of her face with my hand and watched as she licked her lips. My cock jumped in my pants.

"We're waiting," Addie singsonged.

"I hate you right now," Sutton whispered, side-eying her sister. She looked up at me. "Okay, let's do this so they stop."

My eyes drifted down to Sutton's perfectly pouted lips. I could still taste her from our earlier kiss. And the memory of our kisses all those years ago.

Only one way to find out, Brody. You've got to kiss your wife.

I leaned in and pressed my mouth to Sutton's. My tongue swept over her lips, and she opened for me. When I deepened the kiss, she brought her hand to my face, then slid it around to the back of my neck. She dug her fingers into my hair, and I nearly moaned.

The kiss didn't feel fake. It felt fucking amazing, and I never wanted to stop feeling her tongue move against mine in a delicate dance.

We both pulled back at the same time, and when our eyes met, I couldn't help but wonder if she'd felt it. That pull. The longing to be connected as one. That same feeling we both felt all those years ago.

My chest rose and fell as I attempted to catch my breath. One quick glance at Sutton's chest proved she was searching for air as well.

"Jesus. That was one hell of a kiss," Gannon said. "Are you two sure you're not...you know..."

"Gannon," Addie whispered. "Stop teasing."

Sutton blinked a few times, then slowly sat back in her seat. She smiled and said, "See, we can totally pull off passionate. No problem at all." She picked up her fork, cut off a piece of her cinnamon bun, and popped it in her mouth. As if that kiss hadn't rocked her world like it had mine.

I sat back, and when my eyes met Gannon's, I saw the understanding there. He gave me a half smile and then reached for his orange juice. "I suggest your next stop be the parents'. About fifteen people just witnessed the two of you kissing. Rumors are going to start."

"Right. We'll do that as soon as we're done here," Sutton agreed.

"Yeah." It was all I could say.

Addie must have sensed the tension in the air because she quickly launched into something about the wedding and asked for Sutton's advice. They soon got lost in conversation.

"You okay?" Gannon asked quietly as the girls continued to talk.

"Perfectly fine."

Fucking hell. Now I sounded like Sutton.

He nodded. "You never could lie very well, Brody."

Chapter Ten

Sutton

B rody and I agreed it would be best to tell our parents together, all at once. I was hoping that being around other people would keep my dad from going off the rails when we told him the reason behind our quickie wedding.

Janet and Ken were more than happy to meet us at my parents' house for dinner later that evening. We'd told them we had something important to discuss, and I was almost positive they thought it had something to do with Addie and Gannon's wedding.

We walked up the steps of my parents' house, and I paused on the top step.

"What's wrong?" Brody asked.

I closed my eyes and drew in a deep breath. "I'm worried. What are my parents going to think about me when I tell them everything?"

He took my hand in his. "They're going to love you and trust you. Your dad is going to be fine."

I looked down at the rings on my finger and tried to ignore the flutter in my chest. Brody had added the engagement ring to the band after we'd left the bakery. It was a beautiful antique cushion cut with a halo of smaller diamonds encompassing the center stone. Additional accent diamonds went down the shank of the ring. The bands were platinum, and I was stunned that they fit me like a glove.

I couldn't believe Brody had given me these rings. I had assumed he would pick out a plain band for me when he got his own. Instead, I was wearing his family's heirlooms.

"You ready?" Brody asked.

I nodded. "Yes, let's get this over with."

The idea that my parents were about to find out what a *complete* asshole my ex-husband was and how he had actually treated me was not something I was looking forward to.

"Sutton, Brody, come on in. Your parents are already here, Brody," my mother said as she opened the door and kissed us both on the cheeks. I kept my left hand in the pocket of the sweater I'd put on. The evenings were beginning to cool off now that fall was officially here.

"Thanks so much for agreeing to have dinner here at the last minute," Brody said, following my mother to the dining room. "Sorry we're late."

She smiled. "No worries. I brought home some lasagna from the restaurant, and Janet brought over the salad. We just took the bread out of the oven."

The moment we walked into the dining room and I saw my father and Brody's parents, something in me snapped. I started to panic, even as I tried like hell to act totally normal.

"Do you need help with anything?" Brody asked.

My mother beamed at Brody as she answered, "No, you kids sit down. I'm going to go grab the lasagna."

Brody pulled a chair out for me, and I sat. He walked around the table and kissed his mother on the cheek. Then he shook his father's hand, followed by my father's. I wasn't sure why those small gestures affected me so much. I pressed my hand to my stomach in an attempt to calm the flutters that were less from nerves and more from watching the man who was now my husband move around the room.

"You look nice tonight, Sutton," Janet said. "You have a glow about you."

I let out a nervous laugh. "Thank you, Janet. So do you! I mean, you look nice."

She laughed.

My mother walked back in and set the lasagna and a serving spoon down in the middle of the table. "Should we dive in?" she said.

"Let's!" my father agreed.

He reached for the salad—and I don't know what came over me, but I suddenly pulled my hand out of my sweater, turned it so everyone could see, and blurted out, "Brody and I got married today."

Everyone paused. Including Brody.

Okay, so that wasn't how we'd agreed on breaking it to them. We had decided that I was going to tell them about Jack first. The money, the harassment, all of it. But looking at my father...I couldn't do it. His heart attack had been so scary, and the thought of upsetting him was too much. I couldn't do it.

"I'm sorry. What did you say?" my mother asked as Janet gasped.

"Are those Marie's rings?" she said.

Brody looked at my hand, then at his mother. When he didn't say anything, I jumped in. "Yes. He asked me to marry him, and we didn't want to wait, but we also didn't want to rain on Addie and Gannon's big day."

I felt Brody's eyes boring into me. I could only imagine what was going through his head at that moment.

"You asked *her* without asking for my permission?" my father said.

Shit. Shit. Shit.

Brody opened his mouth, but all that came out was, "Ahhh..."

"It was my fault, Dad. I asked him to keep it between us. I knew that once Addie was back, there was a strong possibility Gannon would ask her to marry him, and honestly, Brody and I liked keeping it our little...secret." I turned to Brody. "Right?"

He nodded and smiled. "Yes. I wanted to ask for her hand, sir."

My father narrowed his eyes at Brody. "And she talked you out of it?"

Brody gave a shaky nod. "She didn't, um...well, she was worried, um, that—"

Oh, dear God. Brody can't lie to save his life.

"It was so soon after your heart attack when Brody and I started dating," I said gently. "And, well, we also really didn't want to deal with the gossip since it was so soon after my divorce too."

"Yes, it *is* soon," my mother stated.

I shook my head. "It may seem like it's too soon, but I've had feelings for Brody for a long time."

All eyes snapped to me.

"Then why in the hell did you marry that asshole?" my father demanded.

"Keegan Bradley!" my mother said in a firm voice.

"What?" he scoffed. "It's a damn good question."

Brody and I looked at each other, and he simply raised one brow. It was obvious he was going to let me dig deeper into this lie.

"Brody was in the Navy, and he was older," I said. "I thought at the time that I was in love with Jack, but then Brody came back to Seaside, and things with Jack went sour. Brody was there for me and we...we fell in love."

I turned to Brody. The way he was looking at me made me think for one brief moment that he really *was* in love with me. I silently pleaded for him to go along with me.

"Yes, that's pretty much how it happened," he agreed.

"Why the cloak and dagger, though? Why didn't you tell us?" Janet asked.

"I don't know, Mom," he said. "We wanted to see how things went. Then I realized that I loved Sutton, and I wanted to make her my wife as soon as possible."

I quickly added, "Now felt like the right time."

"Why now?" my father asked.

I drew in a deep breath. "Jack is back in Seaside."

My father's jaw tensed.

"He's been trying to reconcile, and he was being rather pushy about it, so Brody and I decided..." My words faded.

My mother closed her eyes and slowly shook her head before looking at me. "Tell me you didn't get married simply to put off Jack? Oh, Sutton—"

"No," Brody cut in. "We'd been talking about it, but after Addie and Gannon got engaged, we decided to put it on the back burner."

"But then you suddenly eloped?" Ken asked. "Why?"

My heart started to pound in my chest.

"Oh my God! Oh my God!" My mother jumped up. "You're *pregnant*!"

"What?!" My father stood so quickly his chair fell back. He looked like he was ready to lunge across the table and kill Brody.

"Oh my gosh! We're going to be grandparents, Ken!" Janet jumped up as well and started hitting Brody's dad on the shoulder excitedly.

Ken looked confused as hell before quickly pulling away from his wife. "Jesus, Janet, that's my good swinging arm for golf!"

Brody leaned over to me and said, "Do something *now* before your father leaps across the goddamn table and murders me with a butter knife!"

I stood. "I'm not pregnant! But I wanted Brody to move in with me, and I knew that you'd all frown on that."

Both moms deflated into their chairs.

"Oh, for the love...Sutton," my father said. "This is 2022, we're not *that* old-fashioned."

We all looked at him.

He sat down and put the butter knife back on the table. "Thank you, Brody, for respecting my *old-fashioned* ways."

Brody wiped away a bead of sweat and simply nodded.

My father cleared his throat. "Well, so...you're married. Jack is back. And there are no buns in the oven."

"Or shrimp," Ken said with a chuckle.

"Is that all you wanted to tell us, sweetheart?" my mother asked.

I nodded. "Yep. That's it. We're married. Yay! We went to the Justice of the Peace this afternoon, and this is our first dinner as a married couple. We wanted to spend it with our parents."

Janet and my mother both dabbed at the corners of their eyes.

"That is so sweet of you, darling," Janet said as she beamed at me, then at her son.

"Can we eat now? I'm starving." Ken reached for the serving spoon and scooped out a healthy portion of lasagna.

Brody had been a complete gentleman all evening at my parents' house. He'd held my hand, kissed me on the cheek, and played the new doting husband—while I'd fought to keep from crawling on top of him every time he'd touched me. He played the part well. Too well.

When we left to head back to my house, he was silent the whole way. After we walked inside, he still didn't say a word. When I returned downstairs after my shower and found him on the back porch drinking a beer, he still remained silent.

"Are you ever going to talk to me again?" I asked.

He slowly shook his head. "You flat-out lied to our parents, Sutton. It's bad enough we're going to have to put on a show for the whole town, but now we have to do it with our parents as well."

I sat down and reached for his beer. I took a long drink and handed it back to him. "I panicked, Brody."

"No shit."

"I'm sorry. I couldn't tell my parents the truth."

He turned and looked at me. "Sutton, your dad is not going to have another heart attack."

I shook my head. "It wasn't just that," I said quietly. "I failed so badly with my first marriage, and if they knew the whole truth, and that my second marriage was a sham...I couldn't do it. I couldn't stand the idea of seeing the pity or embarrassment on their faces."

Brody stared at me for a good minute before he closed his eyes, drew in a deep breath, and then focused back on me. "Sutton, they wouldn't have felt either of those things."

"Are you terribly angry with me?"

He turned away and stared out into the dark night. "No. But I wish you'd given me a heads up."

"It just kind of..." I shrugged. "Happened. I'm so sorry."

"Did you see the way your father looked at me when your mom said you were pregnant? I never saw anyone grab a knife so quickly in my life. And I've been stabbed *and* shot at!"

I brought my hand up to my mouth at the thought of Brody being stabbed and shot. He smiled and winked, and I couldn't help but return the gesture. "What about *your* dad? He was so preoccupied with the lasagna and not hurting his golf arm, I'm not sure he even realized his oldest son was about to be murdered."

Brody laughed, and it was one of the sweetest sounds I'd ever heard. I loved his laugh. And his smile. The left side of his mouth hitched up more than the right, and it was one of the sexiest things about him.

"Oh man, what an evening," he said with a shake of his head.

"Are you, um, going to go back to the beach house or..." I let my words dangle in the air.

With another panty-melting smile, he said, "I've got an overnight bag in my truck. Sometimes I get called out on jobs where I have to stay the night, so I keep a bag ready to go. I brought it in and put in the guest bedroom while you were showering. I'll go home tomorrow and pack up some stuff."

"Bring whatever you what. It's actually your house, too, now."

He looked at me and winked. "That's right. We didn't sign a pre-nup."

I dropped my head back; it was my turn to laugh. "I've got nothing, so..."

He put his beer to his lips and took a long drink. "Well, I've got about four-hundred-thousand dollars in my main savings, and more sprinkled in stocks and other investments. And you're now the proud owner of a beach house and a couple of jet skis."

I opened my mouth to say something snarky, then snapped it shut. Did he say *main* savings? "Main savings?"

He nodded. "I've got three savings accounts. Each for something different."

"Oh." We sat in silence for a few moments. "Brody, I don't think for one minute that anything of yours is mine. I hope you know that."

"Why? As far as I'm concerned, what's mine *is* yours. We're legally married, Sutton."

"I would never..."

He reached for my hand. "I know you wouldn't. But what I need you to understand is that you don't have to struggle. I want to help you and ease some of your burden."

My brows pulled down in confusion. "Why would you do that?"

"Because I... Because I can, and I want to."

Before I could argue, he stood and handed me the nearly finished beer. "I'm exhausted. I'm going to go ahead and shower, then hit the hay."

I forced myself to smile at him even though I wanted to ask him more. Not about how much he had or owned, but why he would so easily share it with me. Instead, I gave him a soft smile. "Okay. Sleep well."

He smiled down at me, then leaned over and kissed my forehead. "You, too, Sutton. Sweet dreams."

Chapter Eleven

Sutton

The Seaside Chronicle

September 29, 2022

Waves Splash!

Seasiders,

Breaking news coming right from the docks! There's been a marriage. Can anyone guess who tied the knot?

This writer knows...

Fair winds and following seas!

"Welp, I can safely say they've moved on from me and Gannon now!" Addie exclaimed. She was a little too excited for my taste.

I stared at the paper on my kitchen table. "How did they find out?"

"Mindy?" Brody asked before he took a sip of his coffee.

Addie shook her head. "No way it was Mindy. I can't see her gossiping. *Or* being author of the column."

"Who else have you told since Monday?" Gannon asked.

I read the short article once more as Brody replied, "Only our parents, Palmer, and Brax."

"Harlee knows too," I said. "I told her yesterday at work. By the way, the back room is finished now. Well, almost finished. And the, um...products for the loft space come in today."

Addie's eyes lit up. "I'll have to come and buy something for the honeymoon."

Gannon frowned. "Wait, what are we talking about?"

Addie beamed at him. "Sutton's carrying a new line of lingerie, as well as some new styles of clothes."

"And vibrators. Don't forget the vibrators," Brody said with a wink in my direction.

Gannon nearly choked on his bagel. "*What*? You're carrying vibrators in the store?"

"It was Harlee's idea," I quickly stated.

"Harlee? Our sweet little princess of the island suggested you carry *vibrators*?" Gannon asked.

I felt my cheeks heating up. "Yes."

He turned to face Addie. "Is that what you're buying for the honeymoon?"

She giggled. "I wasn't going to, but I can if you want."

Before Gannon could respond, I held up my hand. "Please. It's way too early in the morning for this."

Addie huffed while Gannon and Brody both grinned.

"Okay, Harlee aside, what made you decide to carry that particular line of products, Sutton?" Gannon asked.

I gave him a one-shoulder shrug. "I don't know. She mentioned it, and I guess I realized I was free to carry whatever I wanted now."

Reaching for my hand, Addie gave it a squeeze. "Will you do me a favor?"

Oh my God, was she about to ask me to save her a vibrator? Maybe it wasn't such a great idea to carry personal pleasure products after all. "Please don't ask me to set one aside for you, or to test them out or something."

"I'll volunteer for that," Brody said. "I mean, to help you test them out. We *are* married, after all."

I stuck my tongue out at him and then turned back to my sister.

"No, nothing like that," she said, laughing. "But when you tell Mom and Dad you're selling sex toys, please let me be there."

Gannon attempted to hide his laughter while Brody simply smiled that devastating grin of his.

"Ha ha. I'm seriously having second thoughts about it now," I said.

"No!" Addie exclaimed. "I'm totally kidding. You never know, Mom might be into that kind of thing."

Brody laughed. "Your dad is a lucky son-of-a-bitch, if she is."

"How do you know *your* mom isn't into them, as well?" I asked Brody. I laughed when he gagged.

"God, Sutton, don't give me that visual." His whole body shuddered.

"Have you heard from Jack?" Gannon asked.

I shook my head. "No, but the money is back in my business account."

He nodded. "Nothing about selling his half of the shop to you?"

I'd gotten an update from my lawyer yesterday, and supposedly we could expect the sale to go through in the next few days. I was praying the news wasn't too good to be true.

"Hopefully any day now," I replied. When I caught Brody's eye, he winked again and smiled at me.

The last couple of days had been crazy. I hadn't truly had time to process the fact that I was married once again. Or that Brody was now living in my house. He'd stayed here the last three nights, only going home on Tuesday to pack up some things to bring back. He'd been parking in the back of the house, so I wasn't sure who had seen him coming and going.

"I hope it means Jack realizes there's no hope for the two of you now," Gannon stated.

I frowned. "I don't see him simply giving up, unfortunately. If he hasn't found out about the marriage yet, that is."

Addie gave me a sympathetic look. "I wish I could chat more, but I've got to run over to Dr. James's office. He's starting to pack up some of his stuff, and I told Dr. Bryan I'd take an inventory of all the supplies."

I stood and followed my sister and Gannon through my house to the front door. "Are you still excited about starting this new job in a few weeks?" I asked.

Addie wore a wide grin. "I really am. It'll be different doing the administrative side of things, but I'm glad Dr. Bryan wants me to help assist with patients when he needs help."

"He's so young-looking. It's hard to believe he's a doctor and has a seven-year-old little boy."

Addie nodded. "He *is* young-looking, but I think Mom said he's thirty-five, or around there. His son Charlie is a hoot."

Gannon laughed. "He is that and then some. He seems like a handful."

Addie nodded in agreement. "A little prankster in the making."

"My kind of kid," Brody said.

Addie leaned in and gave me a kiss on the cheek. "Okay, better run. Love you!"

"Love you, too," I said. "Bye, Gannon."

"See you guys around. Brody, I'll call you later."

"Sounds good," Brody said, shaking his brother's hand.

We stood there and watched Gannon and Addie walk down the steps and out to Addie's car. Gannon opened the door for her before going to the driver's side.

I shut the front door and exhaled as I leaned against it.

"Everything okay?" Brody asked.

"Yeah," I said with a slight nod. "But something feels...off."

He gave me a questioning look. "What do you mean?"

I shook my head. "I don't know. I have a weird feeling. Like something big is about to happen."

He raised his brows. "Something good or bad?"

My eyes met his. "Well, if my gut is right—something bad."

Brody leaned down to kiss me on the forehead. It was something he'd been doing a lot over the last few days. "Stop stressing, Sutton.

Everything's going to be fine. I need to get to work myself. You need any help at the store today?"

"No, Harlee and Palmer will be there. I put up a sign that said we'll be closed for half the day. That should give us plenty of time to get the new inventory out."

"Are you excited?"

I couldn't stop a silly grin from spreading across my face. Nor could I ignore the nerves that were bubbling up in my stomach. "I am, but I'm nervous too. It's a huge jump to go from carrying pretty conservative clothing to a bit more flirty and fun styles. Plus, the toys now...I hope I'm not making a mistake."

"Does it feel like a mistake?"

I thought about it for a moment. "No, it actually feels like the right thing to do. Harlee's right, there isn't anything like that here in Seaside, and women shouldn't be embarrassed about wanting to feel sexier."

A devilish smile appeared on Brody's face. "Or feel *good*."

I felt the heat hit my throat and move up my cheeks. "That too."

We stood there for a moment with the air crackling between us. I wanted him to lean down and kiss me like he did on Monday at the bakery after our wedding. The need to have his hands on me was almost too much. Before either of us could do anything crazy, I pushed away from the door and started toward the kitchen. "We both better get a move on."

I felt Brody's eyes on my back as I walked away. A minute or so later, I heard the shower turn on in the guest bathroom, and I had to grip the kitchen counter to keep from running up the steps and joining him in there.

"What's the matter with me?" I whispered.

After pulling in a few deep breaths, I grabbed my phone and headed upstairs to get ready for the day. I started to send a text to Harlee and Palmer saying that I was going to be a few minutes late and they should start without me, when I slammed into something hard.

I stumbled before hands steadied me at my waist.

I looked up to see Brody in front of me. His hands dug into my waist as my eyes widened at the sight of him. His dark brown hair was so wet it looked almost black. One lock hung down in front of eyes, and I had to fight the urge to push it away. Letting my gaze wander, I felt my legs go weak when I realized he was only wearing a towel. Lord help me, it was so low on his hips, I could see that famous V...and I let out a soft moan.

If I remembered anything from that night so long ago—besides how amazing he felt inside me—it was his body. His insanely *built* body. And thirty-two-year-old Brody's body was even more amazing. Broad shoulders, a perfect chest, and abs that I could wash my clothes on.

Don't look down. Don't look down.

Shit.

I looked down.

That perfectly chiseled V led to something I wanted more than I was willing to admit—even to myself. I swallowed hard and looked back up at him.

"S-sorry. I was, um, I was texting, and I wasn't looking where I was going and..."

My eyes traveled over his body once again, and I felt the pull in my lower stomach.

Brody's eyes went right to my mouth, and I subconsciously licked my lips. He leaned down, and I held my breath as I slowly stretched up onto my toes.

Right before his mouth met mine, my phone rang.

I screamed and jumped back, nearly falling on my ass.

I fumbled with the phone to answer it. "Hello? Hello? I'm here. Yes. Um..."

"Are you okay? What's wrong?" Palmer asked on the other end.

Brody silently asked if I was okay, and I gave him a thumbs up before quickly making my way around him and into my room.

I shut the door and dropped back against it. "Give me a second," I told my sister while I closed my eyes and attempted to calm my beating heart.

"Sutton?"

"One. Second."

"Oooookay."

I took in a few deep breaths before I opened my eyes and headed straight into my bathroom. "Sorry, I just ran into Brody, and the only thing he was wearing was a towel. And his hair was wet. Why is that so sexy?"

Palmer laughed. "Did you pull the towel off and take what's now yours?"

"No!" I stated. "He's not mine."

"Um, beg to differ with you, big sister. You're married. He is well and truly yours to do anything you want with."

I could hear Harlee giggling in the background.

"Am I on speakerphone?"

"Indeed, you are!" Harlee stated with a laugh. "I've got an idea. We have a package that got delivered first thing this morning. It contains some goodies in there that you and Brody could try out."

I reached into the shower and turned the water on...to cold. Doesn't that work for women too?

"I'm going to pretend I didn't hear any of that," I said. "I'm jumping into the shower, and then I'll be on my way. Sorry I'm running late."

Palmer sounded thoughtful as she said, "Did the column in this morning's paper distract you? Who do you think knows? Harlee said it could be Mindy. Oh my gosh—what if it's Mitch?"

I couldn't help but laugh. "It's not either one of them. Let me get going so I can get to the store. On my desk in my office is a layout of how I think the rounds should go. If you guys don't mind starting without me, I shouldn't be much longer."

"No worries. We've already started pulling out some of the inventory. Sutton, this lingerie is *amazing*. You helped design it?"

"A few pieces. I helped more with the skirts and tops. Those should arrive today, and I thought we could put them in the very front of the store, maybe even do up a cute fall display."

"I'll be on the lookout in case UPS shows up early. Go get ready, we'll keep plugging along here."

"Thanks, guys. See you soon."

I stripped out of my joggers and T-shirt and nearly yelped when the cold water hit me. Then I soon made a mental note to myself. *Cold water doesn't help put out the fire of desire after seeing one's very hot, naked husband.*

Chapter Twelve

Brody

I was exhausted. It had been a long day of being under the water and welding parts of the new pier that was getting installed near the port authority building. Every part of my body was sore. Of course, that could also be from the intense workout I'd done at lunch in an attempt to stop thinking about how Sutton had looked at me when she'd run into me after my shower.

The only thing that seemed to keep my mind off of her was work. Now I was off and ready to head to Sutton's, take a long hot shower, and climb into bed.

Yet, for some reason, I swung by Coastal Chic first. I saw that the lights were still on, so I pulled around back and entered through the back door. I could hear female voices—and stopped right inside the door when I heard my name. I knew it was wrong to spy on the girls, but I was too curious to walk away.

"Don't be such a prude, Sutton. Take one home, and try it out."

"Harlee, I'm not a prude. And like I said before, I'm not taking one home because Brody's there, and he might hear it."

"And like *I* said before, have Brody join in on the fun!"

A buzzing sound clicked on, and I heard Palmer laughing. "Oh my God. The tip on this one rotates! Why is it rotating?"

I closed my eyes. Jesus H. Christ. They were talking about vibrators.

"Better to find that G-spot with, my dear," Harlee teased. "Now, back to you, Sutton. Close your eyes and picture what happened this morning, and I bet you'll orgasm faster than you can spell it."

"Stop saying that! I wish I'd never told you guys about earlier."

That made me perk up even more. I was suddenly very, very awake.

"Come on, Sutton, it's perfectly normal to be turned on by something like that. You saw Brody *naked*."

"He wasn't naked. He had on a towel."

"Didn't you say you wished it had slipped off?" Palmer added.

Harlee chimed in. "I think we can all agree that under those tight T-shirts and jeans Brody wears, he has an amazing body. Maybe Thomas should start working out with him."

Palmer and Sutton both giggled.

"That's mean, Harlee," Palmer said with a snort. "He's your boyfriend."

"Meh. The sex could be better."

"Maybe it's *you* who needs to bring home a new toy." Sutton giggled.

I closed my eyes. Sutton talking about vibrators was going to do me in right here. I needed to turn around and leave. I shouldn't be listening. This was wrong. So wrong.

"Trust me, I intend to," Harlee said. "I'm really eyeing this rechargeable thrusting rabbit one. I mean, listen to this. It has a bunch of different lifelike thrusting settings. It says it'll rock your clit and vagina with ten different modes. Oh, and you can use it in the shower or tub too! I think you need this one, Sutton."

Sutton groaned. "Why do I need that?"

Harlee grunted. "I'm pretty sure your vajayjay doesn't even remember what it feels like to orgasm with something inside of it. I highly doubt Jackass ever brought you that kind of pleasure."

Sighing, Sutton said, "I never had a single orgasm with Jack while we were having sex."

The other two women gasped—and I smiled.

"*Never?*" Harlee asked.

"Not when he was inside of me. Jack was more of a 'once *he* finished, he was done' kind of guy. He didn't care if I had an orgasm or not."

I slowly shook my head. That stupid fucking dickhead. If Sutton was my wife, I'd be making her come every damn way I could think of.

I paused for a moment.

Sutton was *my wife.*

"That shaft is too small for me. It's only five-and-a-half inches."

"Jesus, Harlee, how big do you want it?" Palmer asked.

"Bigger than that. If I wanted that, I'd sleep with Thomas."

All three girls giggled. Poor bastard. Thomas better get on the ball, or he was going to lose Harlee.

"What about this one?" Palmer said. "It's seven inches in length. Doesn't have all the fancy modes though."

"Oh no, ladies, I have found the crème de la crème!" Harlee exclaimed. "This baby is nine inches long with a nicely sized girth. It has a bullet at the end of it, and you can control the speed."

"Please tell me women are not going to be in here comparing these things," Sutton said.

Harlee scoffed. "Of course they will be. This is an important investment."

"How do you have this whole town fooled into thinking you're a sweet, innocent do-gooder?" Palmer asked.

Harlee laughed. "I can't help it if I like a good orgasm."

Sutton let out a groan. "I'm totally ready to move on from this conversation. It's late, and you two need to head on out. You've been here all day."

"What about you?" Palmer asked.

"I've got a few things I need to take care of, and then I'll be heading home."

"You're sure?" Harlee asked.

It was the perfect time to make my presence known.

"Evening, ladies," I said as I walked into the refurbished back room. All three of them spun around and looked at me. Harlee and

Palmer gave me wide smiles, while Sutton turned white as a ghost and dropped the vibrator that was in her hand. She used her foot to kick it across the room, with Palmer and Harlee doing everything in their power not to laugh.

"What was that?" I asked with my own laugh.

"Nothing!" Sutton quickly said.

Palmer walked across the room and reached under one of the displays of lingerie. My mind instantly pictured what Sutton would look like in one of those sexy numbers.

"It's a vibrator," she said, "and for some reason, my sister thinks they're taboo."

"I do not!" Sutton defended. "If I did, I wouldn't be selling them."

I blinked a few times as I looked at each woman.

Harlee clapped her hands, making Sutton jump. "Right, well, we were just leaving. Good seeing you, Brody."

Palmer hugged and kissed Sutton, then reached up and kissed me on the cheek. "See you later, bro!"

I chuckled. "See you later." Once they left, I focused back on Sutton. Her cheeks were flaming red.

"How long have you been here?" she asked.

I acted innocent. "I just got here. Why?"

"No...no reason." She turned and looked around the room. "How does it look?"

I walked over to a red bra and felt the soft material with my fingers. "Like I'd love to see you in one or two of these."

She let out a nervous laugh. "Very funny."

When our eyes met, I hoped she could see I was far from joking.

Her eyes widened. "Wait, are you serious?"

Before I could answer, the bell above the front door went off.

"Crap, I assumed Palmer locked the front. I'll be right back."

I made my way around the room, trying to force my dick not to get hard. My eyes traveled up the steps to the loft. I wanted to go see the progress on their...*pleasure toy* display, but something kept me right where I was.

Then I heard his voice—and immediately made my way to the front of the shop.

Sutton stood behind the counter, and Jack was walking toward her. Sutton didn't look scared, but she certainly didn't look happy, either.

"Take another step toward my wife, and my fist will be in your face," I said.

Jack froze—then looked in my direction. "Excuse me?"

"Get away from my wife."

"Your *wife*?" Jack asked as he spun his head to look at Sutton. "You *married* him?"

I moved around the counter, and Sutton came closer to me. "You were told to stay away from me *and* the store, Jack," she said. "Why are you here?"

"Are you fucking kidding me? You married this asshole?!"

Sutton nodded. "Yes, Jack. Brody and I are married."

He looked at the rings on her finger, then back at me. He let out an evil-sounding laugh. "You always did want her. But at least I had her first."

I smirked. "I don't think so, Jack."

Sutton stiffened. I knew it was a cheap shot directed at Jack, one I fucking *had* to take against him, but it had ricocheted and hit Sutton as well.

His eyes darkened and he clenched his fists. Turning to Sutton, he hissed, "I knew it was a mistake, marrying you. You were a whore then, just like you are now."

I moved so fast, Jack never saw my fist coming.

Sutton screamed as Jack stumbled back and hit a rack full of clothes, falling to the floor.

"You have five seconds to get out of here or I'm calling the cops," I said. "You so much as even *look* in her direction again, I'll kill you. Do I make myself clear?"

Jack smiled, wiping blood from the corner of his mouth. "Threatening me, huh?"

I took another step toward him, and he jumped up. "Kind of like how you're threatening my *wife*," I said. "Your five seconds are up."

Jack ran the back of his hand over his mouth again, shot a last glare at Sutton, then stomped out the door.

The second it shut, I locked it and headed over to Sutton. "Are you okay?"

She looked up at me and blinked. "You knocked the shit out of him!"

"I wanted to kill him. The second I heard his voice, it took everything inside of me not to put my hands around his neck and choke the life out of the bastard."

She actually smiled. "Thank you. I think he was waiting for Palmer and Harlee to leave and didn't realize you were here."

"Yeah, well, he never was that bright." We stood there for a few silent moments before I added, "I'm sorry I said that...about having you first."

A blush moved over her cheeks. "It's okay. He kind of deserved it."

"I wasn't meaning to insult *you* or anything. I hope you know that."

She nodded.

"I *am* glad I was your first, though."

Sutton bit down on her lower lip, then glanced nervously around the shop. "I need to close out and clean up a bit."

"I can stay, if there's anything you need help with."

"Would you mind breaking down the boxes in the other room? After I close out the till, I can straighten up in there and have the new area ready and open for business tomorrow."

I glanced toward the back. "What about the loft? Is it ready to go?"

"It is, but I've got to be honest, I'm so worried about opening it up to customers."

"Why?" I asked as Sutton stepped up to the register, typed in a few things, then took out the money drawer.

She looked at me and laughed. "Brody, I'm selling dildos in my store. I don't know what in the world I was thinking."

"Who cares? I think you'll be surprised by how well they do."

Sutton shrugged and headed toward the back. I paused at the entrance to the short hallway, and she paused halfway to her office. She turned around and asked, "Why did you stop by the store?"

"I wanted to see you." The words were out before I even had a chance to think about them.

Her eyes widened, and she gifted me with a beautiful smile. "That's so sweet. I'm glad you did...stop by."

I nodded. "Me too."

Our eyes locked for a few moments before she looked down at the drawer in her hands. "I better go take care of this."

I pointed to the back room. "And I'll take care of the boxes."

"Great, thank you."

Watching her walk into her office, I felt my chest tighten. I jammed my fingers through my hair and headed toward the back room.

Jesus, I was falling more and more in love with Sutton—and I had no fucking clue how to tell her.

After breaking down the last box and tying them all together, I brought them out to the recycle bin. I stepped back into the building as Sutton was shutting off all the lights.

"I'm sorry it's so late. You look exhausted, Brody."

"I'm okay. Just glad I have tomorrow off."

Her face lit up. "Do you? I wasn't sure how long it would take us to set up the new space, so I wasn't planning on opening until one tomorrow. Want to grab a pizza and maybe watch a movie together? I mean, unless you're too tired. I'm a bundle of nerves, and I know I won't be able to go to sleep right away. Plus, I'm starving."

I felt a new surge of energy. "Pizza and a movie sound good to me. What kind of pizza do you want? I'll call it in and pick it up on the way home."

Sutton giggled.

Smiling, I asked, "What?"

"It's just weird."

"What's weird?"

"You live with me, and it's our home, and that struck me as strange for a moment."

I stepped closer to her and pushed a piece of hair behind her ear. "I like hearing you say it's our home."

"It doesn't bother you that Jack lived there, does it?"

Her question threw me for a loop, and from the look on her face, I wasn't entirely sure she meant to ask that question out loud. "Not at all. It's your house, and you love it, so that makes me love it too."

Sutton opened her mouth to say something, then shut it. Studying me for a minute, she finally said, "I'll stop and pick up some beer; I don't think we have any."

I closed my eyes and placed my hand over my left pec. "The woman knows the way to my heart."

Laughing, Sutton pushed me lightly. "I *am* married to you, after all. It only took me a day to realize you like to have at least one beer after work."

"You got me there."

We stood there, smiling at each other like two kids who weren't sure what to do next.

"Okay...you still like pepperoni and cheese?" I asked.

"Yep."

"I'll get the food, you get the booze. See you at the house in a few."

"Okay," Sutton said as she set the alarm and then stepped out and locked the door.

We walked in silence to her car, and I opened her door for her.

"Drive safe, Brody," Sutton said softly.

"Same to you."

I shut the door and watched as she backed out and drove away. Turning on my heels, I headed to my truck with a goofy-ass smile on my face.

Chapter Thirteen

Sutton

The second I pulled out of the parking lot, I called Palmer.

"Miss me already?" she asked when she picked up.

"Brody punched the living daylights out of Jack!"

"Wait—what?"

"Oh my God, Palmer, I know this sounds so wrong, and I'm so confused. But I was also *so turned on* watching Brody lunge forward and hit Jack. It was the best thing I've ever seen!"

Palmer giggled. "Lord, you are so weird. What happened? Where did you see Jack?"

"After you and Harlee left, he came into the store. Brody stayed in the back room while I went to see who was there. You forgot to lock the front door, by the way."

"No, I didn't. I locked it, Sutton."

My heart dropped. "Are you sure?"

"I'm positive."

"That means..."

"Jack has a key to the store."

I hit the steering wheel and cursed.

"What if he goes back?" she asked.

"I set the alarm, and I know for a fact he doesn't know the code.

I changed companies, as well as the password and code, when I left him."

"Thank God. Lord knows what that crazy man would do if he got into the store without you there."

I made a mental note to call the locksmith first thing in the morning. "I'll have the locks changed tomorrow."

"Good. Now back to the punching."

"Oh, right. So, I walked out to see Jack standing there. I immediately went behind the counter to put distance between us, and he started going on about how he can't believe I won't drop the restraining order. I wasn't scared, but that's probably because I knew Brody was in the back. The next thing I knew, Jack started to walk toward the counter, and then I heard Brody come out."

"What did he say? What did he say!?"

"He said something like, 'Take another step toward my wife and my fist will be in your face!' Not going to lie, it was hot."

Palmer burst out laughing, and so did I.

"Jesus, Sutton. You want the guy *bad*. So tell him."

"We're friends, Palmer."

"Who are both in love with one another. Anyone who sees the two of you looking at each other knows how you feel. Why can't you see it?"

I sighed. "I know Brody has feelings for me...but I'm not sure they're *those* kinds of feelings."

"Ugh! I really wish someone would punch *you* in the face." She paused. "Hey, did you bring a vibrator home?"

"No."

I must have waited a beat too long to answer because Palmer said, "You are such a terrible liar. Which one did you snag?"

I sighed and dropped my head down on the steering wheel as I waited for the light in front of me to turn green. "The rabbit one."

"I knew it! You should have seen your face when Harlee was talking about it. Are you going to try it out tonight?"

"Are you insane? No! Brody is there, and we're having a movie night."

Palmer whistled. "A movie night, huh? Sounds cozy."

"It's two friends enjoying some pizza, beer, and a movie. That's all."

"Riiiiight. Is that what we're calling it now? I'm calling it a man and wife getting all snuggled up on the sofa and trying out that new toy she brought home."

"Ugh, why do I even tell you anything!"

Palmer laughed. "Hey, I've got to run, but I'll talk to you tomorrow. Have fun with your hubby tonight!"

"Friend. Just friends!"

"Sure, you keep telling yourself that, Sutton. Bye! Love you."

"Love you too."

The call ended, and I pulled into the grocery store parking lot. After grabbing a couple bottles of wine, some beer, and chips and dip, I headed to the checkout.

"Hi, Sutton!" the cashier said.

"Oh, hey, Laney. How are you doing?"

She flashed me a quick smile as she rang up my stuff. "Good. So, I heard a rumor you're carrying some new styles in the store. Is that true?"

I paused for a moment and stared at her. Was *she* the gossip writer? No way. "I am. I've expanded my inventory, and I'm carrying more lingerie now too. It's a new line from a designer friend of mine. I'm opening up the store in the afternoon tomorrow, so please feel free to stop by any time after one if you want to check it out. I'll be open Saturday until two, as well, but I'm closed on Sundays."

Laney smiled. "I'll be there tomorrow! I have the day off. I'm so excited to see what you have. My boyfriend and I are celebrating our two-year anniversary on Saturday, so maybe I'll find a little something for me...and him."

"Happy anniversary. I hope you find something you like."

Laney beamed with happiness. "I'm sure I will. It's nice to have someone local carrying more personal items like that. I hate driving into Portland to go to Victoria's Secret."

"Well, these are all original designs and exclusive to Coastal Chic."

"Fun!" Laney said with a little clap before she told me my total.

"Thanks again, Laney. Hopefully I'll see you tomorrow."

"I'll be there right when you open!"

Once I got home, I put the beer in the fridge and headed upstairs to change. After smoothing my favorite lotion on my arms and legs, I took way too much time figuring out what to wear, and ended up choosing what I would've worn if I was home alone: a pair of leggings and a Seaside High sweatshirt that I'd stolen from Braxton. It was one of my favorite shirts to wear. I pulled my hair up and piled it on top of my head.

When I heard Brody come in the back door, I took one last look at myself in the mirror and then headed out of my bedroom.

"Hey," I said when I saw Brody at the top of the stairs.

"Hey, sweetheart. I need to get out of these clothes, then I'll be back down."

My chest exploded in a flurry at his use of the endearment, though I was positive he didn't even realize he'd said it. An image of almost-naked Brody from earlier this morning popped into my head, and I felt my cheeks heat. I looked down his entire body, then snapped my eyes back up to his. "No problem."

He gave me that crooked smile of his, and I swore he could read my mind—because he leaned in and said, "Thinking about this morning?"

"What?" I said with a nervous laugh. "No. Not at all. I'd totally forgotten about it. It's not like I haven't ever seen you na..."

My last word trailed off as Brody pulled his T-shirt over his head, then headed into his room. With his door still wide open, he turned around and started to unbutton his jeans while staring at me. My legs damn near went out from under me.

I narrowed my gaze at him, then quickly spun on my heels and headed downstairs. I went straight to the freezer, wishing I could crawl inside of it. "That damn man."

After forcing my libido to calm down, I took out some paper plates for the pizza and then grabbed two beers from the fridge.

"I got some ice cream for later," Brody said as he walked into the kitchen.

My eyes nearly popped out of my head at the sight before me. He was wearing sweats—low-hanging sweats, I might add—and a Boston Red Sox tank.

"What are you wearing?" I asked.

He paused while opening the pizza box and looked down at himself. "You're not a fan of the Red Sox?"

I swallowed the lump in my throat. "You have to change."

"Geesh, does your brother know you hate one of the greatest baseball teams of all times?"

I slowly shook my head, closed my eyes, and counted to ten before I focused on him once again. It took all my strength to keep my eyes on his face and not let them drift down to his muscular arms.

Chest and arms. My two weaknesses.

"I love the Sox," I said.

A look of relief washed over his face. "Thank God. I wasn't sure I could be married to a woman who didn't support them."

A warm sensation ran through my entire body, but I ignored it. "Brody, you need to change because...because..." I motioned up and down his body with my hands.

"Because of what?"

"You're showing too much arm!"

He blinked at me several times. "I'm sorry, what?"

"Your arms. Those big, bulky muscles. They're distracting."

The corners of his mouth twitched, and I knew the bastard was holding back a smile. "You mean *these* arms?" He lifted his right arm and flexed.

"That's just mean."

Laughing, he dropped his arm to his side. "Sutton, you want me to change because you don't want to see my arms?"

"You don't have to put on long sleeves. A T-shirt is fine. And change out of those sweats. I can practically see your—" I slammed both hands over my mouth, but my damn traitorous eyes still drifted down to his crotch. "Shit!" I swore as I spun around and faced the other way.

The heat of his body felt like a warm blanket as he walked up behind me—and he wasn't even touching me yet. He put his mouth to my ear. "Are you saying you're turned on by what I'm wearing? Because I can take it *all* off if you want."

I spun back around...and quickly realized that was a bad idea. He was close. Oh. So. Close.

"Brod—um, Brody. Okay, fine, I won't lie. You have an insanely...*fit*...body."

The corner of his mouth quirked up. Then he pulled a Sandra Bullock in *Miss Congeniality*. "You think I'm sexy, you want to touch me, you want to—"

I pressed my fingers to his mouth. "Shh, stop."

He lifted his hand and grabbed mine. When he laced our fingers together, I had to fight to breathe normally. "If you want me to change, I'll change," he said.

I nodded jerkily. "I want you to change."

"My shirt only."

I chewed on my lower lip for a moment, but stopped when his gaze went to my mouth. "Shirt only."

He brought my hand up and kissed the back of it, then ran his tongue over each knuckle. The room felt like it was tilting back and forth, and I grabbed his chest with my other hand.

"Brody," I whispered as I dug my fingertips into his muscles. "The pizza is getting cold."

Dropping my hand, he took a step back, and I felt myself sway. Without a word, he turned and headed back upstairs.

I made my way to the freezer, took out an ice cube, and ran it over my face and neck. "I'm going to need to break out that damn vibrator if the night keeps going like this."

Chapter Fourteen

Brody

The quiet knock on the door made me stop pacing around the bedroom.

"Um, Brody? Are you still coming down for pizza and movie night?"

She was going to kill me.

I walked over and opened the bedroom door and stared down at Sutton. She smiled, and my heart felt like it was going to burst from my chest.

Tell her, Brody. Tell her you love her. Tell her you want her. Hell, pull her into your arms and kiss the living shit out her.

"Are you mad I asked you to change?" she asked. "I don't really know what came over me. It's been a really long day."

I leaned closer and breathed deeply through my nose. "Is that... whiskey?"

She blushed. "I took a couple of shots. I needed to relax a bit. This whole new thing with the store and the vibrators and Jack showing up and having a key to the shop...it's a lot."

"Wait—what? You said Palmer forgot to lock the front door."

"No. I called her, and she said she *did* lock it. I guess Jack still has a key. I have a note to call the locksmith tomorrow."

That motherfucker. I hated the guy.

"But I'm feeling much more relaxed now," she said.

"Good." I motioned for her to head back downstairs. "Is this T-shirt okay?"

She glanced over her shoulder and gave me a thumbs up. "It's perfect. What do you want to watch?"

"I'll let you pick."

She clapped her hands and practically skipped to the kitchen. "Awesome! I've been dying to watch *Bridgerton*! I've read all the books, but I haven't been able to see the series yet."

"What's it about?"

She sighed as she placed a hand over her heart. "It's about this family and how they all find love in each of the books. It's a historical romance, so I hope that's okay. You can pick the next thing we watch."

"Historical romance?" I asked.

Flipping open the pizza box, she took two slices out. "It's a bit cold."

"That's okay. It's my fault for not wearing the right shirt."

She crinkled her nose, and I nearly groaned. Fuck if that wasn't adorable.

"Okay, bring the whole box. I've got our drinks out on the coffee table. You don't need a fork or anything, do you?" Sutton asked.

"Nope, I eat my pizza with my hands."

When Sutton grabbed the bottle of whiskey, I almost said something but then decided to let it go. Clearly, she needed it.

Except, we were only halfway through the first episode when I realized Sutton was getting hammered. Reaching for the bottle of whiskey when she wasn't looking, I quietly put it on the floor next to the sofa.

Sutton finished off the last slice of pizza, then got up and went for the ice cream. When she walked back in with a bottle of wine and two glasses, I knew it was going to be a long night.

She set each glass down, then handed me the bottle. "Will you pour?" She giggled. "I think I might be a bit buzzed."

"You think?"

She nodded and flopped back down on the sofa next to me. By the time the fourth episode started, she had her feet on my lap with her head against the armrest as she finished off the last of the wine.

"Um, Sutton, maybe you should let me make you a cup of coffee, or maybe drink some water?"

"What? No. I'm fine. Totally fine! As you can see...I can handle my alcohol."

I frowned. "I'm not really seeing that side of you, sweetheart."

She quickly sat up and put a hand to her heart. "I love it when you call me that. You haven't called me that in a long time. Well, you did earlier when you got home, but I don't think you realized it."

"Sweetheart?"

Sutton closed her eyes and let out a contented sigh. "But the time before that when you said it, you were..." Her voice trailed off, and she opened her eyes once more. "Brody, can I ask you something?"

I started to rub her feet. "Of course, you can."

She looked like she was debating what to say. Then she sighed. "Did you mean it when you said you didn't love me? That night that we, um..."

"Made love?"

Her brows pulled down, and she scrunched up her nose. "Is that what we did?"

"It was for me."

"That brings me back to my question. Did you mean it when you said you didn't love me?"

My heart jumped into my throat. "I would really rather have this conversation when you're not drunk."

She gave me a weak smile. "I'm not drunk enough that I won't remember. I can hold my alcohol, remember?"

I grinned. "I remember."

"Then tell me again when I'm sober, but tell me now too."

I reached for her hand and laced our fingers together. "No, Sutton. I didn't mean it at all."

Tears built in her eyes, and I leaned forward and cupped the side of her face. "Don't cry, Sutton."

"Why did you say it if you didn't mean it? I would have waited for you."

"That's why. I didn't want you to wait. I wanted you to live your life. Sutton, you were heading off to college. The last thing I *ever* wanted was for you to sit around and wait for me. It was never even certain that I'd come back home in one piece. I had a dangerous job in the Navy. I don't even know how many times I was shot at."

She gasped and her hand flew to her mouth. "What? You were serious when you said you were shot and stabbed?"

I ran my thumb over her cheek. "Yes, I was serious. And that night, with you...I was scared, Sutton."

"Of what?" she asked—then hiccupped.

I chuckled slightly before focusing on her again. "Of my feelings for you. I knew I loved you before we slept together. But after being with you...I'd never felt that way before, and it scared me. That was part of why I told you that lie. The other part was because I didn't think I was good enough for you. And I wanted you to live your life. Have fun in college. I never really thought you'd go back to Jack."

Closing her eyes, Sutton drew in a long breath and then let it out. I nearly coughed at the strength of the alcohol on her breath.

"I wasted all those years with him when what I really wanted was *you*."

My heart slammed against my chest. It killed me that I'd caused her pain. I pulled her onto my lap and held her. "I hate that I was the cause of any pain you might have suffered, Sutton. I'm so sorry."

She rested her head against my chest. "Do you know how many nights I've laid in bed and thought about that night we shared?"

"I have, too, Sutton." I lazily rubbed my hand up and down her back. "I can only hope that someday you'll forgive me."

Drawing her head back, Sutton's hazy eyes met mine. "Forgive you?"

I nodded.

"Brody, even knowing the outcome, I would give myself to you over and over again."

A lump formed in my throat, and I tried to swallow it away.

She brought her hand up and ran her fingers through my hair as her eyes searched my face. "I'm sorry I made you marry me."

I smiled. "You didn't make me marry you. And I'm not sorry we got married. You're the only woman I've *ever* wanted to marry."

Sutton's eyes filled with tears. "I really wish I wasn't kind of drunk."

"*Now* you admit you're drunk?" I asked on a laugh.

She moved in my lap to straddle me. "I said *kind of* drunk. Kiss me, Brody."

I licked my dry lips. "You've been drinking, Sutton. I'm not going to do this when you're drunk."

Her finger traced along my jawline. "I love it when you go a few days between shaves. You're so handsome. It's not fair."

Pressing my forehead to hers, I let out a shaky breath. "Let me take you up to your bed, so you can get some sleep."

She shook her head. "Kiss me like you kissed me the day we got married. At the bakery."

My heart pounded in my chest. Sutton's finger ran down my throat, and my entire body shivered.

"Please, Brody."

I lost the fight to wait. The moment she'd uttered the word *please*, I knew I'd lost the battle.

Placing my hand behind her neck, I gently pulled her to me, sealing my mouth over hers. She pushed her fingers into my hair as she pressed down, grinding against my hard dick. We both moaned, and when she opened her mouth more, I deepened the kiss. I wasn't sure where I began and she ended in that moment. All I knew was that it felt so goddamn *right*.

I ripped my mouth from hers and kissed down her neck, and she dropped her head back.

"Yes...oh God, yes," she moaned.

When her hands went under my shirt, I knew I had to stop this. She was drunk and most likely wouldn't even remember half of our conversation.

"We have to stop," I whispered against the base of her throat.

"No! Don't stop."

I pulled back. "Sutton, we *have* to stop. If I'm going to be with you again, I need to know it's because it's truly what you want and not because you've been drinking."

She blinked a few times, then finally nodded. When she attempted to crawl off of me, she slipped and damn near hit her head on the coffee table.

I jumped up. "Come on, let's get you to bed."

Picking her up, I carried her up the steps to her room. I set her down on her bed, and she closed her eyes, leaning against the headboard.

"Do you need help changing into pajamas or help in the bathroom?" I asked.

She opened her mouth to say something—then fell over onto the bed.

"Sutton?"

When she started to snore, I laughed. "Okay, then. Let's get you under the covers."

I pulled her back up into a seated position and pulled her covers down, then laid her head on the pillow. I drew the covers up and over her. She snuggled deeper into the pillow and sighed.

"Goodnight, sweetheart."

"'Night, Brody. I love you."

My heart felt like it skipped a goddamn beat at those three words. Warmth filled my chest as I stared down at her. I would love Sutton Bradley for as long as I lived, and I knew I'd do anything in my power to keep her happy, healthy, and safe.

I slowly shook my head. No. Not Bradley anymore. "I love you, too, Sutton Wilson. More than you know."

Kissing her on the forehead, I stepped back and gave her one last look before I walked out of her room. I softly shut the door and headed back downstairs, turning off the lights in the kitchen and living room.

After sitting on the sofa, I stared down at my still-hard cock. I could take it in my hand, but that wouldn't satisfy me in the least. I picked up the remote and turned off the TV, then sat in the dark for a few minutes until my phone buzzed. It was a text message from Miles.

A part of me wanted to delete the message without even reading it. Jack wasn't going to be in the picture much longer, so whatever Miles found would be moot at this point. But my curiosity got the better of me, and I opened the text.

Miles: Sir, I found some info on the subject you sent a few weeks back. Still interested?

I drew in a deep breath, then slowly exhaled.

Me: Yes. Send what you've found.

The three dots started to move, and I found myself holding my breath.

Miles: I'll email it all to you, but looks like our guy is into some shady business. He's also a polygamist.

My stomach dropped.

Me: Polygamist?

Miles: Married a Melissa Frankfort his sophomore year of college, then married a Sutton Bradley almost two years later. Divorced from the second wife, but still married to the first. Has two kids with her.

I stared at the text, stunned, then scrubbed my hand down my face. "Motherfucker!"

Once I got over the shock of *that* little bit of information, I replied to Miles.

Me: Send me everything you've got on him, Miles. And thanks.

Miles: Anything for you, Chief.

I tossed my phone onto the coffee table and stared at it. Five minutes later, it pinged with an email notification. Glancing toward the stairs, I closed my eyes.

"I'm so sorry, Sutton. I'm so fucking sorry."

Chapter Fifteen

Sutton

I rolled over, slowly opened my eyes, and then slammed them shut again. "Oh God, my head..."

"Good morning."

Turning at the sound of Brody's voice, I opened one eye and moaned. "It's too bright. My head feels like it's going to explode."

He chuckled. "Here, I have a glass of orange juice, your favorite bagel with cream cheese, and three Advil."

Forcing myself to sit up, I fully opened my eyes. The first thing I noticed was that I was still dressed in what I'd been wearing last night. Thank God. If anything had happened between me and Brody while I was drunk, I would never be able to look at him again.

Brody placed the tray over my lap and smiled. "Feeling it this morning, I take it?"

I let out another moan. "I haven't had that much to drink in I don't know how long. Why did you let me get so drunk?"

His eyes widened. "I tried to get you to slow down, but you weren't having it."

I picked up the orange juice and took a sip, and it made me feel the tiniest bit better.

I looked up at Brody and felt butterflies move into my stomach when I remembered our conversation on the couch.

"Do you remember anything from last night?" he asked as he sat down on the side of the bed.

I took a bite of the bagel and nodded.

"How much?" he asked, his face filled with hope. He clearly wanted me to remember at least some of it.

"All of it."

His brows lifted. "All of it, huh?"

I nodded, then reached for the orange juice and Advil. I tossed the pills into my mouth and drank half the glass. The memory of last night made my entire body feel warm.

A soft smile spread over Brody's face, and I felt my cheeks heat.

"Where do we go from here?" I asked.

Brody reached for my hand and kissed my knuckles. "Where do you want to go?"

I dug my teeth into my lip and shrugged. "I'm not sure. I feel like I need to pinch myself to make sure I wasn't dreaming last night."

"I meant everything I said, Sutton. I've never stopped loving you, and I hate that I didn't have the courage to take a leap with you that night."

My heart hammered in my chest, and I had to blink back tears of joy. I'd waited for so many years, dreamed so many times of hearing Brody say those words to me.

"I never stopped loving you, either," I said. "I feel like we've both been reading each other so wrong the last few months."

He laughed. "I think so. Sutton, I've never been happier than I have this past week. I...want to...date you."

I couldn't help but laugh. "Date me? You're married to me, Brody."

It was his turn to blush. "I've tried for so long to fight my feelings for you, and I'm tired of denying the truth. I think it's safe for me to fall."

"Fall?" I asked with a questioning look.

"That's what it feels like, Sutton. Like I'm on the edge of a cliff, and the only way I can have you is to step off it and fall. That thought used to scare me, but now...I'd fall from the moon if it meant getting to love you every day for the rest of my life."

Tears ran down my face as I felt a sob escape.

"Are those happy tears or...?" he asked.

I took the tray and placed it on the nightstand, then threw myself at Brody. He wrapped his arms around me and held me tight. Just held me. And it was the most amazing feeling I'd ever experienced.

"I love you," he whispered. "I love you so goddamn much, Sutton."

Squeezing my eyes shut, I prayed I wasn't dreaming. I pulled back and looked him directly in the eyes. "I'm not dreaming, right?"

He smiled, and my heart flipped in my chest. "No, sweetheart, you're not dreaming." His eyes fell to my mouth, then moved back up. "I want to kiss you, Sutton."

"Wait! I need to pee and rinse out my mouth!"

After a quick trip to the bathroom, I rushed back to the bed.

After catching my breath, I said, "Then what are you waiting for?"

A smile spread over Brody's handsome face. He slowly shook his head before sealing his mouth over mine.

I cupped his cheek with my hand. It felt like Brody's hands were everywhere on me, yet I needed more.

I pulled away and dropped my head back so he could kiss down my neck. Lord, what was it about him kissing me like that? It drove me to near madness. "Brody. More!"

He kissed back up my neck and along my jaw. "Tell me how far you want to go, sweetheart."

I closed my eyes and smiled. Was it really going to happen? All the nights I'd dreamed of having Brody inside of me again.

It *was* really going to happen. My hangover was slowly slipping away as I looked at my husband.

"I want you—*all* of you."

He reached for my shirt and pulled it over my head, then moaned. "You're not wearing a bra."

His hands cupped my breasts, and I dropped my head back again. When he took my nipple into his mouth, I nearly came undone. "Yes," I hissed, digging my fingers deeper into his thick hair.

His finger and thumb played with my other nipple, and I swore I felt an orgasm building already. My eyes snapped open, and I cried out, "Wait!"

Brody instantly stopped. "What's wrong?"

"I need something."

He looked at me with a confused expression. "Um, okay."

Laughing, I crawled off of him and glanced over my shoulder. "Feel free to get undressed. I'll be right back."

I dashed into my bathroom and spotted it on the counter, still plugged in. Smiling, I picked it up and drew in a deep breath. "You can do this, Sutton. You can totally ask the man you've been fantasizing about for years to use a vibrator on you."

Pulling the toy to my bare chest, I looked up toward Heaven and said a quick prayer that Brody wouldn't think I'd lost my mind, then headed back into the bedroom.

Brody was on the bed, naked. I came to a stop and just stared at him. He was beautiful in every way. From his dark brown hair to his muscular and insanely fit body to his... Oh my. That part of him hadn't changed one bit.

I licked my lips and stared at Brody's dick.

"Sutton." His voice sounded strained. When he reached for his cock and stroked it, my knees shook. "If you don't stop staring at me like that, I'm going to lose it right here."

I jerked my eyes up to meet his hot gaze. "I wanted to...well...I thought you could... I've never..."

Brody sat up. "What's wrong?"

I brought the vibrator out from behind my back—and watched as Brody's eyes lit up, pooling with desire.

A wickedly handsome grin appeared on his face as he lay back down, put both hands behind his head, and asked, "What do you want to do with that?"

Swallowing past the sudden frog in my throat, I answered, "I want you to play with me, using this."

Brody quickly got out of bed and walked over to me. He took the vibrator and set it on the bedside table, then began to take the rest of my clothes off. We stood in front of one another completely naked, but I had never felt so confident in my entire life. The way he looked at me made me feel so, so beautiful.

He cupped my face in his hands and kissed me. It was soft and sweet, and my heart felt as if it melted right on the spot.

"Have you ever used a vibrator before, or..." He frowned. "Has anyone ever used one on you?"

"No," I said, barely above a whisper.

He gifted me with that crooked grin of his. "I love you so much, Sutton Wilson."

A rush of happiness filled my entire body as I giggled. "Say that again. All of it."

"I love you so much—" he kissed the tip of my nose—"Sutton Wilson."

I wrapped my arms around his neck. "I love you more."

He lifted me up, and I wrapped my legs around him. The warmth of his body against my core made me rub against him like a cat in heat.

"Fuck, Sutton."

"Yes, please."

He groaned and gently placed me on the bed. "Lie back."

I quickly moved to the middle of the bed while trying to keep my breathing under control, but it was hard when I couldn't stop thinking of what Brody was about to do to me.

He reached for the vibrator. "Do you have any lube?"

"Do I need it?" I asked as I reached down and felt how wet I was.

Brody closed his eyes. "Jesus, Sutton. If you want me to last at all, you have to stop doing things like that."

I giggled. "Does it turn you on to see me touch myself?"

He stared at me with an expression I couldn't read. I suddenly got worried and began to sit up. But then he moved over the bed and captured my mouth with his. The kiss was hot and passionate and nearly stole my breath away. When he finally withdrew and looked down at me, he struggled to find his breath.

"It's the hottest fucking thing I've ever seen. You have no idea how crazy you make me, and to see you touch yourself...it makes me want to bury myself inside of you for days."

I felt a wide smile spread over my face. "There's some lube that came with it on the counter in my bathroom."

Brody got up so fast, I swore he had superpowers. In an instant he was back and climbing onto the bed. My heart rate kicked up like I was running a damn marathon.

Before he opened the bottle, he spread my legs and slowly pushed his fingers inside me. A look of pure ecstasy appeared on his face, and I loved that it was because of me.

"Brody, that feels so good."

He kissed the inside of my thigh, and I swore he purred. "As much as I want to keep doing this, I really want to play with this thing."

I nodded and tried to say something, but all that came out were excited breaths. Brody opened the lube, coated the vibrator, then slowly pushed his fingers inside of me once again. After he pumped a few times in and out, I grabbed at the sheets and lifted my hips. Then suddenly he was gone.

"No!" I whimpered—but then quickly moaned when I felt him rub my clit with the vibrator.

"Jesus, I'm pretty sure I'm going to come while doing this," he said.

I pressed my hand to my mouth to keep from laughing.

Brody slowly pushed the vibrator inside of me and then pulled it out a bit before easing in a little more. "Do you need more lube?"

"No," I said with a breathy voice.

"It's all the way in, sweetheart. I'm going to turn it on."

Before I could even reply, he turned it on—and I almost jumped off the bed. "Oh my God! Oh. My. God. Brody. Oh God!"

He placed kisses along my thigh as I fisted my hands in the sheets. "Does it feel good?" he asked.

I nodded frantically.

"Tell me how good it feels, Sutton."

The feeling was unlike anything I had ever experienced. All I could do was moan and arch my back.

"Sutton."

"Feels so good. Oh God, Brody. I...I...oh my God!" I could feel my orgasm building, and holy hell was it going to be big. "Brody! Oh God... Yes!"

And then it happened. The gates of orgasm Heaven burst open, and I experienced an out-of-body moment. I was pretty sure I screamed loudly enough for the entire block to hear me. I'd never in my life had an orgasm like that before. I felt my insides pulsing and my entire body shaking with pure pleasure. I could feel Brody watching me as I fell into a blissful moment of utter ecstasy.

"Too much! Can't! Oh God. I can't take it." I started to push at Brody's hands. It felt so good, yet also incredibly intense. "I want you! Brody, please!"

The vibrator was suddenly gone, and I was pretty sure I heard it thud to the floor.

"Condom?" he asked, rubbing his hard dick against my entrance.

"No. Just you."

That was all he needed to hear. Brody pushed inside of me—and I exploded again.

"Jesus! *Brody!* I'm coming again!" I clung to him as he moved slowly at first, then seemed to lose all control.

"Fuck, Sutton...I can't go slow."

I placed my hand on the side of his face. "Don't go slow. I want all of you, Brody."

He mouth crashed over mine as he picked up speed. I wrapped my legs around him and met him thrust for thrust.

"Sutton! Oh God, I'm gonna come."

"Yes. Brody, yes!"

And then, like a perfect dream, we fell together.

Chapter Sixteen

Brody

Sutton traced a circular pattern on my chest with her finger as I held her close to me.

"I don't want to get up," she said. "I want to stay like this for as long as we can."

Glancing over at the clock on her side table, I sighed. "Unfortunately, you have a store to open in four hours."

She lifted her head and rested her chin on her hand, which was flat on my chest. With a waggle of her brows, she said, "There's a lot we could do in four hours."

I laughed and pinched her ass.

"Ouch! That hurt."

"Should I kiss it?"

Her cheeks turned a beautiful shade of pink. "That was amazing, Brody. I never thought I could actually experience an orgasm like that."

"Which one? The vibrator, or me, inside you?"

She kissed my chest. "Both. But I have to be honest, the vibrator nearly sent me to an early grave in the most amazing way."

I laughed and held her closer to me. "How's your headache?"

"It disappeared the moment you kissed me."

"Wow, so I have some kind of magical power, huh?"

She laid her head on my chest and went back to tracing circles. "I guess so. I'm glad we talked last night."

"I'm glad you weren't too drunk to remember it."

Sutton let out a long sigh. "We should probably talk about something else, though..."

"The next position you want to try, or the next toy you want to sample?"

She gently slapped my chest. I swore I had never been so damn happy in my entire life.

Pulling up the sheet to cover herself, she sat up and faced me. Oh shit. Her face looked serious.

"I obviously never wanted kids with Jack, so I was on the pill the entire time we were married. I stopped taking them when we separated. Earlier...I wasn't really thinking when I told you not to use a condom. I swear it wasn't a trap or anything like that—I was just so caught up in the idea of being with you, and I just wanted to feel you. I'm so sorry, Brody. If you're upset with me, I completely understand."

I sat up, yanked the sheet away from her, and pulled her close enough to straddle me. "If you're asking if I want kids, the answer is yes. I want them with *you*, Sutton, and I'm not the least bit angry. If you'd told me you weren't on the pill but were still okay with me coming inside you, I would have died of happiness right there."

Her face erupted into a brilliant smile. I swore she could light up an entire room with that smile. She dug her teeth down into her kiss-swollen lip. It looked like she wanted to say something else but was clearly holding back.

"Stop biting your lip," I said, "that's my job now. Now tell me what's going on in that pretty little head of yours."

"Well, now that we're both clear on where we stand with kids... I'm wondering about those other positions you mentioned."

My heart slammed against my chest. I tilted my head and pushed a lock of hair behind her ear. "Sutton, I don't really want to ask this because the thought of you with Jack makes me physically sick...but what was sex like with him?"

She shrugged. "Pretty plain and simple. We honestly hardly ever slept together after our first few months of marriage. And when we *did* sleep together, it was nothing like how it is with you."

"You haven't been with any other guys?"

Her cheeks turned bright red. "No, I haven't."

Smiling, I kissed her forehead. "I cannot wait until Sunday."

Sutton's brows pulled down in confusion. "Why?"

"Because I'm going to keep you in bed all day and show you every single way I can make you come. With my hands and—" I cupped her right breast—"with my mouth." I glided my tongue across her neck. "And best of all, with my cock."

"Brody," she gasped when I pressed my thumb against her clit.

Rolling over, I worshipped her body for the next two hours, making her come with my mouth and my dick, until we finally had to get up and head to the store.

"All the locks have been changed out, Brody."

Rich handed me the new keys. "Thanks, Rich. I appreciate you coming over here so quickly."

Sutton walked into the storefront, and I couldn't help but smile at her. She had color to her cheeks from a morning full of lovemaking and a round of fucking in the shower that nearly killed both of us. I had a feeling the next couple of weeks would be filled with lots of moments like this morning.

"Thanks so much, Rich, for coming out to get this taken care of," she said.

He smiled at Sutton and looked away sheepishly.

Yeah, I feel ya, buddy. She's fucking amazing. Beautiful. Smart. And she's mine. The entire drive to the shop, she'd held my hand and had talked excitedly about the new items in the store. I hadn't seen this side of Sutton in a long time, and it damn near made me want to burst with pride. I loved that she was taking a chance on a somewhat new direction for Coastal Chic.

And the idea that she might already be pregnant with our baby... no words could describe how fucking amazing that felt.

"It was no problem, Mrs. Wilson."

Did my chest just puff up a little?

Sutton peeked up at me, and I winked.

"You'll tell Lynn we said hello?" Sutton said as we walked Rich through the store and out the back exit.

"Yes, I will for sure."

"Tell her to stop by sometime," she said. "I'll give her a discount for having such an amazing husband."

Rich blushed. "That's so nice of you. I'll let her know."

After he walked out the door, Sutton turned to look at me. "That makes me feel better, knowing Jack just can't come into the store anytime he wants."

I took her hand and pulled her to me. "Me too. You know what I think we should do?"

"Go unlock the door because it's almost time to open?"

Shaking my head, I glanced toward her office. "I think you should pick out another one of those toys up there in the pleasure cave and let me try it out on you."

Sutton started to laugh. "Pleasure cave?"

"Yeah, that's my name for it."

She tilted her head in thought. "I kind of like that, but Harlee and I already named it the pleasure loft."

"That's even better. Now, which one should I use on you in your office?" I asked as I leaned down to kiss her.

Flashing me a saucy grin, she replied, "You pick."

The knock on the back door caused us both to jump.

"Shoot, I forgot Harlee doesn't have the new key," Sutton said. "Looks like we'll have to play in the office later."

I grinned like a fool. "I'm holding you to that promise."

She laughed.

"I'll run to the hardware store and make a few extra keys. How many do you want?" I asked as she rushed to the back door and opened it.

It wasn't Harlee standing there, but Palmer. She walked in and took one look at Sutton, then at me. A huge, shit-eating grin appeared on her face. "Oh. My. God. You two had sex!"

Sutton's eyes went wide, and I simply smiled.

"What? Why would you say that?" Sutton asked as Palmer did a circle around her.

"You have color in the cheeks and a look in your eyes that says you've been thoroughly fu—"

Sutton held up her hands to stop her sister. "Okay, Palmer, you made your point."

Palmer's eyes gleamed. "So? Did you consummate the marriage?"

"What?" Harlee shouted as she walked in through the still-ajar back door

Palmer turned toward her. "Sutton and Brody finally had sex."

Harlee jumped up and down, clapping her hands. She rushed over to Sutton and hugged her. "Did you use a vibrator?"

Sutton opened her mouth, then shut it quickly. All three of them looked at me.

I shrugged. "Hey, I don't kiss and tell."

Palmer and Harlee both squealed and did some weird little jumping dance with Sutton sandwiched between them.

"And that is my cue to go to the hardware store," I said with a smirk on my face.

The two women let Sutton go, and I walked over to her. I placed my hand on the side of her face and looked into those beautiful eyes of hers that were sparkling with happiness. They were so green, they reminded me of a meadow in spring. "Good luck today, and I'll see you in a few."

She nodded and nibbled on her lower lip shyly before I kissed her.

"I love you," I said.

Her hands gripped at my long-sleeve T-shirt. "I love you too."

Harlee and Palmer both sighed, which caused me to laugh and Sutton to shoot them dirty looks. "Have fun, ladies!" I said.

Harlee followed me and called out, "Oh, we will!"

I glanced back and laughed as she waved goodbye, then shut the door behind me. Poor Sutton. She was most likely already getting hammered with questions.

For the first time in years, I whistled as I walked to my truck.

After stopping at the hardware store and getting the extra keys made for Coastal Chic, I swung by the Seaside Grill. When I walked in, I heard Gannon call out my name. I smiled when I saw him and Braxton sitting at a booth.

"Hey, you're just in time for lunch," Gannon said as he motioned for me to sit. I had texted Sutton to see if she was hungry, and she'd said that Palmer had already gotten her and Harlee sandwiches from The Maine Bakery. Apparently the store was packed and Palmer was going to stay and help out for the day.

"Great, have you already ordered?" I asked, sliding into the booth.

"Not yet," Gannon said. When he looked at me again...he paused.

"What?" I glanced from him to Braxton. "Why are you both looking at me like that?"

Braxton leaned in and lowered his voice. "You *better* have slept with my sister and not some random hookup."

I jerked my head back and stared at him. "I'm sorry?"

Gannon let out an unamused laugh. "Don't even try it, Brody. You were whistling when you walked in here."

"So, is that a crime?"

"Look at his eyes. They're spilling all his dirty little secrets." Braxton folded his arms over his chest. "Who did you sleep with?"

I shook my head and dropped back against the booth. "Not that it's any of your business, but my wife."

Braxton and Gannon both grinned.

"Jesus, it's about fucking time. Did you two talk first?" Braxton asked.

Gannon turned and looked at him. "You knew about Sutton and Brody, Brax?"

He scoffed. "Of course, I did."

"And you didn't beat his ass?"

It was my turn to let out a mirthless laugh. "He got one hit in, but only because I told him to."

Braxton pointed at me. "That's a lie. I believe I said I was going to have to hit you, just for my sister's honor."

Gannon slowly shook his head. "You asshole, you said the same thing to me."

Braxton grinned. "I can't help it if you both fell for it."

"I think we should get a free punch at your face," Gannon said.

"Don't do that. He's got such a pretty face," Ruby said as she set down Gannon and Braxton's drinks.

Gannon huffed.

Ruby looked around the table. "Ready to order?" After we gave her our orders, she nodded. "I'll get you your drink first, Brody."

"Thanks, Ruby."

She turned on her heels and headed off.

"So, I take it things are going well with you and Sutton then?" Gannon asked.

I couldn't keep from smiling. "Yeah, things are going good."

My brother and Braxton both grinned.

"I'm glad," Brax said. "You both deserve to find happiness. And just think, you won't have to deal with planning some big wedding like Gannon has to."

Gannon rolled his eyes. "You did luck out on that part."

I shrugged. "We may plan a small wedding later. For now, though, we'll just sit back and enjoy watching you and Addie stress out over yours."

Braxton laughed.

My expression grew more serious. "Jack was back at the store yesterday, harassing Sutton. We found out he still had a key, so I had all the locks changed today."

Braxton's eyes went wide. "What the hell is wrong with that guy?"

I shrugged. "He's a nut case."

"Were you there when he showed up yesterday?" Brax asked.

"I was. He now knows she's married to me, and I gave him a little parting gift as well."

"Tell me it was your fist in his face," Gannon said.

I smirked. "That's exactly what it was."

"Why does he even want her back? They didn't have a happy marriage," Braxton said with a shake of his head. "Why is he harassing her? He fucking *cheated* on her."

I rubbed at the back of my neck and glanced around the restaurant. "I have some more information about him, but I haven't told Sutton yet."

They both frowned. "What kind of information?" Braxton asked.

"The kind that's not going to make your sister happy at all."

Gannon and Braxton said in unison, "Shit."

Chapter Seventeen

Sutton

The Seaside Chronicle

October 15, 2022

Catch and Release

Seasiders,

It seems the newly married couple, Sutton and Brody Wilson, are enjoying married life

while Adelaide and Gannon's wedding is right around the corner. No news on the docks if Sutton and Brody will have a real wedding of their own.

One can only imagine if Mr. Wilson was the cause of the recent changes at Coastal Chic. As reported last week, Sutton is now carrying a sexier line of clothing, as well as lingerie and, well...this article is PG, so I'm not at liberty to share the little secret of the upstairs loft. You'll have to go and check it out for yourself.

Now that Mr. Wilson is officially off the market, people are buzzing that Braxton Bradley should be named this year's Catch of the Season instead. Maybe our newest Seaside resident, Dr. Mason Bryan, should toss his name into the hat. He is, after all, single and handsome to boot.

Speaking of the new doc in town, it's been reported to me by a few lobsters that there seems to be an influx of sick, single women flocking to appointments with the good doctor. I'll keep an ear to the pier for any more information.

Fair winds and following seas!

"Wow," Palmer said with a giggle. "Whoever's writing this really doesn't like Brax."

Addie and I both laughed. We'd all decided to meet for lunch at our folks' restaurant today.

Palmer shook her head. "I still don't understand how they know so much."

I nodded. "Every time someone comes into the store, I wonder if they could be the potential writer. Clearly, they've been in the store if they know about the naughty loft."

"I do that too!" Addie said. "Every time a patient comes in. She... or he...isn't wrong, though. The office has seen a big increase in single women since Dr. Bryan took over the practice."

Palmer leaned back in the booth with a thoughtful look on her face. "What's he like, Addie?"

Addie set her fork down and wiped at the corners of her mouth. "I'm glad you asked. I was actually going to talk to you about something. But first—he's very nice and seems like a great dad. He's had to bring Charlie to the office a few times, but he's such a sweet kid, you hardly even know he's there."

"Why is he bringing him into work?" I asked.

Addie drew in a deep breath. "Dr. Bryan has a great bedside manner with the patients, but he seems to be struggling with trying to balance his work life and home life. He had a live-in nanny before he moved, but she didn't want to relocate from Portland."

Palmer raised a brow. "A live-in nanny, huh?"

Laughing, Addie added, "She was fifty-eight and a widow. I seriously doubt there was anything going on between them. He asked me if I knew of anyone who might be interested in watching Charlie. I mentioned you, Palmer."

"Me?" Palmer asked in a stunned voice. "Why would I be interested? I have a job."

"Jobs, plural," I said with a wink.

She stuck her tongue out at me.

Addie shrugged. "I just thought you might be. Sounds like he'd pay well, and you seemed to hit it off with Charlie when you met him. Plus, then you wouldn't have to keep doing all your other jobs."

"I *like* my other jobs."

Addie blinked a few times at our younger sister. "You like picking up dog poop, Palmer?"

"That's not all I do, Addie."

I cut in before an argument could start. "I think you'd make a wonderful nanny, Palmer. And maybe you could keep a few of your other jobs as well."

Staring at me with a befuddled expression, Palmer slowly shook her head. "You honestly see me as a nanny?"

Addie and I both nodded and said together, "Yes."

She didn't respond, though it was clear the idea was tumbling around in Palmer's head.

"Just think about it," Addie said. "I gave him your cell phone number but told him I'd ask you about it first. I think you should at least talk to him about it."

"A *nanny*?" Palmer repeated.

"You could even take Charlie with you to walk the dogs each day," I suggested.

"Is he in school?" Palmer asked.

Addie nodded. "Yes, he's in kindergarten. Dr. Mason said it was a bit tough on him, since he started the school year in Portland and then had to move a month later."

"Poor little guy," I said.

"Who's a poor little guy?" a male voice called out.

I looked up and felt my stomach dip at the sight of Brody. I slipped out of the booth and reached up on my toes to kiss him. "Fancy seeing you here!"

His crooked, dimpled smile made my insides pulse with desire as he looked around the table. "How's it going, Palmer, Addie?"

"Good," Addie replied.

"It's going," Palmer said, still clearly distracted.

"Want to join us?" I asked.

Brody gave me a pout, and it was the cutest thing I'd ever seen. "I wish I could, but I have to get back. I only took a short break from work to grab some food on the run."

"That's a bummer. Will you be home late tonight?"

"Trying not to be."

"I'll keep dinner simple, just in case you are."

He smiled, then leaned in and kissed me again. "Sounds good, sweetheart. I'm going to go order. I'll stop back and say goodbye before I leave."

I beamed up at him. "Okay."

Watching him walk away, I felt that warm, tingly feeling in my chest I always got when he was nearby.

"It looks like things are going well with you two," Addie said, bumping my arm once I'd sat back down.

"They are," I said, my cheeks heating. "I never knew I could be this happy."

Palmer made a goofy face and placed her hands over her heart. "That's so sweet. You certainly never looked this happy with Jackass."

Addie chuckled, then sobered up. "Speaking of which, I saw him in the grocery store the other day. Took everything I had not to walk up and punch him."

"I saw him too," Palmer said. "I was out walking a few dogs and took them down to the pier. He was there, and he approached me. I never was a fan of his—as you know, Sutton—but something seems *really* off with him lately."

It felt like someone dropped a brick in my stomach. "What do you mean?"

Palmer moved around uneasily in her seat. "I didn't want to say anything because I thought maybe I was just imagining things, but…"

"What happened?" Addie asked while fear suddenly engulfed my entire body.

"He said something that I dismissed at first. But the more I think about it, the more I'm bothered by it."

"What did he say?" Addie urged.

Palmer looked at me as she spoke. "He said he thought it was cute how Brody thinks he won."

"Who said that?"

Brody's presence instantly put me at ease, and I found my voice. "Palmer ran into Jack on the pier. He said that to her."

"When did this happen?" he asked.

"A couple of days ago," Palmer answered. "At the time I just blew it off, but now I'm starting to think it was some kind of warning."

Addie looked up at Brody. "You don't think he would try to hurt you, do you?"

Her words caused my stomach to lurch, and I stared up at Brody in alarm.

Brody shook his head. "No, I think he's all talk. But just to be safe, I think we need to let the lawyer know about it."

"Did the sale of the shop happen yet?" Palmer asked.

I put my napkin down on my plate, my appetite gone. "We're supposed to close on it next week."

Palmer sighed. "Thank God. Then he'll totally be out of your life."

"I think I'm going to head back to the store," I said. "I'm not hungry anymore."

Palmer reached her hand across the table for mine. "I'm sorry, Sutton. I hope I didn't upset you. But when the topic of Jack came up, I remembered that conversation."

I forced myself to smile. "No, no, you didn't upset me. I just need a moment or two. And I really should get back and open up."

As soon as I stood, Brody put his arm around me. "I already paid for your lunch, ladies, so if you don't mind, I'm going to steal my wife away."

I could see the worry etched on both of my sisters' faces.

"Steal away!" Addie said in a sad attempt to sound chipper.

Brody pressed his hand to the small of my back as he guided me out of the restaurant. My mind was so crazy with thoughts of Jack that I didn't even think to say goodbye to my parents.

"Is Harlee working at the shop today?" Brody asked as we headed down the sidewalk. I had walked to the restaurant since it wasn't that far from Coastal Chic.

"No, she isn't. Why?"

The crease between his brows showed he was worried about something.

"You don't think Jack is really stupid enough to do something to you?" I asked.

He shook his head. "Not me."

I stopped walking and faced him. "Me? Do you think he's going to do something to me?"

"I'm not sure, Sutton."

Something was clearly wrong. "Brody, what are you not telling me? I can see it on your face; you have something to say."

He ran his fingers through his hair and sighed. "I've been trying to find a way to tell you...and honestly, I don't really want to."

I swallowed the sudden lump in my throat. "It has to do with Jack?"

He nodded. "I'm not going to tell you here on the street. I'll tell you tonight. Meanwhile, do you think maybe Harlee can come and work with you this afternoon?"

I jerked my head back. "You don't think I should be alone? I have a restraining order against him."

Brody looked into my eyes, and I could see the conflict there. He wanted to tell me it was okay, but he also wanted to have someone with me. "That restraining order hasn't stopped him yet."

A shiver ran through my body. "I'll call her and see if she can work today."

His body instantly relaxed a bit. "Let me walk you back to the shop."

I put my hand on his arm. "Don't be silly, it's in the opposite direction of where you need to be. I'll be fine." I reached up and kissed him on the cheek. "Be careful, and I'll see you later tonight, okay?"

He placed a quick kiss on my lips. "I will be, and I'll see you soon. I love you, Sutton."

Not in a million years would I ever get tired of hearing those words from him. "I love you too."

I watched as he turned and headed toward the waterfront. A sudden feeling of awareness came over me, and I quickly scanned the area, only to find life going on as usual. People walked up and down Main Street, going in and out of the shops. I shook away the uneasiness and quickly headed back toward Coastal Chic.

Pulling out my phone on the way, I called Harlee.

"Hello there!" she said.

"Hey, Harlee. Can you come in and work with me this afternoon?"

"Of course. When do you need me there by?"

"Just whenever you can make it. I'll explain more when you get here."

She paused for a moment. "Is everything okay?"

I chewed on my lip as I picked up my pace. "I think so, but honestly, I'm not a hundred percent sure."

"I'm leaving now. See you in a bit."

"Thanks, Harlee. See you soon."

Later that night, I stared in shock at the copy of the marriage certificate in my hand.

Brody reached for my other hand. "Hey, are you okay?"

I lifted my eyes to meet his. "He was married *already*? Before he married me?"

He nodded. "He got this girl pregnant and asked her to marry him. She was here on a student visa, originally from France. From what I can tell, I think they met when he was there on a trip working with his dad. Then she followed him to the States."

I nodded. "His father's accounting firm has another firm in Paris. I don't know much about it. I never got along with Jack's parents, so we didn't talk much."

"She's a couple of years older than Jack. She graduated the same year she got pregnant, then went back to France to have the baby."

Closing my eyes, I cursed. "Both junior and senior year, he went over there for a few months. Told me it was because of a study abroad program." I shook my head and laughed. "I am so stupid. I can't believe I didn't see it."

"Maybe you didn't see it because you didn't actually care."

Glancing over at Brody, I nodded. "I think you're right. I was always happy when he left to go to France. I never even cared how long he was gone for."

Brody rubbed at the back of his neck with his free hand. "Sutton, sweetheart...why did you marry him?"

I shrugged. "I guess I was simply settling. I couldn't have you, and I honestly had no desire to date anyone else. It was more of a convenience, really. When I walked into the house and saw him with another woman...I can't even begin to explain the relief I felt. That was my out. Yes, I could have divorced him at any time, but I didn't want to look like a failure in front of my parents. Looking back now, I know that was just utter stupidity on my part."

Brody squeezed my hand in his. "I hate that I did this to you."

"You didn't do *anything*, Brody. I made the decision to marry the idiot. But...does this mean our marriage never actually existed?"

"Yes. That's exactly what it means."

"So, did he ever really *legally* own half of Coastal Chic?"

Brody looked shocked. "Shit, Sutton. I never thought of that."

I quickly stood. "If the marriage wasn't a marriage, I wonder..." Racing to the kitchen for my cell phone, I pulled up my lawyer's number.

Brody followed me into the room. "There's no common-law marriage in the state of Maine," he said with a smile as I waited for my lawyer to pick up.

"I might not have to buy out Jack!"

By the time I was finished with the phone call, I was flying high. Brody had scanned all the documents his associate had found on Jack, and under the new circumstances, my lawyer was confident that, legally, Jack had no claim to Costal Chic. I wanted to jump for joy.

"Do you know what I can do with that money if I don't have to pay off Jack?" I said. "I can pay my parents back the money I borrowed from them *and* pay off a huge part of the mortgage on the building!"

Brody reached for me and pulled me close. "I wasn't sure I should dig around in Jack's life, but I'm so glad I did."

I wrapped my arms around his neck. "So am I. What should we do to celebrate?"

He raised his brows. "I can think of a few things that involve you getting naked."

I giggled as Brody lifted me in his arms, and I wrapped my legs around him. I ran my fingers through his dark brown hair, loving how those hazel eyes looked at me with pure desire. "I like the sound of getting naked."

Brody set me down on the kitchen counter and kissed me with slow, languid kisses. There wasn't anything I loved more than kissing him. He took his time, and I could easily get lost in his lips for days.

He lifted the long-sleeve T-shirt I'd put on when I'd gotten home, pulling it over my head and tossing it to the floor. A wicked smile played across his face as he reached behind me and unclasped my bra. He placed gentle kisses on my shoulder and up my neck, until he captured my mouth once again.

I tugged on his hair gently, drawing out a low growl from the back of his throat. He ripped his mouth away and stared into my eyes.

"I love touching your body, Sutton. I love putting my mouth on your silky soft skin and between your legs."

"Brody," I whimpered as he took one of my nipples in his mouth and used his fingers to play with the other. "More. Oh God, I want more."

"Tell me what you want me to do to you, sweetheart."

I placed my hands on the counter and lifted up. Brody didn't need to be told what to do. He quickly stripped off my yoga pants and panties and dropped down. He spread my legs, and my entire body shook with anticipation.

Brody covered my clit with his mouth, and I moaned in pure delight as I pushed back his thick hair with my fingers. He took his time licking and sucking me while I whimpered.

"Oh, yes," I hissed when he moved his tongue over my clit so slowly, I wanted to scream.

"Touch your breasts," he commanded before going back to fucking me with his tongue.

I brought my hand up and played with my nipple as I watched him. "Brody. I want you inside me."

He quickly stood and pulled his sweats down. I loved that he'd gone commando. I reached for his dick and slowly stroked it while he pumped his fingers inside of me.

"God, you're always so ready for me, sweetheart." He took his dick in his hand and rubbed the tip over my clit.

"Yes!" I cried out when he pushed into me.

"Do you want it slow, baby?"

I shook my head, and Brody smiled. He pressed his mouth to mine and moved inside of me hard and fast. It wasn't going to take long before I orgasmed. Brody knew exactly what to do to my body.

"I'm not going to last long, Sutton. I've been dreaming of being inside of you all day long."

His words tipped me over the cliff, and I felt myself pulse around his cock. "I'm coming! Brody!"

"That's it, baby...*fuck*, I feel you squeezing me. I'm going to come, Sutton."

He buried his face in my neck as I wrapped my arms around his. The sound of him calling out my name pulled another orgasm out of me, and I nearly bucked off the counter. Two orgasms back to back. Good Lord, what did the man do to me?

He stayed inside of me, holding me close, as our breathing slowly returned to normal.

"As hot as fucking you on our kitchen counter is, I'm taking you upstairs," he whispered.

Before either of us could move, the doorbell rang—and we both froze.

"Who could that be?" I asked while Brody pulled out of me. I instantly felt the loss of him. He turned and looked at the small monitor he'd installed last week and cursed. It was turned off. He walked over and flipped it on, and all the camera views he'd installed around the house came to life.

My parents were standing at our front door.

"Shit!" Brody and I said in unison. I scrambled to find my clothes, while all Brody had to do was pull up his pants.

"Why are my parents here?" I asked, hopping around on one foot as I tried to get the other one into my stupid yoga pants.

"I'll go answer the door, you get dressed."

I nodded and hopped into the half bath while Brody got himself together and headed to the door. I finally won the fight with my yoga pants, and I slipped my bra and T-shirt back on.

The sounds of parents' voices drifted through the house, and I started to giggle. I was *married*, for goodness sake. Married to the most amazing man, who also happened to be an incredible lover. I mean, just *look* at Brody; no one could blame me for having sex anytime, anyplace with the man.

"Good Lord, Sutton," I said as I stared at myself in the mirror and attempted to fix my hair. I was horny again, simple from thinking about him.

I heard Brody's voice in the living room. "Have a seat, and I'll get you something to drink."

Slipping out of the half bath, I joined him in the kitchen. "What did you say?" I asked as I pulled the lemonade out of the fridge.

"That you ran out to the garage for something."

"Oh, smart!"

He winked, and my belly flipped. "Is it wrong that I want you again?" I asked.

Brody closed his eyes and let out a low groan. "Sutton, I'm not wearing boxers, I'm in sweatpants, and your father is right in the other room. Don't say things like that."

I pouted. "I'm sorry. I'll keep my dirty thoughts to myself."

I picked up the pitcher while he grabbed the glasses. As we headed out of the kitchen, I glanced over my shoulder at Brody. I started to whisper something about the new vibrator I'd brought home just to tease him some more, but then I heard my mother and father arguing in the other room. I shut my mouth and focused on not tripping as I made my way into the living room.

"Hey, Mom and Dad. What are you two doing here?"

They looked at me with surprised expressions. Then Dad cleared his throat. "You invited us over for dinner earlier, when you came into the restaurant."

My mouth opened, then closed, then opened again, but nothing came out.

Brody saved me. "Yep. We're taking you *out* to dinner, actually. To Pete's Place."

Mom perked up. "Oh! Are we dressed okay?" Then she looked pointedly at me.

"I was just about to change," I said. "Lost track of time."

Brody laughed. "Same here."

Motioning for my parents to stay on the sofa, I said, "Wait right here, and we'll get ready."

"Wait, do we have reservations?" Dad asked.

Brody huffed. "Pete's my cousin, we don't need them." He put on a smile and grabbed my hand. "Come on, Sutton. Let's go change."

While I threw on a dress, Brody called his cousin Pete and begged him for a favor. He agreed to let us have a table for four in thirty minutes, but only if Braxton took him and some of his college buddies out on a fishing charter, which Brody agreed to...without asking my brother, of course.

"You realize Brax is going to kill you," I said.

"He owes me one."

Brody slipped a long sweater coat on me as I asked, "For what?"

He pulled my back against his front and kissed me on the cheek. "Trust me, you don't want to know."

If it involved my brother and a favor, I probably didn't. "Ready? How do I look?" I asked.

"Beautiful, as always."

He took my hand, and we headed back downstairs to my folks.

"Okay, we're ready!" I announced. Minutes later, we all headed out the door.

Mom and Dad decided to drive with us, so we took my car and Brody drove. Once we got to the restaurant, Pete himself sat us. He led us outside to the deck, which had been closed-in for the season with heat lamps stationed around, so it was nice and warm. There were only two other tables out there, so it wasn't as loud as the main dining room.

Pete grinned after he asked us what we wanted to drink. "I'll have those drinks brought out as well as some appetizers on the house."

"Aw, thanks so much, Pete!" I said with a smile.

Brody shook his cousin's hand. "Thanks, Pete."

"Sure thing. Enjoy your dinner."

After our drinks and appetizers were on the table, I took a deep breath and got ready to tell my parents what Brody had learned about Jack.

Before I got the chance, though, a strange feeling creeped up my spine. I shivered and reached for Brody's hand.

"What's wrong?" he asked.

I shook my head. "Nothing. I just had a weird feeling, that's all."

"You mentioned you had something to tell us in the car, Sutton?" Mom asked. "Your last surprise threw me for a loop, I won't lie. But I *will* say I don't think I've ever seen you so happy."

My father nodded. "I agree with your mother. Brody, you seem to make my daughter very happy, and for that, I thank you."

Brody's cheeks flushed, and it was adorable.

"You're right. I've *never* been happier, and it's all because of Brody," I replied as I squeezed his hand in mine. "But, Brody found out some information...on Jack."

Both of my parents sat up straighter.

"Oh?" Dad asked with a cautious expression. "What did you find out?"

I took a deep breath, glanced around to make sure no one was listening, and lowered my voice a bit. "He was already married to another woman when we got married. And he has two kids with her."

My mother's face went white, and my father sat back in his chair and folded his arms, his expression thunderous. "I'm going to kill that asshole," Dad growled.

My mother and Brody both said, "Get in line."

I couldn't help but chuckle. "I know it's shocking. But the good news is, it looks like he isn't a legal owner of Coastal Chic, so I most likely will *not* have to buy him out."

"Oh, Sutton!" my mother exclaimed. "That would be amazing."

"I know. I can pay you and Dad back, then put a big chunk down on the mortgage for the store."

My father shook his head, clearly still in shock. "He has *kids*?"

Brody spoke this time. "She was older than him, they met in college, and she got pregnant. He married her, then she went back to France."

Mom gasped. "Is that why he was always going over there?"

I nodded. "I think so."

"Does she know about *you*?"

Shrugging, I replied, "I don't know, and I don't care. We called my lawyer and sent over copies of everything Brody found. We should hear something back soon. I'm hoping early next week."

My father picked up his glass. "This is a reason to celebrate."

We all lifted our glasses and toasted.

Mom added, "Now, let's just hope the little prick goes back to France and leaves you in peace."

Brody choked on his beer as I let out a roar of laughter.

Dad lifted his beer once again. "I'll drink to that too!"

Chapter Eighteen

Brody

Gannon adjusted the sleeves of his tux for the hundredth time while Braxton and I sat on the sofa watching him.

"Gannon, your tux is fine," Brax said. "The weather is amazing, and you're about to marry the love of your life. Why are you pacing and acting like a freak?"

With a sigh, Gannon faced his soon-to-be brother-in-law. "When you marry the love of your life, then you can tell me how to act. I just want everything to be perfect for Addie."

Brax sat back on the couch. "The only thing she cares about is marrying you."

Gannon smiled. "Thanks, Brax." Turning to me, he asked, "Did you do a walk-around? How's it look out there?"

"I did. Twice. Everything's all set up for the ceremony and the reception."

"Heaters?"

Braxton answered, "I checked them like three times. They're working."

Gannon looked back at me. "Ring?"

Patting my tux jacket, I replied, "Right here."

He turned to Brax again. "How's your sister doing?"

He laughed. "Which one?"

Gannon shot him a dirty look. "The one I'm marrying."

"I checked in on her earlier, and she was ecstatic. She was about to put her dress on."

A wide smile spread across Gannon's face. "I can't wait to see her."

"I'm sure she's going to look beautiful," I said.

"I know she will. I just wish my heart would stop pounding. I don't know why I'm so damn nervous."

Braxton kicked his feet up on the coffee table and put his hands behind his head. "This is why I'll never get married."

I glanced over at our confirmed lifelong bachelor. "Why is that?"

"All this 'my heart is racing' and gushing over a dress. All the hassle of a wedding. No, thank you. No woman is worth all this trouble. If I ever do get married—and that's a very, *very* big if—I'm eloping like you and Sutton did."

I shook my head. "Sutton and I got married for completely different reasons. If we'd gone about it the right way, I would totally have had a wedding. Especially if she wanted one."

Gannon started to pace again, and Braxton rolled his eyes at him before focusing back on me. "She doesn't want to have a wedding now?"

I shook my head. "We've talked about going somewhere—maybe Belize or something—and renewing our vows, but no, Sutton doesn't want a big wedding."

"Not even considering the first one wasn't real?" Braxton asked.

I shook my head. "She's not the least bit interested."

"And you're okay with that?" Gannon asked.

I smiled. "I'm married to the love of my life, and it doesn't matter to me *how* we got married. As long as I get to go to sleep holding her at night and wake up holding her each morning, the rest I couldn't give two shits about."

And it looked like maybe I'd get my wish. Everything had finally worked out for Sutton in regards to Jackass. The courts ruled that the marriage was never legal, and therefore Jack had no rights to Coastal Chic. No one had seen him around town for the last week.

I was hoping that meant he'd gone back to France for good, as his lawyer claimed, to be with his *real* family. But I wasn't so sure.

"That's my man!" Braxton held out his fist, and I bumped it.

There was a light knock at the door, and we all turned toward it. The wedding planner poked her head in. "It's almost time. I need the three of you down at the wedding site."

I walked up to my brother and clapped him on the back. "Let's get you married."

He nodded and gave me a nervous smile.

"It's going to be fine, Gannon. Stop worrying."

Thirty minutes later, my brother turned and looked at me. "It's going to be fine, huh?"

A storm had moved over the coastline, and it was pouring. Luckily, there was a contingency plan for bad weather—but not a plan for the sky opening up just as the bride was almost to the groom. Not even joking. One second it was sunny, and then *whoosh*, the clouds rolled in, the wind whipped up, and the storm-of-all-storms started raging. Addie had rushed back inside, and now we were waiting for the backup plan to kick in.

I lifted my shoulders in an "I'm sorry" shrug. "Sorry, bro. But at least there's an umbrella on standby, and your bride is inside now, warm and dry."

Gannon and Addie were getting married at French's Point, which was just north of Seaside. Since the wedding was on Halloween—a Sunday evening—it was rather small, so we'd quickly moved the ceremony into the retreat house, which was a fucking mansion. The reception would still be held in a tent outside. The storm wasn't strong enough to mess with that plan. Thank God.

I smiled as I saw Sutton walking toward us. She was dressed in a beautiful light blue dress that showed off her bod in all the right ways. She looked stunning. Her hair was pulled up with curls framing her face and neck. Every time I saw her exposed neck, I wanted to bury my face in it.

"How's your sister?" I asked when she stopped in front of me and Gannon.

"She's actually good. The spot they found for you two to exchange your vows is beautiful. They've got the guests in there already. Addie is getting her hair fixed up a little, and then we'll be ready to go. I came to get the three of you."

Sutton looked past me to where her brother was sitting at the bar, flirting with some guest at the hotel.

"Do you mind pulling my brother away?" Sutton asked me with a grin.

"It would be my pleasure. I'll see you in a few."

She reached up and quickly kissed me on the lips. "Have I told you how handsome you look in that tux?"

I took a step back and put my arms out. "You like?"

Biting her lip, she said, "I like *very* much."

Gannon sighed, glancing from Sutton to me. "Okay, you get back to my future wife's side, and *you* go get her nearly drunk brother. Let's get this wedding started again."

I saluted while Sutton giggled and started back down the hall. I couldn't tear my eyes off how good her ass looked in that dress.

"Stop undressing your wife with your eyes, and go get my future dumbass brother-in-law," Gannon said.

"You got it, boss."

As I walked up to Braxton, I heard him say to the woman he was flirting with, "I'm sure I can sneak away at some point."

She slid a card his way. "Give me a text."

Braxton took it and slipped it into the pocket of his tux.

"Hate to break this up," I said, "but we've got a wedding to go to."

The woman—who looked at least ten or fifteen years older than Braxton—winked at him when he stood up.

As we walked toward Gannon, I quietly said, "Going for cougars now, are we?"

"Dude, did you see her smoking-hot body? Fuck yes, thank you very much."

We followed Gannon down the hallway as I said, "You seemed a little speechless when you saw Harlee walking down the aisle earlier."

He huffed. "I wasn't speechless."

"Well, between you and Chip, I thought one of you was going to pass out."

Braxton stopped and looked at me. "He likes Harlee?"

"Would you two come on. I still have no idea where Chip is," Gannon bitched.

Before I could answer either one of them, the man himself came walking up with a shit-eating grin on his face.

"What are you smiling about?" Braxton asked, an annoyed tone to his voice.

"Nothing," Chip answered.

I couldn't help but notice how he and Braxton exchanged a heated look, but there was no time to ask questions. "Time to take our places, gentlemen," I said.

We all moved to our new spots in the next room, and soon the music was playing and Palmer was walking down the aisle, followed by my beautiful bride, and then finally Harlee. I snuck a peek at Braxton and tried not to laugh. His eyes were glued on Harlee—as were Thomas's *and* Chip's. Interesting.

Then the music changed to the "Wedding March," and Addie appeared on the arm of her father.

I watched my brother wipe away tears of happiness as he and Addie exchanged wedding vows. Sutton and I kept catching each other's gaze, and I couldn't wait to get her up to our room. I was going to slowly pull that dress off her and worship her body for hours.

The storm stopped just in time for everyone to head over to the reception tent. It was set up beautifully, yet simple. The wood tables were decorated with understated greenery and candles, with classic place settings that added to the elegant décor. I liked that Addie had kept everything modest while still adding special touches throughout the room. It was honestly one of the most beautiful weddings and receptions I'd ever been to, even with the hiccup of the weather.

Hours later, most people had made their way out of the tent, and I scanned the remaining guests for my wife.

"Hello there, Mr. Wilson," Sutton purred into my ear from behind me.

Turning around, I pulled her close. She wrapped her arms around my neck, and I had to fight the urge to move my hands lower than her hips. "Have I told you how beautiful you look?" I said.

She crinkled her nose. "A time or two. Have I mentioned how hot you look in that tux?"

"A time or two."

"Now that the bride and groom have left, I think we should sneak away."

"Don't we need to help clean up?"

She shook her head. "Nope, Gannon and Addie hired a cleaning crew. My folks and yours are at the bar in the main hotel. I think Braxton must have hooked up with someone, because he slipped out of here right after Gannon and Addie."

"He met some lady at the bar earlier, before the wedding."

Sutton rolled her eyes. "Of course, he did." She quickly looked around the room. "Do you think they were here?"

"Who?" I asked as I dug my fingers deeper into her flesh. She smelled like flowers, and I wanted to bury my face in her hair.

"The person who writes the gossip column. I'm dying to see what they write about for Thursday. I mean, as long as it doesn't have anything to do with us."

"If they were here, they're probably going to write about all the single guys who followed Harlee and your sister around like puppies."

Sutton laughed. "Hey, did you happen to notice that Dr. Bryan was here, too? His son Charlie is a total sweetheart. And I saw the good doctor talking to Palmer for a bit."

"I did notice he was here. Is that an issue?"

"It's not. He asked her to nanny for his son. Addie recommended Palmer for the job."

I somehow couldn't see Palmer as a nanny. She seemed too carefree, and she definitely wasn't the type of person to be tied down to one thing. Which was why she currently had a million jobs. I rubbed the back of my neck as I said lightly, "Palmer? A nanny?"

"Yes!" Sutton said, playfully hitting my chest. "You don't see it? She has such a kind and sweet soul. She'd make a wonderful nanny. Not to mention, she'd be super fun."

After I thought about it for a moment or two, I nodded. "Okay, I can see it now. What about all her other jobs, though?"

Sutton glanced over her shoulder to where Palmer was sitting at a table with Dr. Bryan, his son, and two other women I didn't know.

"I'm not sure, but I hope she really considers it. I think they'd make a cute couple."

"Palmer and Dr. Bryan?"

She turned back and raised her brows. "You don't?"

I let out a disbelieving laugh. "Well, considering your sister has sworn off men, and the fact that there's a bit of an age gap, I don't know."

"Not that big of one. He's thirty-five. Besides, you're older than me by five years."

"And Palmer is twenty-seven. That's eight years. What if he doesn't want any more kids?"

Sutton chewed on her lip, and I reached up and pulled it free.

"Stop doing that, or I'll take you into the bathroom and bite that lip myself."

She wiggled her brows. "I say we leave now."

"I couldn't agree more."

Sutton and I made our way around the tent to the few people who were left. Dr. Bryan had already left with this son by the time we reached his table, so I missed the chance to meet him. Harlee and Thomas were gone, and Palmer was helping the cleaning staff pick up.

"Palmer, don't ruin that dress!" Sutton stated as she walked up and took a plate out of her sister's hand. "Come on, we'll walk you up to your room."

"No plans for this evening, Palmer?" I asked.

She shrugged. "I guess I could have a meaningless hookup with one of the three waiters who flirted with me all night. Or the dude who was working the front desk. He slipped me his number."

"Is that what you want? Casual sex?" Sutton asked.

She frowned, and I could see it in her eyes. Palmer was lonely—but she wasn't ready to admit it yet. "Not really. I'll most likely pull out the new vibrator that came in. I told Harlee I'd preview it for her."

I stumbled over my feet, stopped, and put my hands over my ears. "Nooooo. I don't want to hear that kind of stuff, Palmer! Not from you or anyone else."

"What about me?" Sutton asked with a smirk.

"You're different. You're my wife."

She beamed. "I love hearing you say those words."

I drew her body to mine and kissed her.

Palmer pretended to throw up. "Gag me. You two are worse than Gannon and Addie. Take it to your room."

The elevator door of the hotel opened, and we were about to step in when someone called out Palmer's name. She paused, and we all turned to see Dr. Bryan walking toward us.

"Hey, Mason. I thought you took Charlie up to your room?" Palmer asked as Sutton and I exchanged a look.

"Your mom was kind enough to offer to sit with him while we finished talking about the position."

"The *position*?" Sutton said coyly.

Palmer slowly turned and shot her sister a dirty look, and I was positive she also pinched her, because Sutton jerked and moved closer to me.

Mason nodded, oblivious. "Addie suggested Palmer as a possible nanny for Charlie." He looked back at Palmer. "Are you able to grab just one quick drink?"

Palmer was about to reject him—I could see it on her face—when Sutton spoke up. She gave her sister a little nudge. "She'd love to have a drink and talk about it more. She was just talking about the opportunity as we were walking to the elevator."

Mason's face lit up. Poor bastard. He had no idea what he was in for.

"Great. Just one drink," he said. "I know you said you were tired, and I don't want to leave your mom with Charlie for too long anyway. I'm sure she's exhausted."

"How kind of her to offer to watch him for you while we chat," Palmer said, clearly forcing the smile that was on her face. I wondered if anyone else heard the sarcasm in her voice.

It appeared Sutton did. For a moment, I thought she was going to volunteer to take over for their mother. But all I wanted to do was get her to our room.

I wrapped my arm around my wife and guided her to the elevator.

"You two enjoy your drink," Sutton called out as I ushered her away.

Pressing the up button, Sutton and I watched Palmer and Dr. Bryan head toward the bar.

"He is *so* into her," Sutton said with a giggle.

"Why do you say that?"

She turned and gaped at me. "Tell me you didn't see the way he looked at her, Brody!"

I smiled at my beautiful wife and escorted her into the elevator. "He just seemed like he wanted to talk to her about the job. If Palmer doesn't want it, she needs to tell him that."

She blinked a few times and shook her head. "You really don't think he's interested? I mean, you think he just wants her as a nanny?"

With a one-shoulder shrug, I replied, "I mean, I didn't see it. But then, I wasn't paying close attention to them."

Sutton chewed on her nail as she frowned. "But Mom must have seen it, as well, and that was why she offered to watch little Charlie, so Mason could take Palmer to the bar."

"Are all women like this?"

She nodded. "Yes. But now I'm wondering if it's wise for them to have a personal connection, if she's going to be Charlie's nanny. Maybe they should keep it professional."

"Maybe that's all he's interested in anyway."

The crinkle in her brow deepened. "Do you think? Maybe being so madly in love has clouded my judgment."

Smiling, I pulled her body against mine. "Madly in love, huh?"

She smiled back and ran her finger along my jawline. "I am *absolutely* madly in love, and I can't help it if I want my baby sister to find the same thing. I was in her position not that long ago. Ready to give up on all men and live my life alone. The only difference is, Palmer adopted a cat, so she's one step closer to becoming a cat lady."

I laughed. The elevator opened on our floor, and I motioned for Sutton to step out first. With my hand on her lower back, I guided her to our room. Once inside, I took off my jacket, then the cummerbund.

Sutton kicked off her heels and walked over to me. "Let me help you with the cufflinks."

The smell of lavender and some other flowery scent swirled around me as Sutton concentrated on the cufflinks. Once they were off, she started to undo my bow tie. "Did I happen to mention how turned on I am by seeing you in this tux?"

Smiling, I placed my hands on her hips. "*That*, you haven't mentioned. And you were more beautiful tonight than the bride."

She lifted her eyes to meet mine. "That's sweet of you, but Addie looked gorgeous. That gown was made for her."

"She did look beautiful."

I let my thoughts wander as Sutton undid the buttons on my dress shirt. "You're sure you don't want a real wedding?" I asked.

Once again, she paused to look at me. "I had a real wedding, and it was awful. Now I'm married to the love of my life. What more do I need?"

I pulled her body flush against mine. "A proper honeymoon, maybe?"

Her brows rose up. "Now that's something I could get onboard with."

"When and where? We haven't really talked about it."

She looked up in thought for a few moments before a wide smile spread over her face. "What if we just go up the coast and stay in a nice little place on the beach?"

"It's fall, though, and starting to get cooler. You don't want to go somewhere warm?"

She turned on her heels and looked at me over her shoulder. "Unzip me?"

My hands nearly trembled as I undid the zipper on her dress. It still took me by surprise when my body reacted so strongly to Sutton. As if every moment was our first time.

Sutton faced me once again and let the dress fall in a pool around her feet. "Oh, I'm pretty sure we can come up with ways to keep each other warm."

My dick jumped in my pants. "I'm not just sure about that. I know it for a fact."

She giggled and reached up to take her hair down. Her brown locks fell free around her bare shoulders, and then she stood before me in a matching set of white lace panties and a bra, with her hair floating around her.

"Please tell me that's a thong," I said.

"Thong guy, are you?" She turned and gifted me with the sight of her perfectly round ass.

"Fuck, Sutton. You look so damn hot."

"I could put my heels back on and do a few laps around the room if you'd like."

Quickly unbuttoning and unzipping my pants, I kicked off my dress shoes, pulled off my socks, and stripped out of the rest of the tux. After I finished getting undressed, Sutton reached behind her back and unclasped her bra, then slowly pushed her panties down while I sat on the bed, enjoying the view.

Sutton moved toward me and dropped to her knees. She stared at my cock, which was bobbing against my lower stomach, like it knew where her thoughts were.

"Sutton..."

Her eyes lifted and locked on mine. "I want to do this. I asked Palmer for some tips." Pink swept through her cheeks.

"Do I even want to know how that conversation went?"

She shook her head. "I don't think so. But I'm not sure I'll be able to look at a cucumber the same way ever again."

I closed my eyes and laughed. "Damn."

My eyes shot open when Sutton took me in her hand. "You'll tell me if I'm doing something wrong or if it's not what you like?"

"Trust me, I'll like all of it," I said in a strained voice.

Sutton started off by adding a bit of spit and using her hand. Then she took me in her mouth, and I damn near jumped off the bed.

I slid my fingers into her soft hair, trying to focus on keeping myself under control. "Jesus, that feels so good."

She worked her mouth and her hand together, and when she took me in deep and moaned, I almost came on the spot.

"Oh God, Sutton!"

Moving her hand faster, she sucked me harder.

"I'm so close. Fuck, it feels too good."

She kept moving her hand while the other played with my balls. When she picked up speed, that's when I knew I was about to lose the fight.

"Sutton, baby...I'm going to come. You need to stop."

When she showed no signs of stopping, I reached down, pulled her off me, and tossed her onto the bed.

"Brody! That's not fair," she complained as I moved over her and spread her legs. I found her entrance with my hand and slipped two fingers inside of her, causing us both to moan.

"What's not fair is having to watch you move around for hours in that dress. The way your hips swayed...and that ass of yours...I can't tell you how many times I nearly dragged you into a corner to have my way with you."

She giggled, then sucked in a breath when I rubbed my thumb against her clit. "Brody!"

I pressed my mouth to the delicious part of her neck that I loved to kiss. "Yes?"

"Please! I want you so badly."

Moving my fingers faster, I circled her clit until I felt her body stiffen, then tremble, as her orgasm washed over her. Sutton grabbed one of the pillows and covered her face as she moaned and called out my name. Or at least, I was pretty sure she was calling out my name.

When her body relaxed, I moved over her and pulled the pillow away. My mouth found hers, and I kissed her deeply. Her fingers pushed through my hair before she moved her hands down my back and to my ass. She dug her fingernails in, trying to get me to push inside of her.

All I wanted to do was kiss her. Taste the mix of mint and chocolate on her tongue and feel the connection between us. I *loved* kissing Sutton.

She wrapped her arms around my back and purred my name when I moved my mouth down her neck and across her chest. "Brody..."

I covered one of her nipples with my mouth and gently sucked until it was a tight little point. Then I gently bit down on it with my teeth, and Sutton's back arched off the bed as she gasped.

She brought her hand up so she could play with her other nipple, and I smiled. I loved that she wasn't afraid to express what felt good. When her hand slipped farther down, and she started to rub her clit, I nearly lost my load. I pulled her hand away, laced my fingers with hers, and pinned them over her head as I slowly pushed inside of her.

"Oh God, yes. Brody, you feel so good!"

I thrust slowly and easily as I gently kissed her. Our tongues moved in a beautiful dance, and I found myself wishing the night would last forever.

But my wife was losing her patience, and she jerked her hips up, dragging her mouth from mine. "More. I need more..."

I gave her what she asked for, and goddamn if it didn't feel like heaven. "God, Sutton," I panted, burying my face in her neck. "I'm going to come."

Moving my hips slightly, I adjusted the angle, and she let out a gasp. She squeezed my hands tightly as we both came together.

I eventually pulled out and tumbled to the bed next to Sutton. We both drew in deep breaths as I clasped her hand with mine.

"Why does this keep getting better and better?" she asked, letting go of my hand and rolling to her side.

Smiling, I turned and looked at her. "I know this is crazy...or maybe it's *not* crazy...but I cannot seem to get enough of you."

She traced a pattern on my bare chest with her finger. "It's not crazy, because I feel the same way. I crave you like I've never craved anyone before."

I put my arm around her and pulled her closer. When Sutton laid her head on my chest, I felt an incredible rush of love sweep through me. I'd never been so happy in my entire life.

"I have moments when a thought sneaks into my head," she said, "and sometimes I think I'm nuts for thinking it...but it makes me happy."

Kissing the top of her head, I said, "Tell me what the thought is."

She took a deep breath in, then slowly let it out. "Every time we make love, I pray this is the time it happens."

"It?"

She lifted her head and looked at me. "That I get pregnant. I know it's insane, and we probably should be more careful, but the idea of carrying your child inside me...it just does something to me. Makes me feel so..."

"Hopeful?" I asked as I stroked my fingers over her back.

"Yes."

"I feel the same way, Sutton. A part of me wants to keep you all to myself, but another part can't wait to start a family together. I frequently wonder if we'll have a girl or a boy first."

Her eyes lit up. "You do?"

"I do. Of course, I don't really care. As long as you and the baby are healthy, that's all that matters."

Sutton sighed with contentment. Not long after, I heard her breathing become deep and steady, and I knew my princess was sleeping.

I closed my eyes and thanked God once again for the gift of Sutton. I couldn't imagine my life without her in it.

Chapter Nineteen

Sutton

The Seaside Chronicle

November 1, 2022

Keepin' it Real (Special Edition)

Seasiders,

We all know the youngest Bradley sibling must be the most carefree of the bunch. Last this writer heard, Palmer was employed with at least five different jobs. Pet walker, house sitter, vet recep-tionist, nanny, and the least of my favorite, pooper scooper. To each her own, I guess.

Word on the docks is Palmer has caught the eye of our latest new Seaside resident and single dad, Mason Bryan. Oh, his little boy, Charlie, is just the sweetest thing. A little seagull has planted in my ear that Palmer will be Charlie's new nanny...don't worry, Seasiders, I've got my ear to the ground and will keep you updated on this latest development.

Fair winds and following seas!

I took a sip of coffee as I watched Palmer read the special edition of the gossip column.

Her eyes darted up to mine while her mouth opened, then closed. "Does this person have eyes and ears *everywhere*!?"

"It appears so," my mother said. She glanced over at my father, who was happily eating his eggs and toast. We were all set to head back to Seaside in a couple of hours. Addie and Gannon had slipped out early this morning to drive to Boston to catch a flight for their honeymoon.

"Why can't they write about another family? Why is it always *our* family?" Palmer griped as she slammed the paper down. "For the record, I have not agreed to be his son's nanny. And I've never *been* a nanny before."

"That's a clue," Harlee said, sipping her mimosa.

"Isn't it a little early to be drinking alcohol, Harlee?" Braxton asked.

A look of pure outrage moved over Harlee's features before she covered it up with a smile. "Considering you joined us for breakfast still wearing your tux, I think your thoughts on *any* subject this morning don't count. Or at least, no one cares to hear them."

Braxton opened his mouth to reply, but my mother cleared her throat and shot him a warning look.

"It *is* a clue," Palmer said. "That means the person who's writing this doesn't really know us very well."

"Or they simply made a mistake and threw nanny in there among your other current jobs," Brody said with a shrug.

"Oh! Or they did it to purposely throw us off," my mother added.

Harlee pointed at her. "You're a genius."

Mom blushed and waved off Harlee's compliment while Braxton leaned over and whispered something in Harlee's ear.

Next thing I knew, he was jumping and letting out a small whimper. Harlee calmly picked up her drink and smirked before taking a sip.

My father cleared his throat. "Well, I, for one, wish they would stop writing about my daughters. Go after Braxton, at least."

"Hey!" my brother said, shooting our father a wounded look.

Harlee huffed. "From the little they've already written about Brax, it appears they know him very well."

Palmer and I both covered our mouths to hide our laughter while Brody, Chip, and Thomas—Harlee's boyfriend, and one of my brother's best friends—all laughed.

Mom and Dad both rolled their eyes. "Can I not get a moment's peace over breakfast?" Dad groused.

"I knew we should have joined Ken and Janet on that morning walk," my mother mumbled as she lifted her coffee and took a sip, side-eyeing Harlee's mimosas.

"Can we get back to this stupid gossip column?" Palmer sat back in her chair and folded her arms over her chest.

"What's wrong?" I teased. "You don't like being the subject of the gossip mill?"

Giving me a look that should have knocked me out of my chair, Palmer replied, "No I don't. Especially when there's a little boy involved."

"Okay, that is true," I agreed.

Palmer sighed. "Braxton, can't you do something wicked and wild to get them off my scent?"

He winked at me. "Who says I haven't already."

Harlee pretended to gag as Thomas clapped Braxton on the back. He started to say something, but Harlee shot him a look. He quickly pressed his mouth into a tight line and gave Braxton an apologetic smile.

"I think the conversation is turning in a direction I don't wish to be a part of." Mom stood. "Keegan, shall we head on up to the room and finish packing?"

My father looked lovingly at his plate, which had ja few bites left. "But...I'm not finished."

With a look as sweet as can be, my mother replied, "You're finished."

She turned and started to walk out of the dining room while my father stood, threw his napkin on his plate, and glared at my brother.

"Hey, it's not my fault!" Braxton exclaimed.

Dad slowly shook his head, then turned and stormed out. Brody chuckled next to me. "I think your dad really wants to retire. He's seemed to enjoy himself this weekend, being away from the restaurant."

I nodded, then sighed. Turning to Braxton and Palmer, I said, "I really think Mom and Dad should consider retiring earlier. Dad seems so...tired."

"They both do," Palmer added, worry etched on her face.

Braxton nodded. "I agree. I tried talking to them about it a couple of days ago, and I think they *do* want to retire. But they're not sure what they'll do with all that free time."

"Well," Harlee started, "they do have two married daughters now. Maybe grandkids are in the works."

I felt my cheeks heat, and Brody reached for my hand and squeezed it.

Palmer saw the interaction and gasped. "Are you pregnant?" she practically shouted.

"Annnnnd now that will be in Thursday's paper," Braxton said dryly.

Brody laughed while I shook my head. "No, Palmer, I am not pregnant."

She and Harlee both sighed in disappointment.

A younger gentleman came up to the table and asked, "Mr. Braxton Bradley?"

Braxton looked at him. "That's me."

"An urgent message was left for you at the front desk."

Taking the note from the man, Braxton frowned.

"You don't think anything happened to the boats, do you?" Thomas asked.

Thomas and Braxton had been friends since high school. A few years back, Thomas had joined Braxton in running his fishing charter company. Braxton was so well known for his fishing expertise that his charters had grown in popularity much faster than he'd expected.

"I hope not," Braxton said as he opened the note and read it. Then his eyes jerked up to meet Brody's. "I need to talk to you—in private."

Brody seemed confused, but quickly stood and followed my brother, who had already gotten up and walked away.

"Okay, was that weird or what?" Palmer asked as she looked back at me. "You don't think anything happened to Addie or Gannon, do you?"

I swallowed the sudden lump in my throat. "I...I hope not."

"Let's not jump to any conclusions." Harlee gave me a smile that didn't quite reach her eyes.

Looking in the direction where my brother and husband had walked off, I got up.

"Where are you going?" Palmer asked.

"To find out what's happening."

It didn't take me long to find Brody and Braxton in a corner, talking quietly. They both looked angry—and worried.

"What's going on?" I asked as I walked up to them.

They exchanged a look, then Brody nodded to Braxton.

"Chip left early this morning to head back to Seaside," Brax said, "and as he was driving into town, he saw smoke."

My heart started to pound. "What was it?" I pressed my hand to my throat, feeling like I was going to get sick. "Please say it wasn't the restaurant!"

Braxton shook his head. "No, it wasn't the restaurant, Sutton."

"Then what *was* it?" I asked in a panic. Brody reached for my hand and squeezed it. "Coastal Chic?"

"It was Brody's beach house...or, I guess, it's both of yours now."

My legs felt weak, and I took a few steps back. "Oh my God, what happened?"

"I don't know. Chip said the fire department was there, and that they'd tried to call Brody, his parents, and Gannon but couldn't reach any of them."

"Our phones are all up in the rooms because Gannon and Addie asked us to keep it a phone-free event," I said. "They wanted us to be present in the moment. I doubt anyone has their phones on them right now. Gannon and Addie might be on the plane already."

"Do they know how it started?" I asked.

Braxton shook his head. "I don't think they know yet."

"We need to find my parents and head back home," Brody said.

All I could do was shake my head.

"You two go pack," Brax said, "and I'll let everyone else know while I try to find your parents."

"Thanks, Brax." Brody's voice sounded void of all emotions. His face, though, showed the sorrow he was clearly feeling. The memories that were in that house for Brody and his entire family... I couldn't even imagine the loss.

I jumped when Brody took my hand in his. "Come on, let's go get packed," he said.

"Arson?" I asked, sitting on the sofa and covering my mouth with my hand. I felt like I was about to throw up.

"Are you sure?" Ken asked, holding Janet's hand.

Bobby Jackson, the fire inspector, nodded his head. "It was started on the porch with an accelerant. It spread quickly, and by the time it was called in, there was no way they could save the structure. I'm really sorry, Brody. I wish we could have done more."

Brody reached his hand out for Bobby's to shake it. "I'm just glad no one was hurt. The house can be replaced."

Janet sniffled, and Ken ran his hand up and down her back soothingly. "Brody's right," he said. "I'm also glad no one was seriously injured while fighting the fire."

"What if you had been living there?" Janet asked the question I'd been running over and over in my head.

He smiled tightly at her. "I wasn't, though, Mom. So we don't even have to imagine it."

Janet nodded and wiped her tears. I quickly stood and rushed to the downstairs bathroom in Ken and Janet's house.

I could hear Brody's footsteps behind me. I barely made it to the toilet before I threw up.

Brody knelt next to me, holding my hair back and gently rubbing my back. I thought about how I'd watched his father do the same thing for his mom only moments ago.

"Hey, are you okay?" he asked.

I fell back onto my ass and buried my face in my hands as I started to cry.

Brody engulfed me in his arms and held me while I let out all the fear and anger I'd built up over the last few days.

"Shhh, it's okay, sweetheart."

"Who would do such a thing?" I could see he had someone on his mind but didn't want to say it aloud. "Brody, who do you think it was?"

"If I'm being honest, I'd say Jack."

Gasping, I stared at him. "Jack? He's in France though. I mean, that's what his lawyer said—that he was going back to his wife and kids."

Brody nodded. "I didn't want to say anything because I didn't want you to worry, but Brax was almost certain he saw Jack on his parents' yacht. The one that's docked at the marina."

"Has anyone gone to see if he's there?"

"I mentioned it to the Seaside Police. They're going to investigate."

"When?"

"Yesterday, after I spoke to them."

"And you haven't heard anything since?"

Brody shook his head and tucked a piece of hair behind my ear. "Not yet."

"We should go see for ourselves then."

His eyes went wide. "Are you crazy? First, you still have a restraining order on him. Second, Brax wasn't a hundred percent sure it was Jack. It could have been someone else. His father even."

I shook my head. "Don and Melinda aren't in Seaside."

His brows pulled down as he frowned. "How do you know that?"

"They stopped by the store the other day to say they were leaving town that evening. They wanted to tell me they were sorry for all the problems Jack had caused me, and for any part they might have played in it."

"I wish that family would just leave you the hell alone."

I forced myself to smile. "Me too. What does your gut say? Do you think Jack is still in Seaside?"

Brody shook his head. "I think he left with this tail between his legs. Come on, let's get you up and get some water to rinse out your mouth."

"Can we stop by the police station on the way home and ask if they've checked on your tip yet?"

He gave me a sweet smile. "Yes."

Brody and I stayed at his parents' house for dinner after Janet begged us not to leave just yet. Brody had emailed the fire inspector's report to his insurance agent. After they went through the house, Brody planned on tearing the rest of it down. We would decide what to do with the property later. We all decided to wait to tell Gannon and Addie about it until they came back home. There was no reason to spoil their honeymoon.

Later that night, as Brody pulled into the driveway of our house, I had the strangest feeling that someone was watching us. A shiver ran down my spine. It was quickly chased away by the warmth of my husband's hand on my lower back as we made our way into the house.

But before we walked in, I glanced over my shoulder and did a quick sweep of the backyard. It was dark, so I wasn't sure what I expected to see.

"What's wrong?" Brody asked.

I forced a smile as I looked at him. "Nothing. I'm just tired."

"Me too. Let's take a shower, and then I'll give you a massage."

"I like the sound of that."

Chapter Twenty

Sutton

Two weeks had passed since the fire. The police had checked the marina, and not only were there no signs of Jack, but they discovered that his parents had sold their boat. Their house was also up for sale, and Jack's dad had closed his accounting firm in Seaside. No advance notice, nothing. Just shut the doors and that was it. It was clear that the Larsons were no longer making Seaside their home, which was fine by me.

The door to the store opened and the bell rang as Palmer came walking in. "Did you see the article today?"

I nodded. "I did!"

Palmer pulled the newspaper out of her jacket and flipped it open. "I have to read it out loud. I've never laughed so hard in my entire life!"

The Seaside Chronicle

November 17, 2022

Master Baiter

Seasiders,

Our runner-up for Catch of the Season, and our now-default winner because the real winner went off and got married, ran into a bit of trouble this past week.

I was told from some reliable seagulls at the marina that Mr. Braxton Bradley was attempting to show off for some clients (female, I might add) and ran into a bit of bad luck. You see, he fell off his own boat. The boat he charters to take people out to fish. The man responsible for keeping people safe on the high seas...fell off his own boat. I don't know about you, but I hope those ladies demanded a refund.

Word on the docks is that Braxton tripped and twisted his ankle, which caused him to fall in. This writer believes it was something simpler.

Karma.

After all, there's a reason Mr. Bradley was the runner-up for Catch of the Season. One has to wonder what he's doing with his free time at home these next few days.

I'm just saying...

Fair winds and following seas!

Once Palmer finished reading, we both started to laugh.

"I think my favorite part is the title of the article," she said. "Master Baiter! This person *really* doesn't like Brax!"

I wiped the tears away as I attempted to draw in a breath. Once I had the giggles under control, I let out a long sigh. "Oh, man. Brody and I laughed our asses off this morning when we read that. Has anyone heard from Brax since it came out?"

Palmer giggled again. "I texted him after I read it, but he didn't text back."

"What did you text him?"

She pressed her lips together to keep from laughing again. She pulled out her phone and hit a few things, then turned it for me to see.

It was a text that asked, "Are you busy?" And under it was a gif of what looked like a guy jacking off.

"Palmer! You did not!"

She started to laugh. "I did! Needless to say, he *still* hasn't responded."

"Poor Brax. Brody sent him a 'how to masturbate without hurting yourself or anyone around you' article after he saw that."

Palmer started to laugh all over again. The bell above the door rang and Harlee walked in. She took one look at us—and cracked up too.

"I take it you read the article?" I managed to get out while I was laughing.

"It was the first thing I read this morning. I think the writer of this article and I should meet. We could be BFFs."

We all started to laugh again until I couldn't breathe.

"I needed that," Palmer said with a sigh.

"Hey, what's going on with you and the nanny job?" I asked as I followed Harlee back to my office. She put her purse in the locked drawer while I took mine out. She was going to close the store for me today, so I could have the afternoon off.

"I just don't know if I can give up my other jobs," Palmer said. "I love working at the vet clinic, and I value my days at the pet shelter. I mean, I could still do a few hours at either place in the morning, since Charlie's in school. The poop-scooping business isn't a big deal. I can schedule that on the weekends."

Harlee leaned against the doorframe. "It sounds like you've been thinking about it, at least."

Palmer nodded. "I have. It's a steady paycheck, and it could be fun. The only problem is...Charlie's dad."

I raised my brow. "You don't like him?"

"Addie said he's one of the nicest guys she's ever met," Harlee added.

"Oh, I like him. That's the problem. Have the two of you *seen* the man? He's hot as hell, and he has an amazing body. But do I really want to work for a man I'm physically attracted to?"

"I thought you swore off all men?" I asked with a wink.

"I have," Palmer returned. "But after Addie and Gannon's reception when we went to the bar to talk, my mind was...well, let's just say I wasn't thinking of fun games to play with Charlie. More like the fun games I wanted to play with his father."

Harlee and I both laughed.

Palmer frowned. "So you see, I really don't think it would be a good idea. Besides, I heard he's found someone else."

"What?" Harlee asked. "He hired someone?"

"Addie said he hired a high school student to help him out."

"For now," I added. "He needed someone quickly, but according to Addie, it's only temporary. He's still hoping to hire a permanent nanny."

Palmer shrugged. "Why don't *you* do it, Harlee?"

Harlee's eyes nearly popped out of her head. "Me? In what universe do you honestly think I'd want to be a nanny?"

Palmer followed Harlee back toward the front of the store. As Harlee started to straighten up the clothes on one of the displays, my sister made her case.

"You volunteer in the children's ward at the hospital. You organize the toy drive every Christmas. You plan all the kids' events at the holiday boat parade. You were *born* to be a nanny."

Harlee looked over at Palmer. "That's different. I get to spend a little bit of time with them, then I get to leave. I don't have to stay for hours every day and take care of one of them. I wouldn't even know what to do with a five-year-old kid."

Letting out a disbelieving laugh, Palmer asked, "And I do?"

"I'm going to head on out. Harlee, you sure you don't mind closing up alone?" I asked.

Harlee gave me a soft smile. "I'm positive. Will you please go and do something for yourself for once, Sutton?"

Palmer turned to me. "Where are you going?"

I felt a smile spread over my face. "I'm going to Seaside Spa. I've booked a facial, a manicure, and a pedicure. Then I'm going to stop by the restaurant and surprise Mom and Dad with dinner at Pete's Place."

"Mom will love that," Palmer said.

"Do you want to come with me to the spa? I'm sure they can probably work you in."

Palmer reached for the newspaper that was still on the counter and put it into her bag. "I wish I could, but I'm working at the vet clinic this afternoon. Matter of fact, I need to get going. Enjoy your afternoon at the spa though!"

I laced my arm with my sister's. "I'll walk out with you. I parked out front today."

After saying goodbye to Palmer, I slipped into my car and headed to the spa. As I pulled in and parked, I got a text from Brody.

Brody: I'm off for the rest of the day. Was going to swing by the store.

Me: I'm at the spa, remember? After I'm finished here, I'll pick up my mom and dad and meet you at Pete's Place.

Brody: Enjoy your spa day.

I frowned at his reply. It wasn't like Brody to keep it so short and simple, and he always closed his texts with an *I love you.*

Me: I love you!!!

Brody: Love you two.

I stared at the reply and felt a rush of cold through my entire body. "That's how Jack would spell two."

Before I had a chance to hit call, someone knocked on my window and I jumped, nearly throwing my phone into the backseat. I glanced over and saw it was Kimberley, one of Palmer's friends. Harlee and I once thought she might be the writer of the gossip column, but Palmer swore she wasn't the sharpest tool in the shed.

I tossed my phone into my purse, grabbed it, and opened my door. "Hey, Kimberley. I forgot you worked here. How are you?"

She beamed back at me. "I'm doing great! Are you here to pamper yourself this afternoon?"

"I am."

"Come on, I'll walk you in."

After I'd checked in, the receptionist walked me to the locker room. "Pick a locker. Each one has a robe and slippers in it."

"Thank you," I said as I pushed the door open.

"Sure thing. Once you're finished, come out here and they'll call your name. There's water and tea if you'd like some."

Smiling, I headed into the locker room, ready for an afternoon of pure relaxation.

Chapter Twenty-One

Brody

I walked into Seaside Grill and immediately spotted Barbara talking to Addie and Gannon. When she saw me, she rushed over, with Addie and my brother hot on her trail.

"Hey, I thought we were meeting at Pete's Place?" I asked as I bent down to kiss Barbara on the cheek. "I waited there for a bit before I realized no one was showing up."

"Why aren't you answering your phone?" Gannon asked. It was then I finally noticed the worried looks on all of their faces. Keegan came walking out of the kitchen and looked relieved to see me as well.

"Is Sutton with you?" he said. "Why haven't you two been answering your damn phones?"

"Keegan, calm down," Barbara said, a concerned tone in her voice.

Addie approached her father. "Dad, take a deep breath and don't get upset. I'm sure there's an explanation."

I looked at all of them and frowned. "I lost my phone. Well, honestly, I think someone stole it."

"Then you haven't spoken to Sutton?" Addie asked.

"No," I said with a shake of my head. "Not since this morning. I thought the plan was for her to pick you guys up, and I'd meet you at the restaurant."

Barbara put her hand to her mouth.

"What's going on?" I asked, dread filling me.

Gannon stepped forward. "Sutton never showed to pick up her parents. We called Harlee, and she said Sutton and Palmer left the store together. Palmer was heading to work and Sutton was going to the spa."

"Palmer went to the spa to see if maybe Sutton got held up for some reason," Addie added. Then her phone rang. "It's Palmer."

I instantly felt a sharp pain in my chest. Turning to Gannon, I whispered, "Something's wrong."

"Don't freak out, Brody. It could be nothing."

I grabbed his arm and pulled him away. "Something is *wrong*. My phone just happens to go missing this afternoon, and now no one can get a hold of Sutton?"

He frowned. "What are you saying?"

Before I could respond, I heard Addie say, "What do you mean, her car's still there but they haven't seen her?"

Barbara started to cry, and Keegan pulled her to him. "Someone call Braxton, *now*," he said.

"I will," Ruby stated as she quickly pulled out her phone.

I made it to Addie in two large steps. "What's going on?"

She looked to me, then Gannon. "Palmer, come to the restaurant. Yes, now!" She hit End and took in a deep breath. "I think we need to call the police."

It felt like someone reached into my chest and squeezed my heart. "Why, Addie?"

Tears filled her eyes as she fought to stay calm. She looked over at her parents, then back to me. "Kimberley said she walked Sutton into the spa. The receptionist showed her to the locker room and told her where to go to wait for her facial. But after almost fifteen minutes of waiting for her to come out, they went in to check on her. Sutton wasn't in the locker room. She never changed or anything, so they assumed she left without telling them. But Palmer said her car's still in the parking lot."

"Oh my God! Where is she?" Barbara called out.

Turning to Gannon, I said, "We need to call the police. Give me your phone."

Gannon handed it over, and I dialed 9-1-1. "Addie, don't you have that Find My Friends app on your phone?" I heard him ask.

Addie's eyes widened. "Yes! It's not that one, but another tracking app. We all have it."

"Pull it up!" I barked just before the dispatcher answered. After quickly telling her everything I knew, she said someone was on their way to the restaurant and to stay put.

I hung up, then walked over to where Addie and her mother were looking at her phone.

The door to the restaurant opened and Harlee walked in. She smiled when she spotted everyone—then frowned when she saw the way we were all looking at her. "What's wrong?"

"Have you heard from Sutton?" Addie quickly asked.

Harlee's eyes darted around to everyone before landing on me. "No. Like I told you on the phone, not since she and Palmer left the store earlier this afternoon. What's going on?"

Braxton walked in with two cops, and for the next few minutes, I felt like I was inside a cramped box looking out as they asked everyone the same questions.

As an officer interviewed Palmer—who had gotten there right after they did—I got up and started for the door.

"Brody, where do you think you're going?" my brother asked.

"I can't just sit here and do nothing!"

Addie walked up and shook her head. "I can't figure out why this location thing isn't working. It says her location hasn't been updated in an hour."

"Then either her phone is off or she doesn't have a signal," Gannon said somberly.

"But her last location doesn't make sense. Why would she be down at your beach house, Brody? It's not even there anymore."

I snapped my head to look at Addie. "What?"

She turned her phone and showed me. "That's the last location it gives for her, but why would she be down there?"

As if Braxton read my mind, our eyes met and we both said, "The fishing hut."

"I think I know where she is!" I shouted to one of the police officers. "Addie, tell him where it's located!" Running out of the restaurant, I heard Gannon and Braxton behind me.

"Shouldn't we let the police handle this, Brody?" Braxton shouted as we all piled into my truck.

"If that's where she is, I'm not waiting. They can follow us there." I pulled out onto Main Street and floored it. If a cop tried to pull me over right now, there was no way I was stopping.

"What makes you think she's at the fishing hut?" Gannon asked, hanging on as I squealed around a corner.

"It's where we were first together."

"Okay, but again, why would she go there and not tell anyone?"

It was Braxton who answered. "Jack must have her. He probably brought her there because he somehow found out that's where Brody and Sutton went all those years ago, the night of the bonfire. He's sick enough to do something like—"

Gannon threw up his hands to make him stop talking. "Wait, wait, hold on a second! Jack isn't even in town anymore."

"I think he is," I said. "I think he's been here the whole time, waiting. I also think he started the fire at the beach house."

"Holy fuck," Gannon said softly. "What makes you think that?"

I looked at my brother, then back onto the road. "You forget what I did in the Navy, Gannon. My job was intelligence. A week after the fire, I got tired of waiting for the police to figure it out, so I took matters into my own hands and had someone hack into the camera footage on the pier the morning of the fire. There was a man walking on the beach who looked a hell of a lot like Jack, but I couldn't be sure. Then I remembered that one of the houses farther down the beach also has security cameras. They finally got back to me yesterday—and their footage showed the same man walking away from my beach house the morning of the fire. At first I thought I was just letting my emotions get in the way, but I was going to talk to Sutton about it after dinner tonight anyway. After this? I'm *positive* it was

Jack. He's been here in Seaside the whole time, just waiting to make his move."

"I'm going to fucking kill him," Braxton snarled.

A similar growl sounded from the back of my throat. "Not if I get to him first."

We pulled up to the ruins of the beach house, and I'd barely put the truck in park before we all piled out. Braxton had never been in the military, but he copied Gannon and me as we got down low and made our way toward the fishing hut. I could see a light shining from under the door. The windows all faced out toward the water, so even if the curtains were drawn back, no one would see us coming.

In the distance, I heard police sirens.

"Fuck. They're going to alert him," I whispered.

Gannon put his hand on my shoulder and squeezed. "I'm on it."

He dropped back, and I knew he was calling dispatch to tell them not to come in with sirens on.

Braxton and I kept making our way to the fishing hut. I crept up along the side and peeked in through a crack in the curtains. My heart dropped at the sight before me.

Sutton was on the bed, and she appeared to be...out of it. She was having a hard time sitting up and keeping her eyes open.

Turning back to Braxton, I motioned for him to go to the front door and I'd go around to the back. I couldn't see where Jack was, and I had no idea if he was armed or not.

As we both made our way around the building, I heard vehicles pulling up. I probably only had a few seconds to do this before they came running in with guns drawn—and crazy-ass Jack might do something horrible to Sutton in the chaos.

Once I got to the back door, I let out a whistle that sounded like a bird. Braxton replied twice in return. Thank God! He remembered the silly cops and robbers game we used to play as kids. I'd whistle back twice when I was ready, we would count to five, then we'd both enter.

Whistling twice, I counted as my heart pounded in my ears.

One.

I'm going to kill Jack.

Two.

I'm coming, Sutton.

Three.

Please be okay.

Four.

I'm here, sweetheart.

Five.

We kicked in both of the doors, which caused the police to start running down the pier, yelling out. None of that mattered—because the first thing I saw was Jack sitting in a chair, a gun on the table next to him.

I knew what Braxton would do first—go to his sister.

I dove toward Jack and knocked him to the ground, along with the table.

"I've got the gun!" Braxton called out as I wrestled to get Jack's arms behind his back.

I looked up when I heard a loud commotion and saw my brother running in with three cops behind him.

"Get Sutton out of here!" I shouted to Gannon.

Braxton handed the police the gun while I held Jack. Now that more people had entered, he suddenly stopped fighting me.

One of the officers walked over to me and bent down. "Sir...sir, we've got this now. You can let him go." I looked at the cop, and he simply nodded. "I've got him, sir."

Focusing back on Jack, I leaned down and whispered in his ear, "You better hope they lock you up somewhere far away where I can't get to you—because otherwise I'm going to *kill you.*"

"He's threatening me! Did you hear him threaten me?!" Jack called out as I put my hand on his head and pushed myself up, muffling his words.

"I didn't hear a thing," the cop said. He took my place and put Jack in handcuffs.

I rushed out to the pier and straight to Sutton. "Is she okay?" I asked Gannon, dropping to my knees and pushing her hair back from her eyes so I could inspect her face.

Sutton opened her eyes slightly and moaned. "My head...it feels like I have a massive hangover."

The relief that rushed through me at that moment nearly caused me to cry. I pulled her out of Gannon's arms and into my own. "It's okay, sweetheart. It's okay."

As if the reality of the situation finally hit her all at once, Sutton wrapped her arms around me and started to sob.

Gannon stood, turned to face the cops, and shouted, "We need an ambulance!"

"It's pulling up now, Gannon," one of the cops said as they escorted Jack out of the fishing hut.

"Brody," Sutton whispered, her face buried against my chest. She sounded broken.

"Shhh, it's over. You're safe."

I looked up at Gannon and Braxton, who both had the same expression on their face. Relief mixed with pure rage.

When the paramedics rushed down the pier, I almost pushed them away, but I knew that Sutton needed to be checked out.

"Don't leave me!" she cried when I pulled back from her.

I shook my head and swallowed the lump in my throat. I took her hand in mine and didn't let go, not even as they loaded her on a gurney, pushed it down the pier, and transferred her into the ambulance. When I sat down next to her, I said, "Never. I'll never leave you, sweetheart."

The door to Sutton's hospital room quietly clicked shut behind me before I turned and headed to the waiting room. Both sets of our parents and her siblings were all waiting for an update.

When Barbara saw me, she jumped up. I glanced at Keegan and saw that he looked exhausted. I wanted to ask him how he was feeling, but I knew he would rather hear an update on his daughter.

"She's sleeping comfortably," I said. "Jack didn't hurt her except for a few scrapes and bruises when she attempted to fight him off. He drugged her and carried her to his car. Luckily, she still had her purse with her phone inside it."

"And even luckier that the stupid idiot didn't plan on us tracking her phone," Braxton said.

I nodded. "He, um...the doctor said Jack didn't...hurt her in the fishing hut, either, so she's okay in that regard." I clenched my fists as I thought about what I would have done to him if he'd touched her.

"How's she doing emotionally?" Barbara asked.

I gave her a weak smile. "It's Sutton. She's stronger than any woman I've ever met. The only complaint she has is a massive hang-over. And that she missed all the fun."

Small chuckles filled the room as I watched Keegan let out a long breath.

My mother walked up to me. "And you, darling? Are you okay?"

I nodded. "I'm fine. Aside from the fact that I want to kill him"

From the corner of my eyes, I saw Braxton nod.

Keegan clapped me on the back. "I'm just glad she's okay and that none of you got hurt."

"Thank God we kept that stupid app!" Addie stated as she hugged her mom.

Braxton stood and motioned for me to follow him.

"What's up?" I asked when we reached the hallway.

He glanced over my shoulder to make sure no one was listening before he looked back at me. "I've got a couple of friends who work at the police department. I can arrange for us to be alone with that asshole."

I raised my brows. "Really?"

Braxton nodded. "All we have to do is—"

"Nothing. All you need to do is *nothing*."

I turned to see Gannon standing there. "The last thing either of you need is to end up in jail and for Jack to somehow get off because you two idiots snuck into his cell and beat the shit out of him."

Braxton and I exchanged a look.

Gannon sighed. "Guys, I get it. I do. If someone took Addie and drugged her, I would want to rip them limb from limb. But right now you have to think about Sutton. This wouldn't be helping *her*, only the two of you."

I scrubbed my hands down my face and groaned. "Fuck, you're right. It's just...every time I see her on that bed, knowing that he manhandled her, I just want to..." My voice trailed off.

Brax nodded. "I know. I feel the same way. And I'm sorry if I let my emotions get the better of me and dragged you into it. It's just—"

I shook my head at him. "You don't have to explain, Brax. I get it. Believe me."

Gannon walked up and put his arm around our shoulders. "Let's just focus on Sutton right now, okay?"

My stomach did a weird flopping thing whenever I thought about her. Despite the circumstances, I couldn't help but smile. "Right. Sutton is who we need to focus on. I'm going to head back into her room. She might be awake now. They said she can have visitors, but I want to talk to her first."

"Of course, dude," Gannon said. "Go talk to your wife. Take your time."

I hit my brother on the side of his arm. "Thanks, Gannon, for keeping our heads in the right place."

Braxton smiled, but I could tell he still wanted to pay a visit to Jack. I'd leave that up to him, but I wouldn't have any part in it. Gannon was right. I needed to focus on Sutton. Now more than ever.

"I'm going to head on back," I said. "I'll come out and let you guys know when you can see her."

Gannon nodded and motioned for Braxton to follow him, and they headed back toward the waiting room.

Drawing in a deep breath, I returned to Sutton's room. When I opened the door, she looked over at me sleepily and smiled.

"Hey, you're awake," I said, moving toward her. "How do you feel?"

She gifted me with a soft smile. "I feel better. Whatever they gave me is taking the headache away. Thank goodness."

I sat down on the edge of the bed and took her hand in mine. "Do you want anything? Are you hungry or thirsty?"

"Maybe something to drink. A chocolate milkshake?"

Laughing, I lifted her hand to my mouth and kissed the back of it. "You're craving a milkshake, huh?"

She nodded. "Oh, a cheeseburger sounds good, too, if you don't mind."

I pulled out my phone and sent Braxton a text asking if he could go get Sutton what she wanted. "Mind if I slide in next to you and hold you?"

Sutton scooted over some, and I lay down next to her. She reached for my hand, and we laced our fingers together.

"I'm so sorry this happened," she said softly, resting her head on my chest.

"Sutton, none of this was your fault. I just wish we'd known for sure that he was still in town."

"I don't even know how this could've happened."

I ran my thumb over her hand as I cleared my throat. "Earlier this afternoon, someone stole my phone. Turns out it was Jack. He pretended to be me and texted you. You replied, telling him you were going to the spa. I'm not sure if he already knew, or just got there before you did. There's a back door, and we assume that's how he got in. He snuck into the locker room and waited for you."

She frowned. "Yes…I remember walking into the locker room and going over to a locker. Someone grabbed me from behind. I tried to fight them off, but they put something over my mouth, and the next thing I knew, I woke up in the fishing hut. I saw Jack sitting there at the table. He had a gun…and then I heard the doors crash open and saw you and Braxton. I don't really remember much after that."

I kissed the top of her head. "That about sums it up. The police are pretty sure Jack is the one who started the fire at the beach house. We were able to find video from some security cameras that show him walking away from the property after it was set on fire."

She covered her mouth with her hand. "Why would he do that? And why would he take me?"

I shook my head. "That part, I *don't* know."

"And why bring me to the fishing hut?"

That bothered me as well. It was as if Jack knew about Sutton being there with me in the past. "Sutton, did you ever tell Jack about us? About our night at the fishing hut?"

She shook her head, then quickly stopped. "Okay, so my headache isn't all the way gone."

I held her closer. "He didn't touch you though, right?"

"No. I do remember him saying something in the locker room about he just wanted to talk. I have no idea what he really wanted."

"Considering he'll be charged with arson and kidnapping, I don't think Jack is going to be a problem for you any longer." She looked up at me, and I could see the worry in her eyes. "I swear to you, Sutton. As God is my witness, he will never be able to hurt you again. *Never*."

Snuggling into my chest, she sighed. "I believe you."

"There is something we do need to talk about though, sweetheart." My heart started to beat faster in my chest as I prepared to tell her what I'd learned earlier.

"You sound serious. Is everything okay?" Sutton pulled back and looked up at me.

Smiling, I leaned down and kissed her gently on the lips. "While you were still sleeping, the doctor came in to talk to me. They ran some tests just to make sure you were okay."

Sutton's brows slowly drew down, and her expression turned to one of worry. "Is everything all right? Did they find something wrong?"

"No, they didn't find anything wrong. Just the opposite. I guess one of the things they checked for were hormones—pregnancy hormones."

Her eyes widened and she whispered, "Brody, what are you saying?"

I could feel the tears building in my eyes as I tried to keep my voice steady. "We're going to have a baby, Sutton."

She reached up and pressed her mouth to mine, tears spilling from her eyes. She kissed me hard and fast, then pulled back. "I'm *pregnant*?"

Nodding, I placed my hand on the side of her face. "Yes. They did a sonogram to check the baby. Everything's fine. He said you're not very far along and probably weren't even aware you were pregnant yet."

She wiped her tears away, a sob slipping free. "I *didn't* know. I mean, I'm a few days late, but I wasn't thinking much about it just yet."

"I didn't tell anyone. I wanted to tell you first, and since you're not very far along, I thought it might be best to keep it between us for a while."

Sutton blinked rapidly. She still seemed a bit shocked. "Pregnant?"

With a soft chuckle, I kissed her softly on the mouth. "Pregnant."

"That might explain my sudden craving for a cheeseburger and a chocolate milkshake. Speaking of which, where's my food?"

This time, I laughed outright. "I texted Braxton to get it for you."

She searched my face with her eyes. "How are *you* feeling about this?"

I smiled. "How am I feeling? I've never been so happy in my entire life, Sutton. I mean, I'm not going to lie, I'm also scared, nervous, and worried. All those emotions are kind of wound up in one big ball."

She giggled, then moved her hand down to her stomach. "I can't believe we're pregnant. We're going to have a baby!"

"What!"

Sutton and I both turned to see Braxton standing in the doorway, holding a milkshake and a bag from the Seaside Grill.

"So much for keeping it to ourselves," I whispered. I pointed at Braxton. "If you so much as utter a word to anyone, I'll break your other ankle."

He frowned. "First off, I *twisted* my ankle, dickhead. And second, I won't tell a soul—but holy shit! I'm going to be an uncle!"

Sutton and I looked at each other and smiled before I leaned down and kissed my wife.

Chapter Twenty-Two

Sutton
November

Warm arms engulfed me as I stood on my parents' widow's walk and looked out over the bay.

"Thought I might find you up here," Brody whispered against my ear before he placed a kiss on my neck.

"I just needed to get away for a few minutes."

Our two families had decided to celebrate Thanksgiving together, since it made it easier on all of us. Brody and I had yet to tell anyone about the baby, and I was glad it was still our little secret. Well, ours and Braxton's. My mother did keep giving me telling glances and smiles, almost as if she knew but wasn't going to say anything until we did.

"How are you feeling?" Brody asked as he turned me around and looked lovingly into my eyes.

My morning sickness had started almost as soon as I'd gotten out of the hospital. It felt like my body realized the secret was out, so now it was going to start displaying all the signs of pregnancy. The morning sickness had grown worse over the last week.

I placed my hand on Brody's chest and gave it a pat. "Better, now that I had some of that ginger candy you bought."

"I'm telling you, that New Dad group the doctor told me to join on Facebook is going to come in handy for both of us. John in Lubbock shared that little tidbit with me."

I let a small chuckle slip free. "Well, thank John in Lubbock for me. It really does calm my stomach."

Brody's eyes fell to my mouth, and I reached up and pressed my lips to his. Our tongues moved lazily in a tango before we drew back and rested our foreheads together.

"I love you so much, Sutton. Sometimes I swear I feel like this is all a dream, and I'm going to wake up and none of it will be real."

I reached behind him and pinched him on the ass, causing him to let out a little squeak.

"See? You're not dreaming."

He laughed, then rubbed his nose against mine. "Are you happy, sweetheart?"

I placed my hand back on his chest before running it up and behind his neck. I played with the hair at the base of his neck. "I don't think I've *ever* been this happy. I was thinking, though, about the property on the beach."

"Yeah?"

I stared at the buttons on his shirt, then lifted my gaze to meet his. "What would you think about building a house there for us? I know I've tried to make our home fresh and new, but the idea that Jack once lived there makes me feel uneasy now. I want to raise our kids in a house that's ours. *Only* ours."

Brody tilted his head, and that smile of his that I loved so much appeared on his face. Dimple and all. "I love the idea of building a house there for us. The property is completely cleared now, so it's a blank slate. Do you have any idea what kind of house you want?"

"Nothing too over the top. Just a sweet little house where we can raise our family. There are so many memories in that spot, and I think having our kids grow up near the water would be great."

"I agree. We can meet with an architect whenever you're ready to get things going."

"Seriously?" I asked, my cheeks straining from how wide I was smiling.

Brody wrapped his arms around me tighter before sealing his

mouth over mine and kissing me so deeply my knees felt weak. When he pulled back, I sighed with happiness.

"Seriously. I'll do whatever it takes to make you happy, Sutton Wilson."

I raised a brow. "Anything?"

"Anything."

I slowly moved my hand down to his jeans and unbuttoned them.

He caught my wrist with his fingers, and the wicked gleam in his eyes made them sparkle. "What are you doing?"

"I've suddenly had a craving hit me, and it's a strong one."

Laughing, he dropped my hand and let me unzip his pants. I slipped my hand into his boxers and found him already hard.

"We can be fast, Brody."

He smoothed his hand up and under my dress. Pushing my panties to the side, he slipped his fingers inside of me and moaned. "You're so wet already."

I nodded. "I want you."

He looked toward the steps before he focused back on me. "Turn around."

I did as he said. Then I looked over my shoulder and watched him push his pants and boxers down just enough to take himself in his hand. I licked my lips as I lifted my ass toward him.

"I'm going to fuck you from behind, sweetheart. It's going to be fast and hard. Do you want that?"

Nodding, I nearly whimpered. "I want that."

Brody positioned his dick at my entrance and pushed in so fast, I gasped and then moaned.

"You have to be quiet," he said, gently biting down on my shoulder.

"Move, Brody. Move!"

He started off slow but then quickly picked up his pace, nearly making me purr like a damn cat. I could feel my buildup already starting.

"Brody," I gasped as his hand came around and cupped my breast through my dress. Then he slid it down, and the moment he found my clit, I came undone. Brody followed right after.

He laid over my back and attempted to get his breathing under control as he looked around again. "Hopefully no one down on the street can see us up here."

I turned around and smiled at my handsome-as-hell husband. He was looking for something to clean off with. I pulled off the thin scarf that I'd wrapped around my ponytail and handed it to him.

Brody dropped to his knees to clean me before he cleaned himself. Then he stood and got his pants situated.

"Feeling better?" he asked with a wink and a smile that said he knew how good he was.

"Much better. I'm ready to face everyone again."

Brody put his arm out, and I took it. We slowly made our way out of the window's walk and soon found ourselves in the middle of our two blended families.

Addie and Gannon were off in a corner with their heads bent toward one another, talking quietly. From the way my sister was smiling, I was sure it was a good conversation. Palmer was helping my mother with the rolls that they'd soon put in the oven. A sign that dinner was almost ready.

Ken and Janet were deep in conversation with Braxton and his date, Jennifer, whom he had met on a charter that she and her family had booked last month. I wasn't sure how serious it was, since my brother didn't do serious. He claimed they were just having fun. Jennifer lived about an hour inland, so maybe it was a good arrangement for them both. Brody said it was all about the sex, but it was interesting that he'd brought her home to meet everyone.

My eyes swung back to the kitchen, where my mother was humming a song as Palmer brushed butter over the rolls before she put them in the bottom oven. And all the while, my father stared at the turkey that was roasting inside the top oven.

Smiling, I placed my hand over my stomach and thought about how our family was slowly growing. Addie hadn't said anything, but I was pretty sure she and Gannon wanted to try and start a family soon—if they weren't already. My mother wanted grandchildren. And maybe if she knew at least one was on the way, it would help her and my father decide to retire early. At least I hoped so. They both deserved a break.

"Do you need help with anything?" I asked as I stepped fully into the kitchen.

My mother glanced up and smiled. "Will you put the plates on the table?"

"Sure!"

"I'll help," Brody said, picking up the stack of plates. We headed into the formal dining room. My father had put in the two leaves, so the table was extended to its full length.

"We have a couple of extra plates," I said, looking at the table that sat twelve.

Brody appeared to be counting in his head. "There's eleven of us. Your mom must have just grabbed too many plates."

"I did no such thing." Mom came walking in and placed a salad on the table with four different types of dressing.

"Who are the other two plates for, Mom?"

The doorbell rang, and my mother's face exploded into a grin. "Palmer! Will you please get that for me!"

My mouth fell open. "Mom, you didn't."

"Didn't what?" Brody asked. "I'm missing something."

"I don't know what you mean, Sutton," she said innocently.

Palmer rushed by and headed to the front door. I brought my hands to hips, but before I could say anything, I heard Palmer's surprised voice.

"Mason! What are you doing here?"

Brody started to chuckle. I hit him in the stomach, shot my mother a look that said I knew what she was up to, and then made my way into the foyer. Dr. Mason Bryan stood there with a pie in his hand and Charlie by his side. His smile had faltered a little by the time I came rushing around the corner. Then a look of confusion washed over his face.

"Your mother invited Charlie and me for Thanksgiving dinner. If I messed up..." Dr. Bryan's voice trailed off.

When it was clear Palmer wasn't going to say anything, I stepped in. "No, of course not. We were expecting you both." I bent down and smiled at the little boy. "Hey, Charlie, how are you?"

He smiled, and I saw that his front tooth was missing. It was the cutest thing ever. "Hi, Mrs. Wilson."

"You can call me Sutton."

Charlie smiled even wider. "Hi, Sutton!"

I stood up straight and saw Palmer taking Mason's coat. At least she'd gotten over the initial shock of seeing him.

"Dr. Bryan! You and Charlie made it. I'm so happy!" my mother gushed as she swept into the foyer, wrapped her arm around Mason's, and escorted him into the house.

Meanwhile, Brody knelt next to Charlie. "How about you and me finish setting the table? Want to help with that?"

Charlies eyes lit up as he took Brody's hand. "Daddy says I'm a big boy now, so I think I can help."

Brody laughed and started to head off with Charlie. I turned and looked at my sister, who watched them walk away. I wasn't sure how to read the expression on her face, but one thing was clear—Dr. Mason Bryan had thrown my baby sister for a loop.

"I'm stuffed!" Addie said as she collapsed into one of the chairs on our parents' back screened-in porch. The space heaters were going so that anyone who wanted to sit out here wouldn't freeze to death. "Everything was so good."

Harlee—who had stopped by for dessert like she'd done every year for as long as I could remember—stepped down into the room and asked, "Is it just me, or is Jennifer a little..."

"Ditzy?" Palmer finished for her.

"Well, I was looking for a nicer word to describe her, but yeah."

"I don't think Brax is with her for her intellectual attributes," Addie stated with an eye roll. "I'm pretty sure she was playing footsies with him under the table."

Palmer laughed. "I think she was playing with *something*, but I'm not sure it was his foot."

Harlee fake gagged.

"I didn't need that visual," I said, shivering.

"What in the world was our mother thinking by inviting Dr. Bryan?" Palmer crossed her arms over her chest and shot a questioning look at Addie.

"Hey," Addie started, putting her hands up to ward off any accusations. "I had nothing to do with it."

Palmer raised one brow.

Addie glanced away. "Fine. I might have had *something* to do with it. I felt bad for them, Palmer. They had nowhere else to go, and it's Thanksgiving. I wanted Charlie to have a big dinner with lots of dessert. Plus, I knew he'd love being around Brax, Gannon, and Brody. And I was right. I mean, they all played video games with him, and now Charlie and Brody are playing a board game. How sweet is that?"

I felt my heart warm as I thought about watching Brody with Charlie all afternoon. He was going to make such an amazing father.

Palmer gave a one-shoulder shrug. "I mean, sure, I see your point. But why didn't she tell anyone he was coming?"

"Maybe it was an open invite, and she told him to just show up if he wanted," Harlee suggested.

Palmer chewed on her lip. "Maybe."

I leaned forward and reached for Palmer's hand. "Hey, why does Dr. Bryan, I mean, Mason, being here have you so out of sorts, Palmer?"

"It doesn't. I was just surprised to see him."

Addie glanced toward the door to the house, then back at us. "He's been interviewing people for the nanny position. The girl who's been watching Charlie is graduating high school early this December and planning on going to Europe before she has to come back and start college. I just feel so bad he hasn't been able to find anyone."

We all looked at Palmer.

She raised her hands. "Oh, no. I already declined. Do not try to guilt me into taking that job."

Addie pretended to be surprised. "What? I'm doing no such thing."

Palmer rolled her eyes. "Uh-huh. Sure, you're not."

At that moment, Jennifer walked out onto the porch. "Hi, ladies! The guys are all talking sports, so I thought I'd track you down and see what you're gossiping about!"

"We don't gossip," Harlee said.

Jennifer's friendly grin faltered. "Oh, well... am I interrupting? I can leave."

Addie gave Braxton's date a warm smile. "You don't have to leave. We were just discussing how Dr. Bryan is looking for a nanny."

"Oh yeah! He mentioned that, and I told him I might be available for the job."

Both Palmer and Harlee sat up, suddenly taking a bit more interest in the conversation.

"Are you a nanny?" Harlee asked.

Jennifer shook her head. "No, but I do love kids, and I went to school for early education. I want to be a kindergarten teacher."

"You have a college degree?" Palmer asked in a surprised voice. I saw Addie kick her, and Palmer jerked, then rubbed at her ankle.

Luckily, Jennifer missed all of it. "Yep!"

"You'd make a perfect nanny," Addie said, clearly not seeing the daggers that Palmer was sending through her death stares.

"Is...is Mason...I mean...is Dr. Bryan going to interview you for the position?" Palmer asked.

Jennifer bounced in her seat, her breasts nearly popping right out of her tight shirt. "I think so! I gave him my cell number. He's hot, too, so there's that. I might get a little bonus working for him... if you get my meaning."

Palmer snarled her lip up in disgust while Harlee asked, "Wait, aren't you dating Brax?"

Jennifer let out a laugh that sounded like nails going down a chalkboard. "Brax, serious about dating? That's funny. We're just friends."

"Friends?" Harlee repeated.

Jennifer nodded, smiling down at her perfectly manicured nails. Then she looked Harlee right in the eye. "Fuck buddies. I like his big co—"

I jumped to my feet. "Okay...well, I think we need to steer this conversation in another direction before my Thanksgiving dinner comes back up."

Not five seconds later, Brax poked his head into the sunroom. "Jennifer, you ready to leave?"

She jumped up. "Yes, I am!" Turning back toward us, she waggled her brows and then waved goodbye. "Thanks for the conversation, ladies." Brax put an arm around her waist as they headed for the door.

"I'll see you guys later?" Braxton asked, glancing around the room. His smile seemed to slip for a moment when his eyes landed on Harlee. He quickly removed his arm from around Jennifer's waist.

"See you later," Palmer and Addie said at the same time.

"Bye, big bro." I blew him a kiss and his smile came back.

Then he looked at Harlee again. "See you around, Harlee."

She pulled out her phone and focused on it intently. "See ya around."

He gave a quick nod, then ushered Jennifer away.

"I'm pretty sure I threw up in my mouth a little." Addie covered her lips and gagged.

"Same," Palmer and I both said before we all fell into a fit of laughter.

Once we'd all calmed down, Palmer stood. "Well, I think I'm going to go see if Mom and Dad need any more help, then head on home."

Harlee followed suit. "Same. My dad asked me to look at some things for the paper, then I need to start organizing stuff for this year's Christmas boat parade. We're still opening an hour early tomorrow for Black Friday, right?" Harlee asked me.

"Yep! But don't worry if you can't make it in that early. Palmer will be there to help out too."

"Are you kidding me?" Harlee said. "I want to watch all those women go crazy over the naughty loft sale. Plus, I saw a new toy come in, and I want to snag one before everyone else does."

Addie shook her head and chuckled. "One of these days, your dark side is going to get exposed in the gossip column."

Harlee scoffed. "That'll never happen. Why do you think I do all this volunteer stuff?"

"You evil genius," Palmer said. Both women let loose an equally evil-sounding laugh before they walked out of the sunroom.

I exhaled and then stood. "Well, I'm exhausted. Think I'll track down my husband and head on home."

Addie nodded in agreement. "Same here. Being pregnant really zaps the energy out of you, doesn't it?"

"It really does."

I froze when Addie gasped. Then I quickly turned and faced her.

"I knew it! I *knew* you were pregnant!" she said.

I rushed over and put my hand on her mouth. "Shut up! We don't want to tell anyone yet. And how did you know?"

"Please, everything is heightened. My sense of taste, smell—even *lies*!"

"Wait, why..." My eyes went wide. Then I grabbed her hands, and we both started to jump up and down.

"Addie!"

"Sutton!"

"How far along are you?" I asked as I pulled her back down on the love seat.

"Six weeks. You?"

"*Shut up!*" I nearly screamed. "I'm seven weeks."

"When's your due date?" Addie asked.

"July eleventh. Yours?"

Tears filled Addie's eyes. "July twenty-second!"

We hugged one another and started to cry harder.

"Sutton, we're going to have babies at the same time! And they're going to be so close!"

I drew back and wiped away my tears. "I can't believe we're both pregnant. When did you find out?"

Addie grinned. "Just today! We went to the doctor to confirm it. I haven't been feeling well and missed my last period. You?"

"When I was in the hospital. They found out during some tests they ran."

"Oh wow, you found out pretty early then."

I nodded. "I was only a couple of days late for my period, which isn't unusual, so I didn't even think to take a test."

"Morning sickness?" she asked.

"Ugh, yes. You?"

She shook her head. "Nothing too bad. Just feeling some nausea, but that's about it."

"When are you going to tell Mom and Dad?"

"Not until I'm past the first trimester."

I laughed and dabbed at the corners of my eyes. "Us too."

"What are you two doing out here?" our mother asked as she stepped down into the sunroom.

Addie and I both tried to act normal as we wiped away any last tears.

"Oh, we're just comparing notes as married sisters," Addie mumbled.

Mom smiled, glancing between us both. "That's so wonderful. To think that two of my girls are both married women and soon-to-be mommas."

My smile fell, and Addie sucked in a breath. I tilted my head forward and tried to pretend that I was confused. "I'm sorry...what... what did you say?"

Addie just let out a nervous laugh.

Mom crossed her arms over her chest and raised one brow. "I knew the moment I saw you both. Don't worry, your secrets are safe with me." She walked up and pulled me into her arms, hugging me tightly. Then she did the same to Addie. After wiping away a few tears, she drew in a deep breath and clapped her hands. "I better go make sure your father didn't fall asleep in his chair. You know how that hurts his neck."

And just like that, she swept out of the room, leaving Addie and me standing there with our mouths open.

"It has to be some kind of weird mom power because I'm pretty sure Janet knows too," Addie stated.

I nodded, letting what just happened sink in. "Do you think we'll get special powers like that some day?"

We turned and looked at each other. A slow smile spread across Addie's face. "I sure as heck hope so!"

Epilogue

Palmer

The warmth of the sunlight hitting my face caused me to stretch and open my eyes—and then I quickly sat up and looked around the room.

Everything from the night before came rushing back.

"Oh no," I whispered as I closed my eyes tightly and prayed it was all a dream.

I opened one eye and saw that I was still in a room that *wasn't* my bedroom. My other eye opened—and I had to fight the urge to flee as fast as I could. One look at myself and I felt my heart drop to my stomach. I was naked. I *never* slept naked. A light blue sheet was pooled at my waist, and the cool air made my nipples tighten.

Or maybe it was the memory of last night. Or the man sleeping in the bed next to me.

The bed moved, and I held my breath. I heard soft breathing coming from my left.

Slowly turning my head, I saw him lying there. A deep pool of want and need hit me so hard, I nearly gasped. Then reality reared her ugly head.

"What did you do, Palmer?" I whispered to myself, right before I realized I needed to get the hell out of there.

I carefully slipped out of the bed and began to quietly search for my clothes. Once I'd found everything but my panties, I rushed into the bathroom to get dressed.

Tiptoeing back into the bedroom, I held my breath and quickly headed to the door. I carefully opened it and slipped out. I sped down the steps and to the back door. Just as I opened it, I heard someone call my name.

"Ms. Palmer? Are you gonna make me breakfast?"

And that, ladies and gentlemen, was when the panic hit. Turning, I forced myself to smile as I looked down at the little boy I was nannying.

"Morning, Charlie."

The Seaside Chronicle

January 1, 2023

The Lucky Angler (Special Edition)

Seasiders,

Word on the docks this morning is that Palmer Bradley had a sleepover last night.

All I can say for now, my little fishes, is that judging by the flush on her face this morning at The Seaside Grill, this writer would venture to guess it was a very enjoyable sleepover.

More to come…

Fair winds and following seas!

The End…for now.

Look for *Lost to You* coming out November 1, 2022.

Other Books by Kelly Elliott

The Seaside Chronicles
Returning Home
Part of Me -
Lost to You - November 1, 2022
Someone to Love - January 3, 2023

Stand Alones
*The Journey Home**
*Who We Were**
*The Playbook**
*Made for You**
*Available on audiobook

Boggy Creek Valley Series
*The Butterfly Effect**
*Playing with Words**
*She's the One**
*Surrender to Me**
Hearts in Motion (releases on March 22, 2022)
Looking for You (releases on May 3, 2022)
Surprise Novella TBD
*Available on audiobook

Meet Me in Montana Series
*Never Enough**
*Always Enough**
*Good Enough**
*Strong Enough**
*Available on audiobook

Southern Bride Series
*Love at First Sight**
*Delicate Promises**
*Divided Interests**
*Lucky in Love**
*Feels Like Home **
*Take Me Away**
*Fool for You**
*Fated Hearts**
*Available on audiobook

Cowboys and Angels Series
Lost Love
Love Profound
Tempting Love
Love Again
Blind Love
This Love
Reckless Love
*Series available on audiobook

Boston Love Series
Searching for Harmony
Fighting for Love
*Series available on audiobook

Austin Singles Series
Seduce Me
Entice Me
Adore Me
*Series available on audiobook

Wanted Series
*Wanted**
*Saved**
*Faithful**

Believe
Cherished*
A Forever Love*
The Wanted Short Stories
All They Wanted
*Available on audiobook

Love Wanted in Texas Series
Spin-off series to the WANTED Series
Without You
Saving You
Holding You
Finding You
Chasing You
Loving You
Entire series available on audiobook
*Please note *Loving You* combines the last book of the Broken and
Love Wanted in Texas series.

Broken Series
Broken*
Broken Dreams*
Broken Promises*
Broken Love
*Available on audiobook

The Journey of Love Series
Unconditional Love
Undeniable Love
Unforgettable Love
*Entire series available on audiobook

With Me Series
Stay With Me
Only With Me
*Series available on audiobook

Speed Series

Ignite

Adrenaline

*Series available on audiobook

COLLABORATIONS

Predestined Hearts (co-written with Kristin Mayer)*

*Play Me (*co-written with Kristin Mayer)*

*Dangerous Temptations (*co-written with Kristin Mayer*

*Available on audiobook